REPRISAL

REPRISAL

ETHEL VANCE

Little, Brown and Company · Boston

1943

813.52
5+1r
70552
July, 1970

Chapter 1

WHEN Françoise reached the Rue Keréon she got off her bicycle and walked. She noticed that very few people were on the streets and that a number of shops had been closed and the iron shutters drawn. She passed no one she knew and as her rain hood shaded her face she hoped no one would recognize her. Only a man leaning against the wall of a house stared at her as she passed.

The Rue du Parc along the river was nearly deserted. Two empty coal barges were moored alongside the quay. There were no children playing in the steep little park on the opposite bank. Only the old priest who always walked there in the afternoon, reading his breviary, was shuffling his feet in the dry leaves, stopping to look disconsolately now and then at the Gothic patterns of bare trees against a white sky. By the bridge a solitary German soldier paced back and forth.

Françoise propped her bicycle outside a shop and took off the little wire basket that hung on the handle bars. As she went in a pale girl of about sixteen got up politely from a chair. The girl looked at her with eyes that were sleepy but suddenly grew alive with excitement.

"Good day, Alice," Françoise said.

"Good day, Mademoiselle."

"I came to get some paper, if you have any. Any sort will do, though I'd rather it had no lines."

The girl scarcely seemed to hear what was said. Then she gave a quick sigh. "Yes, Mademoiselle," and she turned to the shelves behind her. After a search among a few odds and ends she found an old school exercise book. She held it out. "It's all we have left," she said.

Françoise nodded and opened her little purse.

"They say that Monsieur le Ministre is writing a petition," the girl said. "Is it true? Everyone also says that a petition from Monsieur le Ministre won't do much good now."

"How is your aunt?" Françoise asked, giving her the money. "I hope she's not ill again."

"No, no," the girl said eagerly. "She's in church. She spends all her time there. You can't pry her out even for meals."

"She's a good woman," Françoise said rather luke-warmly.

"She says only God can save them now," the girl said, her eyes shining, "and that perhaps He has turned from us all because of our sins."

Françoise put the exercise book in her basket. "Tell her not to give up hope so easily," she said. When she was outside her face flushed with exasperation. "The idiot," she murmured.

She walked her bicycle slowly through the fine drizzle that had begun to fall. She was chilled and the handle bars were cold and slippery, but she was in no hurry to reach the shop of Madame Simmonet. Usually it was a pleasant place to be but it would not be pleasant today.

It was a shop full of smells that seemed to linger, though the commodities that produced them had long since vanished, smells of spice, coffee, chocolate. Just as Madame Simmonet herself mysteriously remained fat and full of bustle though everything that might have kept her well and produced energy was gone.

Madame Simmonet had a capacity for working small miracles. Only last Thursday she had said, "Listen, Mademoiselle. I had a great piece of luck. I found at the bottom of an old bin in the storehouse a beautiful little box of pure cocoa. How it got there I can't imagine, unless an angel left it or it dropped out of some wrappings a long time ago. Now I'm going to get it to my boy somehow. My God, the way they feed them there, nothing but potatoes and a kind of horrible powder that turns into soup. But because Mademoiselle has been so kind and brought the chicken for him last month and the sausage I'm going to take out a little of the cocoa for her."

Françoise tried to refuse the cocoa but Madame Simmonet insisted so warmheartedly that in the end she accepted a little of it shaken into an envelope. It seemed that to do less would have deprived Madame Simmonet of a genuine pleasure.

When she came to the shop she saw a sign in the door, CLOSED BECAUSE OF THE EVENTS. But she could see through the glass top of the door Madame Simmonet, leaning with both elbows on the counter. She tried the door. It was open and she went in.

Madame Simmonet glanced up at her very quickly from under her bushy, auburn eyebrows and then looked down at her hands on the counter.

"Good day, Madame Simmonet."

"Good day, Mademoiselle."

Françoise felt suddenly weak and afraid of Madame Simmonet. She had expected acute anxiety, perhaps despair, but this was even worse.

"Madame," she began.

"What did you come for?" Madame Simmonet said harshly.

"To see if I could be of any help."

"You came also for more cocoa, I have no doubt."

"No, Madame. How could you think I would come for that!"

"It is gone," Madame Simmonet said. She did not look up at Françoise. Last week she had also promised to write out a receipt for a sauce using peanut oil. She thought of that and added, "There is no peanut oil. And there is no sugar. There is nothing, absolutely nothing."

Françoise stood before her like a culprit and made no answer. Her attitude seemed to infuriate Madame Simmonet, who cried, "Why should some people have all the luck? What do they do to deserve it, I ask you?"

Françoise turned slowly toward the door. "Madame Simmonet," she said, "I understand what you feel. Believe me I do. And my father is doing all he can."

"Is he indeed!" cried Madame Simmonet. She came suddenly, heavily, around the counter and put her face close to Françoise's. Her eyes were swollen from crying. "But they don't take the son of Monsieur le Ministre," she said.

There was such hate in her that Françoise shrank back. "Oh, Madame," she exclaimed, "I am so sorry."

It was no use. She hurried out.

There was Jeanne Peguinot to be visited, the shoes to be collected and the laudanum to be bought. Which should she do next? She did not feel equal yet to Jeanne Peguinot though she lived near by, so she went past the cathedral square where Jeanne lived and on up the Rue Elie-Fréron and the Rue du Sallé and into a little Place where Bouchaix's shop, no more than a cupboard, was tucked into an ancient house, blackened with age. He did not live here but went every night to his own hideous little brick and plaster house a few kilometers outside the town. There he had a small garden of cabbages, an arbor to sit under in summer, and there he lived a bachelor life, in the old days drinking a great deal more than was good for him or than he could afford. As Françoise saw his shop and the outline of his head inside the dirty window she was thankful that he was a bachelor and moreover had no relatives nearer than a brother who owned a fishing boat at Audierne. Except for a few cronies he had no friends in town and presumably was not closely affected by the terrible happenings.

When she went into the shop it was almost too dark there to see, but Bouchaix, who had fixed her father's shoes, lining them with green felt cut from the old billiard table, held them toward the window for her to look at.

"Fine work," she said. "He'll be very pleased."

As he leaned near her she saw that his eyes were very congested and she smelled alcohol. She was astonished. That anyone could get alcohol these days, least of all a poor man, was hardly to be believed. But he gave a loud hiccough and she saw that he was slightly drunk. He was a man of fifty or more, weathered from his youth spent at sea, and he had one of those beaten, blurred faces almost without character, but he was a powerful man and even his hair had a look of being tougher and more resistant than the average.

"Monsieur Bouchaix," she said, "have the police been questioning you?"

He looked at her dumbly, took a few steps backward, and sat down in a little rush chair. He gave the impression of being unable to stand on his feet.

"Did they question me! All morning," he said.

"Could you tell them anything?"

"Not a thing. Why should I have any information? It's my bad luck to have been sleeping near by — that's all. I said to them I heard absolutely nothing, but that's because I sleep soundly. And why do I sleep soundly? I said to them. Because I have a clear conscience."

"I should think you might have heard something."

"Well, I didn't. And I didn't see anything either. The first I knew of it was the next morning when I came into town and heard it like everyone else."

He turned the shoes, which he still held, around on one hand, examining them. "I have no paper to wrap them in," he said. "Do you mind taking them as they are?"

"Not at all."

She felt in her purse for money and gave it to him. He took it indifferently and laid it on his bench. He hiccoughed again and said, "Not that I wouldn't have done it myself if I could. Not that I wouldn't have done it. . ." He choked his words and knotted his hands together as though twisting something soft.

"But I wouldn't dare," he said bitterly. "I'm a coward. That's what I am. That's why I left the sea. Because I'm a coward. Yes, it took a better man than I am to do it."

"Monsieur Bouchaix, you must be careful. I wouldn't say that sort of thing." She turned to the door and he lurched up again to open it. She put her hand kindly on his arm: "Don't talk to anyone for a while, especially now that you're a little drunk."

"Yes, I'm drunk," he said craftily, "but not so drunk I don't know what I'm saying. Mademoiselle, you don't know what happens to men who go to sea. They're the ones who get into trouble. And they don't care either — the fools. But not old Bouchaix, who saves his money and buys his house and keeps his mouth shut."

She opened the door. "Well, be careful," she repeated. Her bicycle was leaning against the black wall. Bouchaix put the shoes into her basket. He was so unsteady he pushed the bicycle and it nearly toppled. He caught the handle bars and looked down at it, staring with bloodshot eyes as though it were suddenly a frightful thing that he should be holding her bicycle and looking at it. She saw that he was frightened beyond all reason. She took her bicycle from him and turned away. But are all of them as frightened as this? she thought.

Now it was Jeanne Peguinot's turn. She lived in the Place Corentin, where she and her husband had a small restaurant and souvenir shop. Jeanne used to be a cook for the Galle family and Françoise had known her for many years. The restaurant had a specialty of *chaussons aux crabes* and had been patronized in the old days by tourists, so the Peguinots had gone in for local color, dressing the little maids in peasant cos-tume and furnishing the rooms with old carved-oak dressers. Even now there were a few postcards and guide books in glass cases, some *faïence* plates and dolls in peasant costume. The windows were tightly closed to keep out the cold and the air was musty.

Jeanne Peguinot sat opposite Françoise. Between them was the big chair where Peguinot always sat, but it was empty. The old woman wore a gray sweater and a wool shawl wrapped around her and held under her elbows. She sat perfectly still and fixed her tight old eyes on Françoise. Françoise had brought her a covered tin milk pail with milk for her grandson who was about fourteen months old. His mother was dead and the Peguinot boy, Jean, was still a prisoner of war in Germany.

"How is the baby?" Françoise asked.

"Well enough."

A fretful cry came from the next room and the old woman gave a little flick of her head like a horse shaking off flies. She didn't want to talk about the baby now.

"I have no news for you, I'm afraid," Françoise said, "except that as you know my father saw the Kommandant this morning and he promised to do nothing until Monsieur Schneider comes."

"Monsieur Schneider!" the old woman said contemptuously. "You mean Monsieur Edouard?"

"Yes. He arrives tonight."

The old woman considered this a moment, her eyes bright with attention. Then she said, "Everyone said Monsieur le Ministre had written him to come, but I said to myself, if Monsieur Edouard disturbs himself, it will be a miracle."

"Just the same, he is coming."

"He's a big man now, I suppose."

"Very. He's the Vichy representative to Paris, the ambassador, you might say."

"What does that mean?" The old woman gave another expert flick of her head, tossing off Monsieur Edouard's pretensions. "Do we have an ambassador from one French town to another? Next we'll have an ambassador from Rennes to Rouen, what? That's nonsense."

"Still, that's what he is."

The old woman looked at her as though she thought

there were a trick to it somewhere and didn't want to be taken in by it. Her face was like a brown scrubbed potato and her mouth was hardly to be seen in it but the narrow twist of it showed a sort of derision.

"And I remember well," she said scornfully, "when this Monsieur Edouard was no more than a species of valet to Monsieur le Ministre."

"He was his secretary," Françoise said.

"It's the same thing, what?"

They sat in silence and Jeanne Peguinot tucked her shawl tighter under her elbows.

"Perhaps," Françoise said, "Monsieur Edouard will have some word of your Jean. We wrote about him you know."

"A fine return my boy will have — if he ever comes," Jeanne said fiercely. "His wife dead and perhaps my old man gone too." Then she began to talk rapidly. "That Marie of his was no use anyway. She was never serious. I said to her, 'Don't run around like that in all weathers, getting your feet wet.' 'It's to hear the radio,' she told me — the radio the Tesslers had in the back of the shop — 'It's to hear news about Jean.' Always that radio! Or that's what she told me. So she began to cough and cough, and pretty soon she began to cough blood, and then she was dead. And in the end it's my old man who gets in trouble over a radio too. Why did he have to listen to those

English broadcasts? They're all lies, those broadcasts. They're only to stir us up and keep us working for them — as always. And what difference does it make if an old fool does listen? They don't have to give him six months in prison, do they? And if he hadn't been in prison then this wouldn't have happened."

She closed her eyes and tears trickled from her lids.

Françoise leaned over and touched her hand. "There is still the baby," she said. But she knew it was only a sentimental expedient to bring up the baby. An emaciated, sickly, crying baby, demanding constant attention and thought, is not really the consolation it is imagined to be.

Jeanne opened her eyes. Then she said crisply, "That's not enough milk you brought this time."

"It's all I could get. I had to borrow that. Tulipe is not well."

"Tulipe? Ah!" She shook her head. "That's bad. What's the matter with her?"

"We don't know. She won't eat. Maurice thinks it's the feed. Yves is afraid it may be tetanus. The Moriers lost their last cow by tetanus."

"You must get the veterinary."

"Yes, we've sent for him."

"What a misfortune!"

They were silent again and the old woman, never taking her fierce, bitter eyes from Françoise's face, rubbed the back of her hand along her nose and sniffled. Françoise would have liked to go but she knew that her physical presence for a decent interval of time was a due that Jeanne felt her misfortunes exacted. She sat quietly. The air was icy-cold but it seemed to be filled with exhalations of old age and exhaustion. She felt giddy. It was hard to draw a deep breath and her gaze wandered uncertainly around the room.

Suddenly Jeanne leaned toward her and said, "Mademoiselle, it's necessary that Monsieur le Ministre do something."

Françoise threw up her hands. The wrists felt brittle and weak. "But my poor Jeanne, he is doing all he can."

The old woman repeated in a louder voice, "No, no. He must do something."

"But what can he do that he hasn't done already?"

"Who am I to tell a man like Monsieur le Ministre what he can do?"

"But you don't understand!"

"Yes, I understand very well. We all understand." Jeanne reached out and clutched Françoise's hand tightly. It was like having a knotted cord drawn around it. "We all understand that Monsieur le Ministre was a friend of *theirs*, that he helped to make the peace with *them*, and that even if now *they* don't like him *they* will still listen to him. Besides, there's this Monsieur Edouard who used to be glad to sit at the table and eat the food I cooked. He's a big man now, you say. Well then, let Monsieur le Ministre speak to this species of valet of his and make him help us. Why, don't I remember when I went to Paris to cook for Monsieur le Ministre that this Monsieur Edouard had only two shirts, one to wash and one to wear, and he jumped to his feet each time Monsieur le Ministre came into the room?" Jeanne laid one finger along her nose and her eyes grew sly. "And how did he get so rich, with race horses and newspapers and such things, if not because of Monsieur le Ministre's help? No, he will listen now to whatever Monsieur le Ministre says."

It appeared that even Jeanne thought these humiliations were to be as lightly taken as they were tossed out, that Françoise must inevitably accept for her father the contempt or the half-grudging admiration of the people of the town, whichever they chose at the moment to give. They did not hate André Galle. It was impossible to hate him. Most of them said, "He's an idealist, what?" as you would say, "He's an idiot, it can't be helped." But they knew that this "idiot," this "idealist," had once had power and more money than they had, and still might have a little of both left over. It was not so certain, but still, he might. And so he might have something they could use. And they had themselves to protect and they had their legitimate cunning.

That morning she had waited with Yves in the
carriage before the Kommandantur. A group had
gathered outside, many of them relatives of the men
involved. As André Galle came out he stood a moment on the steps, his face very pale under its gray-
ing ruff of reddish hair. They knew when they
looked at him that the interview had been painful
but not hopeless, and a slight breath of relaxed tension came from them. André, feeling this, smiled
slightly and nodded to reassure them.

Then a woman who was crossing the square
stopped on the edge of the crowd to see what was
happening. She carried a basket but she wore a faded
black skirt that somehow suggested a larger place,
perhaps even one of the working quarters of Paris.
Her face was gaunt and white and gray strands came
down from her hair. She spoke to someone, questioning him. Suddenly she called out in a raucous
voice, "Traitor! Traitor!"

Everyone turned and the man she had spoken to
took her arm and pushed her hastily toward a side
street. But she became beside herself. She shook her
fist at André. "He has always betrayed the people.
Let him remember the Café Oriental," she shrieked.
Then she suddenly gathered up her black skirts and
ran off down the street. No one followed her. Everyone stood still, even the German soldiers on the steps
of the Kommandantur.

André looked after her with a puzzled expression as though he half recognized her.

A rumble began to form in the crowd. At first it sounded dangerous but almost at once there came an undertone of falseness. The Café Oriental — what nonsense was that? No one had ever heard of it. And then the grotesque scuttling away of the woman, whom no one knew. And André's expression of puzzlement. The noise changed to one of contempt, and a man somewhere gave a foolish loud laugh. They had already decided what use was to be made of André Galle.

Françoise, remembering this, looked at Jeanne Peguinot and hated her. What had Jeanne ever done in all these years but take from the Galle family, blindly and instinctively, whatever she could get? There was an insufferable superiority in her refusal to see anything in them but a source of exploitation. She was stupid with a bodily stupidity and her fierceness was a bodily, sucking fierceness.

"My father will do what he can," Françoise said bitterly.

The terrible old eyes finally left her face. It was a permission to leave. Françoise's will had plainly given in to hers, so she could now be trusted to pass on her insistence to the man who had power to help.

Françoise got up to go and Jeanne got up too. But suddenly the old woman broke, from weakness and from having accomplished her object. She put her hands up to her eyes and began to wail feebly. "They have no right to do these things to us," she cried. The scant tears dripped down her cheeks once more. "They have no right. They poison our lives with their piggeries. They are like pigs and they make us like pigs, too."

Françoise stopped and looked at her in despair. She agreed absolutely. And in comparison with these things Jeanne's claim on the Galles was an entirely respectable one, had been already recognized as such, and had endured a long time. She hesitated. Then she felt in her purse and brought out a hundred-franc note and laid it on the table.

"Please buy something extra for Peguinot," she said, "or the baby. Whatever you have a coupon for."

The old woman took her hands from her eyes and looked down at the money.

"Thank you, Mademoiselle," she said, and her voice was angry and clipped as usual.

"Good-by," Françoise said and went out.

She walked until she came to the pharmacy of Monsieur Costard on the Rue Keréon. It was closed but she rang the emergency bell and almost at once he let her in. It was quite dark and very cold. Monsieur Costard had been reading in a chair close to the window. He looked like an ancient wax figure in which all the veins had been painstakingly modeled and he wore a muffler wrapped up to his chin. There was a faint smell like paregoric about him.

Françoise dropped into a chair by the counter and said, "Monsieur Costard, how goes the throat?"

He shrugged and made no answer. His throat was hopeless and he knew it. Then he said in a whisper, "You want the laudanum?"

"Yes, if you can spare it. My father is having terrible neuralgia. Sometimes he doesn't sleep all night."

"Yes, I have some for him. Tell me, what does he think will happen?"

"He has sent for Monsieur Schneider. He will come tonight and see what can be done. But Monsieur Costard, these things can't go on."

"No," he agreed. "But they will, I'm afraid."

"But can't the man be found? Surely the police are looking for him."

"Oh, yes. But it's not easy."

"They've questioned many people?"

"Yes. Even me." He smiled faintly.

"But you think they've learned nothing?"

"They haven't learned much."

She watched him as he stood before her holding his muffler against his throat.

"But someone did it," she said anxiously, "someone who had a reason perhaps to pick on that particular man. Was he a bad one — as *they* go?"

"I don't think so."

"It seems so incredible that no one even heard the shot. There are a few houses not too far away, the little Relais Fleuri for instance, and Bouchaix's house, which is only a few hundred meters from the place."

Costard shrugged. "People don't run out these days to see who has been shot." Then he added, whispering with difficulty, "It may be as you say, someone with a special reason for hatred. There was a struggle, you know. It seems the fellow was clutching a button in his hand, torn from a coat undoubtedly. That should be a clue for them, but nothing has come of it. And another thing — there was a woman's black-cotton stocking in his pocket."

"A stocking?"

"Yes." He smiled a ghostly little smile. "Very sentimental, these Germans."

Françoise smiled too. Then she said seriously, "But no one would acknowledge the stocking?" It seemed dreadful to her, the black-cotton stocking, the pathetic token of the respectability of some working girl. There was a girl at the Relais Fleuri, such a thin little wretch. And then Madame Buisson, sixty at least.

"What about the Relais Fleuri?" she suggested, without conviction.

"He may have come from there. But everyone there

absolutely denies it. And at that hour! And then that half-starved girl could hardly be the one, or Madame Buisson. No," he whispered, "it is a mystery. I've come to believe it must have been a stranger, some unfortunate or other passing by." He closed his eyes a moment and the lids were so thin the dark eyes seemed to show through. Then he said, "But you want the laudanum."

He went behind the glass screen where his prescriptions were made up. He turned a light on and the shadow of the filigree top of the screen sprang lace-like on the white ceiling. The chilly clink of glass and the faint sound of his movements suggested precision and care. He came back with a tiny bottle.

"Hot applications sometimes help," he said.

"Yes," she said, "sometimes I heat cloths and hold them against his face. But you know — with fuel so scarce — "

He stood looking down at her. "What a pretty girl you are," he whispered.

Françoise tried to keep tears from her eyes. "Oh come now. I'm an old maid."

He looked at her and shook his head. His eyes lit with a ghostly twinkle.

"What became of that young man who visited Rusquec once, or was it twice? You came here one day. It was a pleasure to see you together."

"Oh, that young man." She herself spoke in a

half whisper. "That was Simon Astley, an American. He's gone." She shrugged her shoulders. "Who knows what became of anyone?"

He looked at her gently but almost with mockery, as though the mischances of youth, seen from this distance, were not only touching but a little comic.

"I have a present for you," he said. "Wait a moment." He walked back of the screen and to a room behind.

She waited, turning the laudanum bottle around in her cold hands. The shop was filled with the whitish glow of the light. She read the lettering on two beautiful old pharmacy jars: C. ROSARUM —V. FUS-CUM. On the chair where he had been sitting lay a book and she could read the title from where she sat. It was *The Art of Being Poor*. In the midst of a very anguish of deprivation it seemed that Monsieur Costard read of being poor as though it were an exceptional accomplishment which he cultivated willingly and with grace.

When he came back he had a tiny carton with a picture of a cow in a mountain meadow. "It's chocolate," he whispered, putting it into her hand.

"But Monsieur Costard, you mustn't. There are so many others."

He closed her fingers around it. "No, no, for you. Because it's such a pleasure to give it to you." His voice was almost inaudible.

She said, "Thank you," and she added, "The laudanum — how much is it?"

"Fifty francs."

She took out the money and paid him.

"Good-by," he said. "Try the hot applications."

"Yes, I will."

Now she had finished all her commissions and it was after four o'clock. She wanted to get home before dark. She left the shop and went down the Rue Keréon and the Rue Chapeau Rouge. In the Rue Douarnenez she got on her bicycle and came quickly to the edge of town. She followed the road past the scattered houses and finally reached the open country. About four kilometers from town she passed the house of Bouchaix, standing solitary and grotesque in the midst of sodden fields. A little farther on came the fork that turned to the left past the abandoned park of the Château de Prat-an-Ros, leading to Audierne and the Point du Raz. Somewhere between this fork and the Relais Fleuri the murder had been committed. She passed the Relais Fleuri, a little country restaurant with a leafless arbor and wooden benches. A sign dangling from a tree said ONE MAY BRING ONE'S FOOD. There was no sign of life about the place: the shutters were already closed and it had the desolate look of a place meant for summer seen under a winter-evening sky.

She went through the darkened, shuttered villages

of Kerbagen and Plonéis, the land mounting steadily
so that at times she had to get off and walk. Beyond
Plonéis she took a dirt road to the right. It was dark
now and thick fog from the sea drowned the rough
rolling country and the shaggy, low woods. The
dripping thorn hedge beside the road was a dim
shape. She climbed another small hill and stopped at
the top to rest. She was completely exhausted, not
only from physical fatigue but from hopelessness. To
be in motion accentuated the futility of the effort it
cost her, because at the end of the way she was no
further along and there had been no real objective.
She leaned heavily on her handle bars, quaking with
sudden nerves and weakness.

"I'm hungry," she said in an astonished voice. She
considered this for a while. She went over minutely
what she had eaten that day: coffee made of dried
beans and a dash of chicory, very thin milk, a piece
of bread, no butter, no sugar, and for lunch, soup
of cabbage and carrots, and one egg. They were very
lucky to have eggs. The chickens they still had laid
fairly well. They were very lucky to live in the
country, too. But then they gave so much food away,
to people in town and to the men at the camp for
political prisoners. They even mailed it to friends
in other places.

And now one of those crises of hunger that seemed
uncontrollable had suddenly come over her. The

chocolate in her basket became an immense object, with all the force and seduction of a major temptation. Excuses fluttered through her: Blaise is younger and stronger than I. He doesn't need it. And Father won't eat it. Everyone was so difficult today. Everyone but Costard was cruel. Costard was not cruel because he is dying. He has learned to live in the midst of death. And the others haven't, not even old Jeanne. But then Costard hurt me too, because he spoke of Simon. He spoke of him in a terrible, light-hearted way, as the dead, who have nothing, would speak of the living. He spoke as though he knew we were both dead together, and that only Simon was alive, somewhere infinitely remote, beyond all reach.

She snatched up the carton, tore it open, and pushed the chocolate into her mouth. The slow delight of it melted on her tongue, trickled down her throat, and brought such an assuagement that she felt no concern or pain, for Simon, the hostages, or her father.

The pleasure of it quickly vanished. She found that she felt nauseated.

Serves me right. No, how silly to make a moral issue of it — it's simply that the system needs so much sugar. Don't always be a Jansenist.

But in spite of the slight nausea she felt stronger. No chemical change has yet taken place, so it is only a matter of hope. My stomach, my liver and pancreas are capable of hope. Why not I?

If I am not dying like Costard, I am living in a half state, diminished. I can't think clearly so I must make everything as simple as I can. It is like the times when I'm sick and have a low fever. I imagine I am thinking deep thoughts and they turn out to be nonsense. I am losing my memory and at the same time I have hallucinatory periods when the past and the present are blended.

And lately there has been a sharp decline. Something vital in me has jarred loose. It is again like a sickness. Suddenly without feeling much worse I am aware, by an obscure series of warnings going out from some center in me, that the point of danger has been reached. I do not feel worse but I am certain that I am worse.

Better get along home. The darkness, the wet fog, the solitude — above all the solitude — will do me harm. I have only to coast down the hill almost to the stone gate. Then there are the avenue, the old elm trees, and the house beyond.

Standing there in the fog Françoise could see nothing, yet she felt suddenly the nearness of her home: all that it was of stone and wood, the earth around it, all the physical solidity and dimension. She felt at the same time the subtle change that had come into it.

But what was the change? Was it even sure that there was one?

Three days ago she had opened the window just before daybreak and looked out to see a long streak of red behind the hill where she now stood. The hill was dark but she knew every fold of it lapped in dry bracken. She knew where to see the dim chapel sunk at its foot. The figure moving darkly toward the stable was Yves going to milk the cow. Faint noises from the kitchen were the sleepy voice of Colette, the drowsy tapping and clink of kitchen-ware. The birds were beginning their delicate, harsh piping. What was different? From all these things fear rose like a smoke and passed through her. It was the fear of the familiar grown strange. As though what she saw were about to become transparent and reveal terrifying processes. It was the fear of revela-tion.

She tumbled back into bed and lay there shaking. Then she dozed a little.

As she suddenly roused again and looked around at her window it all seemed as usual. The bare branch of a tree swung against the pane. It was light outside, a windy November morning. She could smell burnt chicory and beans from below. Everything was solid, with its natural dimension, fixed in its natural place. She felt a great lazy relief. She slept heavily for half an hour, so heavily she didn't hear the telephone.

When Colette brought her coffee she said, "Mademoiselle, it seems that something terrible happened in the night. Monsieur le Ministre wants to see you at once."

Françoise didn't wait to question her. She threw on a dressing gown and ran into the hall. Her father met her at the foot of the stairs. His face was pale and drawn.

"They have shot a German sergeant," he said. "He was found early this morning lying on the Douarnenez road just this side of the fork. He had been shot in the stomach."

"Who did it?"

"No one knows. But they have already taken twenty hostages. They took them from the camp for political prisoners. Among them are Yves's brother Jacques, and they have taken the young Simmonet boy, too, and old Peguinot. If the police can't find the murderer in three days they will all be shot."

Perhaps that was it. A catastrophe of this kind would affect everyone living here. It might cast a palpable sense of calamity and terror before it. Yes, that must have been what she had felt in the early morning hours. And yet it could not have been that.

This message was more than a warning of calamity. The terror it had held was not the terror of death. But already the quality of it had grown dimmer and during the day she forgot it entirely.

But now, standing on the hill in the mist and darkness, she felt it again, not in its full intensity but rather in a sudden memory of fear. She threw her head back to receive it, to let it penetrate her with knowledge. But it passed. She waited a moment, then got on her bicycle and coasted down the hill. And there was the stone gateway with its urns and the high tunnel of elms beyond.

Chapter II

FRANÇOISE, taking off her overshoes and raincoat in the hall, looked at André through the open doors of the library. He sat before an iron stove that had been set into the seventeenth-century fireplace. There was a rug over his knees because the fire had not yet been lighted and beside him a reading lamp cast a glow on his beautiful, thin hands. He had been writing and sheets of paper were scattered on the table, but now he had heard her, knew that she was outside, and sat with an expectant, patient look.

For a moment she didn't go in but lingered in the hall, hanging her raincoat over the back of a chair, fussing with the packages in her basket, looking at André through the door.

If he were only very large and robust, she thought. If he were only not so finely made and so small, not sick so much of the time. Since the defeat she had grown so sensitive about him that she was constantly seeing him in all the various cruel and careless ways in which others would see him: —

*So that's the fellow who went to all those con-
ferences and made so many speeches before the
League. He actually seems to have thought that
peace and understanding, those spiritual states, could
be achieved by sordid political means!*

*He wasn't very realistic, was he? He'd better have
thought more of our security and tried to make the
proper alliances for us.*

*He'd better have cleaned up things at home, in-
stead of letting the reds run the country.*

*Called himself a Socialist, did he? Well, you'll
have to explain that one to me all over again. When
the poor devils of Spaniards were fighting the bloody
Fascists he didn't talk about helping them, at least
not loud enough for anyone to hear.*

*He's a compromiser and an appeaser, that's all.
And what did that get him? What did it get any
of us? He's a failure. A public and irrevocable failure, and so he is my scapegoat. Everyone's scapegoat. He is his failure and mine.*

*Then all of them together: And my God! What
a funny little fellow he is!*

She went in quickly, holding her packages, and
leaned over to kiss him on both cheeks. "Congratu-
late me. The billiard-cloth idea was a great success.
Just look at the shoes."

"Good. Did you hear any news in town?" he
asked anxiously.

"No news. No one has been arrested. No one has confessed. What are you doing?"

He spread his hands over the paper and looked down at the sheets. "I may have been wasting my time. I have been making out a full report. But Edouard will feel better about it if he thinks I have gone to the maximum of trouble. I ran out of paper though."

"I got a notebook for you. It was all they had left. And I have the laudanum too."

"Good. I'll save it for the worst neuralgia of all."

She leaned over to see what he had written. He had covered pages with his precise writing and she saw he had taken as much pains as when in the old days he was preparing one of his cases for the Cour d'Assises.

"Let me change your shoes now," she said. "You are still wearing those frightful slippers. Your toes are out." She kneeled down and exchanged them for the pair she had brought. "A very funny thing," she said. "Bouchaix was drunk."

"Really?" he said absently. "Where did he get it?"

"I don't know. But I told him he had better be careful. He was half-frightened and half-boasting of what he'd like to do. I saw old Jeanne, too."

"What did she say? How does she take it?"

"Exactly as you would expect. She said I hadn't

brought enough milk and that you must do something."

"Ah." He smiled faintly but he was only half listening, his mind on something else. Pressing his fingers into the corners of his eyes he gave an audible sigh. In the anxious watch she kept on him, his gestures too had come to have an exaggerated poignance scarcely noticed in the time of his success, such as a habit of running his finger along his chin, the very careful way he handled his papers — as though he not only took satisfaction in the work but felt also an innocent vanity in the beauty of the hands — his laugh, high-pitched, eager and with a faint suggestion of a whinny: these things of no importance yet so intimately himself he did now in a prison of despair. Each familiar gesture made its evocation of the past and told her that he was a beaten man. She almost wished he could stop being entirely himself and become colorless and transparent, without any individual character or eccentricity. She wished he could stop being lovable.

"Are you very worried?" she asked.

"Yes. I'm worried. Several things worry me particularly."

"What are they?"

"Well, first of all, I'm afraid I was a little hasty in sending for Edouard."

"Why do you think that?"

"Because it's not certain at all that he'll help us. We don't know Edouard very well now."

"He can't have changed so much."

"We parted on the worst possible terms and it's been a year since we've seen him. Besides, it's he who has a certain power now. Our positions have changed."

"But he answered your telegram at once. Would he have done that if he hadn't intended to do the best he could?"

"I don't know. I sent for Edouard almost through habit. He might have answered through habit."

"Well," she said, trying to speak lightly, "then perhaps he'll do what you ask through habit."

As André didn't answer she said, "After all, it's a terrible thing. He'll see that it must be stopped as much as we see it."

"Let us hope so."

This uncertainty about Edouard surprised her. It had seemed perfectly natural at the time to send for him. It was the first thing they had both thought of, not because Edouard was now powerful but because whenever there was a question of handling people they were accustomed to let Edouard do it. André, with all his concern with humanity, had little skill with human beings. He was at bottom — Françoise was convinced of it — a little afraid of them. He was always trying to understand them. He turned his power of reason upon them and examined them, their origins and their environment, he deduced their probable thoughts and motives and resultant conduct. But when he had completely clarified them they would often do something unpredictable, something obscure and wanton, something illogical.

Edouard was not afraid of them. He never tried to understand beyond the point where it was necessary for him to handle them. He accepted cheerfully everything they did, the worse the better, the more illogical the better, because the greater their flexibility the easier it was for him. He said once to André, "Really, old fellow, when I hear you explaining someone to me I wonder if you really consider yourself as a fellow human being."

And André was speechless with astonishment. But still he looked on Edouard's powers with a little awe, as one would look on a minor magician, one who could make a mango tree grow from a seed, or momentarily defy a natural law by swallowing fire or edged swords.

Before she could ask him more about Edouard he looked toward the door and said, "Where is Maurice?"

"I don't know. Isn't he here?"

"No. He's not been here all afternoon. I've rung once or twice and only Colette has come."

"Isn't he at the barn? Is Tulipe worse?"

"Yves says Tulipe is better. Maurice is simply not about."

"Then he's with Blaise. They've gone to Douarnenez."

She rang the bell. It tinkled emptily and in a moment Colette came clumping down the hall. She put her head in the door. "Mademoiselle rang?"

"Yes. Where is Maurice?"

"Mademoiselle, he hasn't come back yet."

"Where has he gone?"

"I don't know, Mademoiselle."

"We want the fire built now. We must get the room warm before Monsieur l'Ambassadeur comes. You'd better build a fire later in his room too."

"Yes, Mademoiselle." She went off.

Seeing André's worried face Françoise said, "I don't doubt they've both gone to Douarnenez. Blaise will bring back fish for tonight. If he doesn't there will be no dinner."

"It seems to me," André said, "that we might manage to get fish without Blaise spending all his days at the port."

"Blaise likes to be with the fishermen," Françoise said. "You know when he had his yawl he used to be there all the time. He knows them all. And I suppose to be around a port and see boats leaving, even fishing boats, makes him feel a little less a prisoner."

Just then they heard Blaise's voice outside. He came along the hall and looked in the door. "Good evening, everyone."

He was not in the least like his father. He had a big bony nose, full lips, prominent, strong-looking blue eyes. There was bright color in his cheeks, he wore high boots and a reefer coat.

"Blaise," said André, "where have you been?"

"Look!" He held up three dangling herring and two soles. "I helped Pierre with his boat. The oil is miserable stuff and the engine fouls up. We took off the cylinder heads and cleaned out the carbon. He gave me these."

He dangled the fish toward them. The sight of the fish, the strong briny smell, distracted them an instant from what he was saying. The sight or smell of food stirred little flickers in them all, as though on some long way they had to go they had taken a first step.

"And then I missed the damned bus," he said, "and had to get a lift back in a cart. Françoise had the bicycle."

"Was Maurice with you?" André asked.

"No. Why should he be?"

"Take the fish to Colette, will you?" Françoise said. "She'd better clean them right away. Tell her not to mind about the fire till later."

"And come back," André said. "I want to talk to you."

Blaise looked questioningly at Françoise as he used to when he was a child and a scolding was coming. Then he assumed his exaggerated look of innocence, his what's-this-all-about-I-haven't-done-a-thing look. He went off with his fish.

André got up and stood before the stove, his hands behind his back.

"You are worried about Blaise?" Françoise said.

"Yes, I am."

"But why? Has he done anything?"

He took a few steps before the stove. Then he said, "What do you think about Blaise?"

"I don't quite know what you mean."

"He's changed a great deal, hasn't he?"

"For the good, I should say."

"For the good? That may be. I want to hear why you think so."

"But you know what I mean. Must we go over it all?"

She took a chair on the opposite side of the stove and reached down into her knitting basket. She picked up the sock she was making and began to work on it. It went very slowly because it was being made of odds and ends of wool as she was able to find them.

"I want to hear," André insisted, "I want to hear what you think about Blaise. What does he believe in now?"

"Well," she said, "first he believed in nothing, because everything he saw disgusted him. At sixteen one can be very furiously disgusted." She smiled faintly but André did not smile. He waited anxiously for her to go on. "Then he believed in everything: revolution, the New Europe, youth, regeneration. That was a disillusion too — " She hesitated to say more because it was obvious that what Blaise had believed at this time had been a simple, violent, and concrete reflection of what André believed. And nothing is more painful than to realize what forms our beliefs can take in those we influence.

"And what does he believe now?" André insisted.

"Now? He is in a changing state. He works, that's all. He works all day."

"Well," André said, "he cleans out fishing boats and he works about the farm. But who does he talk to, what ideas does he get?"

"I don't know. He works with men who are working. Perhaps they don't talk much or think much. Work of that sort is a safe way to fill in a gap between beliefs. Let's not complain of that."

It struck her that not for over a year had either she or André shown any interest in what the other believed. At one time their disagreements had been an agony. Now they felt themselves condemned, and their beliefs had no substance. But Blaise — that was different.

They heard just then a whistle in the hall. Blaise used to whistle but for a long time he had moved around in sullen silence. The only sounds of the house were footsteps, or low voices. Now he whistled, and this whistle made a shrill, serious little piping. It was someone who discoursed to himself about a thing that was sharp and new in his mind.

"It's Blaise," she murmured.

André was also listening and he also heard something in Blaise's whistle. His face grew more grave.

Blaise came in and stretched himself out in a chair, his long legs straight before him.

"What's up?" he said. "What did you want to say?"

Now André hesitated to begin. He took a few steps back and forth and ran his finger along his chin. Finally he said, "Maurice wasn't with you this afternoon?"

Blaise appeared surprised. "No, I've already said that. I think he's with the vet. He went to get him in one of the carts and he must have driven him back."

"Surely Yves can look after the cow. He's our farmer; that's his affair."

"Yves is no good. Personally, I think he's going

crazy. You ought to hear him talk! And these last three days he's been absolutely ga-ga."

"Really, Blaise!" Françoise exclaimed. "The man's brother has been taken as a hostage. He will be shot if something doesn't happen to save him."

"Well, you know as well as I do," Blaise said, "that Yves has been queer a long time. No one but us, or rather, no one but Father, would have kept him. But what's all this about old Maurice anyway?"

"I'm only surprised that you seem to spend so much time with him lately. What you suddenly find to talk about with Maurice I can't imagine."

"We don't talk much," Blaise said. He shot an amused look at Françoise. "He talks to *me* every now and then. He likes to explain about 'those gentlemen' who ruined the country. You know, the politicians, the bankers, the big industrialists! But mostly we don't talk, we work. There's a lot to be done here, though you both seem to forget it every now and then."

"I don't like to interfere with your associates," André said. "I feel you are old enough to pick them for yourself. You like boats. You like to be with fishermen and that's natural. I'm sure they're decent fellows. In any case, I can't inquire into all of them. But when it comes to Maurice I feel it's my duty to tell you something."

Françoise, watching Blaise, saw with a slight shock

that while he took care not to move a muscle, not to change the direction of his eyes, not to lose his smile, his whole body stiffened visibly.

"The truth is," André said quietly, "that Maurice is a murderer."

In spite of the second's forewarning Blaise grew pale and his eyes wavered. Françoise was so disturbed that she looked away from him as though that would make André, too, look away. And André did look away. She did not even realize what he had said. In her instinct to avert what seemed to be like a collision she said, "Why, that's impossible." After she had said it she realized that truly she did not believe it and she repeated with conviction, "It's not possible."

Blaise gave a low whistle to express incredulity.

"It's true, nevertheless," André said. But he spoke so reluctantly that it seemed he would add nothing to it.

"He's been with us since before I was born," Françoise said.

André nodded. With his hands behind his back he began to pace up and down. Finally he said, "You both know why I have always felt myself under such deep obligation to Maurice and why I have put up with him in spite of his faults, which are very tiresome at times. But I'll remind you that in 1914 he saved my life, that in carrying me under fire to a field dressing station he himself was so badly hurt that he lost a foot. All this you know. One does not forget a thing like that. I've never forgotten it."

He stopped. He bit his under lip and ran his finger along his bearded chin.

"But what I've never told you," he said, "is that when the last war began Maurice was awaiting deportation. He had been convicted of murdering a man."

Blaise gave another long whistle and shook his head. He was beginning to smile, as though he wished them to see he thought this was absurd.

André said, "Maurice was very young, only eighteen, and he had just been brought up to Paris by a Madame Chantemesse to serve as *valet de chambre*. He was a rough, ignorant boy. Some older servant in the household, the butler I think it was, undertook his initiation into the life of what was evidently a rich household very slackly run. There was considerable opportunity for graft and plenty of occasion for loose morals. You know what sordid underworlds we sometimes have in our own houses. There is no use telling it in detail but the petty tyranny and bullying, the cheating and viciousness that went on below stairs, finally culminated in a genuine attempt at corruption on the part of this butler. Maurice, refusing to conform, was accused of stealing something. He became enraged with the wrong done him, got a knife from the kitchen, and chopped the man up as though he'd been wood."

André stopped but no one spoke. He waited a moment, then went on, "Well, that's the story. He was let out with many others when Paris was threatened. He fought bravely. After the war I got a pardon for him. The crime, after all, had a few extenuating circumstances. There was his youth, and the proven attempt at corruption. At any rate, I took him into my service. I meant it as a temporary thing until someone else could be found to employ him, but he managed somehow to stay on. Your mother became attached to him. He was very devoted to her, especially when she was so ill. I never regretted having taken him."

Blaise gave a sudden laugh. Françoise found his laugh shocking. He had gone too far in recovering from the fear she had seen in him. With his hands in his pockets he was looking brightly and impudently at André. "What a story!" he exclaimed. "It's got everything — crime, heroic rescue, pardon — "

"Blaise!" Françoise exclaimed. "That's not in very good taste, is it?"

Blaise ignored her. "It's a classic," he said, "even to the ending. Now he's the old family retainer; insults the guests, chases the maids, and is the only butler in Finistère who knows how to make an American cocktail. The cocktail is the modern touch

— brings it up to date and keeps it from being too much of the crucifix-of-my-mother genre."

André had listened with a look more of anxiety than annoyance. When Blaise finished he said, "I am thinking now of discharging him."

"Oh!" Françoise exclaimed, and she added incredulously, "You wouldn't do that!"

"But it's equivalent to committing suicide!" Blaise cried, his impudence fading a little. "We can't get along without him, as he'll be the first to point out. Besides," he added more earnestly, "he just won't go."

"Surely," Françoise said, "you won't discharge him because he killed a man twenty-seven years ago, when you've kept him in your service ever since."

"The qualities he had twenty-seven years ago can't have altogether died, and the truth is — " André spoke as though it humiliated him to say this — "the truth is, they seem now to be a danger to us."

"What made you think of them now? Why did you think they'd be a danger?" Françoise asked.

André said, "Because of one or two curious things that have happened. I'll tell you what they are, but first I want to say that I hope you find them of no consequence. Don't imagine I'd get rid of Maurice willingly. There is only one thing that would make me discharge him and that would be a conviction that he is a menace to one of you."

"To one of us!" Françoise cried.

"In these days," André said, "we infect each other sometimes without meaning to."

He looked at her pleadingly. She saw that he still avoided looking at Blaise.

"You know I don't sleep well," he continued. "Three nights ago I got up and came down here for a book. It was after three o'clock. I heard someone walking along the terrace, then I heard him open the door into the back hall. I had my torch and went to see who it was. It was Maurice. He was muddy and disheveled. He was stupefied, apparently, at seeing me. He turned back, snatched open the door, and looked out again as though someone else were out there who shouldn't be seen. Then he closed it carefully behind him."

Blaise said quickly, "He'd been out to see Tulipe."

"Tulipe was not yet sick. Besides, that's not the explanation he gave me. He said he'd been to see a girl."

"Surely," Blaise said, "he has a right to some privacy."

"It's not a question of his privacy. It's a question of the safety of all of us. Suppose he had been picked up by a patrol. Suppose he were even seen by someone else who chose to report it. Would the story of the girl go down very well? Would it even be listened to?"

"Well, he wasn't picked up, and apparently no one saw him."

"That isn't enough, and you don't seem to grasp the significance of what I'm saying. The night a German is murdered, a short distance from where we live, Maurice, whom I know to be a murderer, is out on some mysterious errand."

It seemed to Françoise that Blaise had made a rapid recovery, but he was still not himself. It is seldom possible entirely to recover naturalness under shock, but one can often find some substitute. He was now much too bright, too defensive and too garrulous.

He said, "There may have been any number of people out that night, and if Maurice's murderous instincts were going to reappear, isn't it reasonable to suppose they'd have come out long ago? The truth is Maurice has no hatred of Germans. He doesn't exactly chum around with them but you know that he lays all the blame for our troubles elsewhere. Besides, I happen to know he *has* got a girl. He does go out to see her."

"Who is she?"

"Really I haven't asked him. Take my word for it though. He does speak of her every now and then."

"It's not that girl at the Relais Fleuri?"

"No, no," Blaise repeated with vehemence. "That girl is fourteen. A horrid little sickly thing. Do you think a man like Maurice would go after her?"

All this about the girl sounded false and silly.
Blaise seemed to realize it. He watched André, then
said suspiciously, "What made you think of her?"

"I believe the German had been there that night."

"Don't they all deny it?"

"They would anyway. But there was no other place
on that road where he could have been."

Blaise said, "For a lawyer you must know the case
against Maurice is thin."

André took a few more steps without speaking. It
was clear he disliked what he had to say because it
was in the nature of a betrayal of Maurice. But it
seemed that he shrank even more from something in
Blaise's reception of it.

"There's another thing," he said. "We had a large
fat hare for dinner about two weeks ago."

Françoise smiled at the unexpected triviality of
this, but she glanced at Blaise, and saw he was not
smiling. "Well, so we did," she said.

"Where did it come from? All those we had in
the hutch have died, been eaten, or given away."

"We caught it in a trap," Blaise said quickly.
"Maurice and I. I can show you the trap," he added.

"Marie cooked it, didn't she?"

"Yes, or Colette. I think Marie was sick that
day."

"But Maurice skinned and cleaned it for her."

"I think so. Colette doesn't like that part."

"The hare, however, wasn't thoroughly cleaned. I got a piece of shot in one mouthful. Now I want to ask you, Blaise — " he turned directly toward him — "what I should have asked you at the time: what has become of the shotgun?"

Blaise said nothing. He stared at André with his hands in his pockets, not moving.

"The retention of arms," André said, "is punishable with death. I spoke to Maurice long ago about the shotgun. I know how he liked to hunt several days every year, though after his dog died I thought he had given it up and perhaps sold the gun. But I asked him about it. He told me it had been stolen some time ago."

Blaise said, "Well, the truth is, he hid it. You can't imagine him giving up a piece of property, can you, for all that he likes to fancy himself a Communist? As for the hare, the traps were no good. We hadn't caught a thing except a few weasels. But we'd seen this fellow, a big fat one, loping around in the cabbage bed as bold as you please. I knew Maurice had a gun. He had taken it out one day to oil and clean, so I got it from him and shot the hare."

"You shot it."

"Maurice didn't want to. He said it was dangerous. I think Maurice is afraid of that gun. Actually I can't remember his ever having shot anything with it."

André stood rubbing his forefinger against his chin. He wanted to be reassured. Françoise saw him make an effort to be more natural, to speak without too much strain and emphasis.

He said, "Where is the gun now?"

"Well, Maurice said we'd better bury it again. He said he didn't dare turn it in at this late date, though we thought of that. So at this moment it's buried again."

"Is this true?"

"Yes, it's true."

It sounded true. It had been said simply and with conviction.

Then Blaise added, "You were right to trust Maurice. I shouldn't have laughed at that, because I know him too. He's more than trustworthy: he's got good sense. Do you think he'd be such a fool as to take a gun out and shoot a German for no special reason, take a risk like that for so little?"

André nodded. He seemed relieved by the change in Blaise's manner as much as by what he said.

Blaise said more earnestly, "You can't believe he'd do a thing like that, a senseless thing, and let others take the punishment? There are things that you instinctively know don't fit a man. Murder, perhaps. When you told us that story I *could* believe it, though it did strike me as — well, as too complete, as though if someone had to fit a murder to Maurice it would be just that murder. Still, I believed it. But I'll bet you can't believe the other."

André sat down and clasped his hands loosely. His last uncertainty seemed to be showing in his hands.

Blaise said his final word. "If you send him away now it will seem that we distrust him, and then other people will."

Blaise had said at last what André wanted to hear. And moreover he had become what André wanted him to be.

"I won't do anything at this time," André said, and his voice was firm and relieved.

He took up his papers again and Blaise went over to the table and began to turn the pages of an old *Illustration*.

A moment later Françoise, glancing up, saw a smile on his half-turned face, a smile so obviously self-congratulatory and slightly derisive that she could hardly believe it. Hearing Maurice's scraping step in the hall André looked up and he also saw it.

Maurice appeared in the doorway. Because he had hurried he was still putting on his coat, and looking solemnly from one to the other he caught the lapels, straightened them on his shoulders, and deliberately buttoned his striped waistcoat. He was giving a picture of the man who has been summoned from something important because of a whim, a caprice.

"Monsieur le Ministre rang?" he said.

"Yes," André said drily, "some time ago. I want a fire built here. And I want you to drive into town in time to meet the eight-o'clock train from Paris. Have you your permit?"

"Yes, Monsieur le Ministre."

Maurice waited a second to see if there were more orders. He did not look at Blaise and Blaise began to turn over the pages of *L'Illustration* again. Assured that there were no more orders, Maurice left, going slowly down the hall.

André sat down and picked up the notebook Françoise had brought. "I'd like to do a little more work," he said, "before Edouard gets here."

"We'll leave you," Blaise said. He got up and starting toward the door stopped. "I suppose," he said, "there is no question but that Edouard can arrange everything?" His whole tone had changed again. He spoke in a childish, cajoling way.

André said, "You mean about the hostages?"

"Yes."

"I think he can have the executions held off again for a time."

"But only for a time of course."

"In the end," André said deliberately, "the criminal must be caught."

Blaise hesitated. Then suddenly remembering Françoise he gave her a flicker of a smile, quite different from the one she had seen a moment ago. It was consciously, limpidly, conspiratorial. It said that he had just played an innocent joke on the old man, and that she knew it — a ritual smile, not entirely honest. He saluted her impudently with one finger and went out.

She heard him whistling down the hall. André, who had begun to write in the new notebook, said without looking up, "You see why I am concerned about Blaise."

"Yes," she said hesitatingly, "but I wouldn't be too concerned about him. It's obvious that he is rebellious. That is only to say that he is still alive. Some of his rebellion he takes out on us. It's much safer that way."

"Yes," André said, "but he is like a heap of inflammable material waiting for a spark."

"Maurice is hardly the spark!" she exclaimed.

As he went on writing she said, "How very strange about Maurice! I could hardly believe it. And yet, as Blaise says, it does fit somehow. It's a clue to things in him that I've wondered about."

But André didn't want to talk any more about Maurice. He nodded but went on writing. Françoise knitted in silence.

The thing which worried them both and which they did not dare speak of was that Blaise had been whistling now for three days.

Chapter III

SHE WENT to the kitchen to give orders for dinner.
Colette, the housemaid, cooked for them while Marie,
Yves's wife, lay in bed with a wasting grippe. At
present she reflected the horror that had stricken the
town and the whole countryside. All day she had
been running out to talk to Yves and Marie, and she
had spent a long time fixing a little bundle of food for
Yves to take to his brother at the prison camp. At
noon she rushed in to say, "They have all been shot.
Someone passing has just told me." It was hard to
convince her that it was not true and she became quite
incapable of getting the lunch. When Maurice scolded
her she burst into tears. He retorted by singing rau-
cously the Chevalier song of the man who, having
been born on a rainy day while his mother peeled
onions, had wept all his life. Finally he slapped her
and she rushed in to tell Françoise about that. Françoise had a difficult time making peace.

Now Colette had to get dinner for Edouard and
Françoise was determined it should be a good one,
to put him in the best humor possible.

As she explained what must be done, Colette looked apprehensively toward the door, as though the terrible and dreaded Monsieur Schneider might be coming in. "He will be furious," she said, not listening to the instructions, "because Marie isn't here to cook for him. I said to her, 'If you have any feeling for your brother-in-law you'll get up and manage it somehow.'"

She stood by the table on which lay the fish, some herbs, a few tiny mussels, some mushrooms, a tablespoonful of butter, and a cup of wine. She looked at them hopelessly and added, "Is it true that Monsieur Schneider can save everyone if he wants to?"

Françoise knew that this fish, these mussels and mushrooms and wine would never come together in a suitable form. She said irritably, "Of course he can save them. But you must remember to call him Monsieur l'Ambassadeur and you must be certain not to burn the fish. As for the sauce, I'll attend to that myself."

"I'll do my best," Colette said. She was getting ready to weep again.

Gluttony, thought Françoise, looking at the fish, is one of Edouard's weaknesses. It is actually one of the seven deadly sins. It ranks in the estimation of the Church with lust, with envy, and with sloth. But the necessity for order, for decency and harmony, in the running of a house is one of my weaknesses.

I don't believe it has ever been classified as more than a weakness. Martha got off lightly after all. Say it is rather a matter of taste. I wonder then why I haven't given it up, if only from sheer lassitude. I've given up so many things. Sin is a big word. I don't know whether I have many sins to give up. But I imagine a sin is much more easily given up than a taste.

She went upstairs to have a bath and rest. She carried a little jug of hot water with her, which was all she dared take to wash in since Edouard must be sure to have enough on his arrival. She washed bit by bit in the cold room. Extreme personal cleanliness was another of her tastes, and every day she practised expedients and economies to have enough warm water and soap for bathing. Now she put on a bathrobe and lay down. She hoped to be able to sleep. For the evening before her it was not only necessary that Edouard's water be hot, the house warm, the dinner good, but that she be as refreshed and full of strength as possible. It was necessary that all of them appear as much like their old selves as possible. Edouard would deeply resent any change in them that suggested calamity, martyrdom or reproach.

The carriage crunched along the drive outside. That was Maurice, going to the train, but it would be an hour before they came back. That ought to be time enough for a rest.

But she couldn't relax, she couldn't sleep. She went

on thinking of the fish sauce, imagining the in-
gredients one by one as they met and blended. She
thought of the people in town, of Madame Simmonet,
of Jeanne and Monsieur Costard, of Bouchaix, with
his unaccountable drunkenness and fear. She thought
of these things with the new undercurrent of uneasi-
ness that was growing in her till finally she exclaimed
aloud, "How extraordinary that we should have a
murderer in the house!"

At first it had seemed a story André had decided to
tell in order to astonish them or to prove a point.
Then all at once, as Blaise said, it fitted Maurice exactly.

She had known Maurice all her life. Ever since she
could remember he had been a part of the house.
Everything that was coarse, unhappy, and cruel in
him she had accounted for and explained in other
ways, such as that he had been an ill-treated and
neglected little peasant, that his qualities were related
to good ones, to loyalty, courage, and a capacity for
taking life seriously and depending only on himself.
She had lacked the real clue.

André, however, had the clue, and the more she
thought of it the more remarkable it seemed that,
having it, he had been willing to keep Maurice.

When André was very young his passionate, youth-
ful concern with the problem of human progress crystallized into a faith natural to the age he lived in. In the

thirteenth century his faith would have taken another form; in his time it became a belief in the principles of International Socialism. He did not think these principles would be easily acceptable. He knew what it meant to struggle with acute nationalism — was not he himself deeply a Frenchman? — he knew the terrific problems that face highly industrialized and organized societies, and he recognized the fatal tendency in each creature to retrograde, which is always neck and neck with his urge toward betterment.

André began by studying law, was admitted to the Paris bar, and after practising for a time became a Socialist candidate for the Chamber. He was never very skillful in using the machinery of politics, perhaps because from the first he distrusted it, knew it was not good enough. He never became a successful parliamentarian, but he did have a political career, with some of its necessary evasions and compromises. He was first elected a Socialist deputy. After the war there were periods when he was out of office, during which he returned to his law, but again he was elected, became Senator, was three times Minister, and many times a delegate to the League.

As he lived more deeply in this political world he began to be discouraged by the repeated failures of Socialism. He saw it either used unscrupulously by clever politicians as a cover for power politics, or

reduced to ridiculous impotence by ineffective ideal-
ists. The failure of the Popular Front was only the
end of a long series of failures and compromises that
began in 1914. Even the rise of Hitler and the mis-
named National Socialism of Germany were no more
disillusioning to him than Communist Russia's abuse
and perversion of Socialist principles to enslave its
people.

The worst was that he himself, as his discourage-
ment grew, had lent himself more and more to these
compromises and had shared responsibility for these
failures. This morning a woman had called out, "Remember the Café Oriental." André, at first puzzled,
had evidently realized almost at once what she meant.
As they drove back to Rusquec he talked to Françoise about this incident. He said the woman had
probably been the girl who sat behind the *caisse* of the
Oriental long ago when it was the rendezvous of the
extreme young Socialists and the Hervéists, as they
were called. All the way home André talked sadly
and nostalgically of those days. He told Françoise
about his first client, a young Syndicalist, a man involved in an incident of a miners' strike in the North.
Then he fell into a sadder silence. The woman had
called him a traitor. What is a traitor but a man whose
faith has weakened? The gradual weakening of his
own faith had been marked by the changes from those
early friends, those early clients, by the political shifts

he had felt obliged to make, even by the accumulation
of some wealth.

But, Françoise thought, he obstinately kept Maurice
with him, because Maurice was a man who had been a
victim of social evils and who remained an uncompro-
mising proletarian, and Maurice was a secret gauge to
the faith that had weakened in him.

But still there was his horror of violence — the
horror in his voice when he said that Maurice had
chopped another man as though he had been wood.
Even as a symbol of the people, even through grati-
tude, Maurice remained a murderer, the man committed to violence.

André's faith in peace, Françoise thought, grew
stronger when his other faiths failed. In 1914 he had
fought even in spite of his parliamentary immunity.
His patriotism had proved stronger then, as it had for
the majority of the Socialist party, though it was also
true that later he had supported the International
Socialist conference of Zimmerwald even while the
armies were locked on the Western Front. That conference failed. And for years André thought of peace
only as an essential part of the goal they must reach.
But as Europe, after a period of hope, began to move
so relentlessly toward disaster, as Socialism degener-
ated into a struggle for power, André believed more
and more that peace was not the goal but the foundation, the essential and neglected foundation, of all

progress. It had been taken as an end finally to be reached, but it was actually the beginning. Without peace all other effort would remain forever hopeless. So at the time of the Spanish War he watched, with despair but without lifting his voice, the death of the Republic. And even the direct threat to France only strengthened his determination, because he was convinced that nothing in France would survive another war — this France, so precious but so underpopulated, so economically lagging, half in the climate of the nineteenth century, and suddenly pathetically incapable of her great rôle as creator of ideas. No, not even hope would be able to survive another war.

So for another reason he kept Maurice. Because a man can hold not only beliefs but instincts that may be at variance with them. And for a long time, faced with the nearly insoluble dilemma of war, he had guessed or obscurely felt that one kind of man is not enough for any effort. In the long slope of human betterment there are bound to come crises so irrational as to seem from extrahuman causes, as say even spots on the sun, where reason and the lucid mind seem often of no avail. In these mysterious tests it might be that a man like himself had no deciding power. That power might lie with a simpler man, one whose more elemental instincts would seize the essentially elemental character of the menace and who, seizing it, would be ready to take any risk.

And over and above all this, and perhaps in the end unexplainably, he simply liked Maurice.

Then suddenly another illumination came to Françoise. André, while he told the story of Maurice's crime, was trying to convince himself of something. But it was not what she had believed at the time. She had felt then that he told it so that she and Blaise would say just what they had said: that it was non-sense to suppose Maurice would commit murder again and in these circumstances, that he was certainly innocent of any connection with the German's death.

Perhaps that was what he wanted to hear. It had appeared that it was. And yet — not quite. There was something else worrying him. What was it? What was it? Her mind groped and suddenly stumbled on the truth.

He was afraid Blaise had done it. Yes, it was actually that. He was afraid that Blaise was the reckless one, the rebellious one, the one who would risk anything, so he told himself and them the old story of Maurice he had kept hidden so long, to reassure himself and to say to them, "See, the true man of violence is some-one else and he alone is really capable of it."

But Blaise had known that story already. He must have known. Or if he did not know exactly that story he knew something else, and something that put the forgotten murder in a different light.

Françoise got up and turned off the light and opened

the window. The mist was still thick but the moon had come up and forms were beginning to show as darkness slowly drained away. She could see the loom of the barn, slightly distorted by mist. It looked like a low, formless barrow, covering generations of ancient dead. Over her head the old weather vane gave a hoarse croak as it swung slightly on its rusty shaft.

She shut the window quickly and turned on the light again. She couldn't lie down. She wandered aimlessly around the room, looking for something it suddenly seemed to her she must find: a key, or something, lost that morning.

What idiocy, she said to herself. Exactly the same reasons hold good for Blaise that he himself gave us for Maurice. He also had no motive, he also would not risk so much, for such a mediocre triumph. He also does not fanatically hate Germans, even now. Or does he? It's hard to tell. He has grown so bitter and secretive about all he does. But then murder, deliberate murder, a shot in the stomach — and an untried boy like Blaise. And there's the other reason against it, the final one. He would never let innocent men suffer for his sake. He knows Yves's brother, he knows young Simmonet, old Peguinot, as well as I do. No, it's all unthinkable.

She caught her hair in both hands and drew it up tightly off her forehead. She stood in the middle of the room trying to remember that thing she was looking for: the key to the chapel. It should be on a ring with other, smaller, keys and a large cardboard tag attached to it. It lay in the top drawer of a chest of drawers. It was clearly marked in her handwriting *Chapelle St. Herbaud*. This morning before going into town to see the Kommandant she had an impulse to go to the chapel for a few moments, but the key wasn't on the ring. Where had she seen it last? It was months since she had been in the chapel. She opened the top drawer of the chest and began to search fretfully under the heaps of underwear, gloves, scarfs, odds and ends. It was not there.

Simon's letter was there, in the top of a glove box. She had wished to go to the chapel in order to spend a few moments in one of the last places she had seen Simon. It was not really the last. They had left the chapel and were sitting on the stone wall outside. There they had said good-by. She touched the letter with her finger. No use to reread it.

I really should throw it away, she thought. One letter. She closed the drawer and dropped on the chaise longue.

Sometimes, she thought, I don't think of Simon for days and days, but now, to take my mind off this dreadful thing, I'll allow myself to think of him. Because he is being wiped out of me. Finally nothing will remain of him. What was it that I thought he meant? It's hard to know now. It's only tiring to remember. Everything has faded.

It must be very fortunate, she thought, to be killed suddenly in the flush and pride of life, killed by a blow that brings an instant ending. But this slow rot! The blood flows thin and the fibers of the brain open like a leaky basket and hold nothing, the bad or the good, the true or the dream. Only a few instincts remain, the poorest and the most simple. For a while they fight back, but only for food, for a little more breath.

Suddenly a relief came to her. She clasped her hands over her head and closed her eyes and dropped into a twilight of drowsing. It was a deep and expectant twilight, like that in a theater before the curtain goes up. It was not cruel and had no terrors. It seemed natural, of the earth and the works of man. How charming, she thought, what a charming place I'm in! What will happen when the streak of gold under the curtain becomes full day?

She was suddenly strong and light. She was walking across the Place Vendôme.

Chapter IV

She was walking across the Place Vendôme and Simon came up behind her. "Wait a moment." They stood together arm in arm under the bronze shaft in the exact center of the matchless order of the city. This place was a precious stone cup, always holding various weathers, opaque or luminous, sparkling sometimes with sun or frost. Today it held warm vapor through which the soft May light touched the severe, lovely buildings, the white-and-gold chair in a window, a painting by Cézanne of a boy in a wide hat, a jar of cold cream. These things and the square itself seemed a tribute to the Roman conqueror on his shaft. The world that enjoyed them was even at this last hour the one he had made. The man who was to destroy it had not yet looked on the Place Vendôme.

Simon, holding her arm, drew a deep breath. "Place Vendôme 29," he murmured. They walked slowly toward the Ritz.

"Don't you ever paint anything else?" she asked him.

There were twenty-eight canvases stacked against

the wall in the Rue Fürstenberg, every one of them the Place Vendôme.

"It's a series," he said. "I'll paint it out finally. Twenty-nine may be the last. Besides, I've decided to become a fashionable portrait painter."

"Have you really! Since when?"

"Since last night. I was looking fixedly at old Lady You-know and I suddenly saw exactly how I intend to paint her. I want to call it 'The Eloquent Skull.' "

"I can see you'll be in great demand."

Inside the Ritz they stopped before the Van Cleef and Arpels showcase.

"Let's decide what I'll buy you when I get all that money. How about the ruby leaf?"

They looked seriously at it.

"It will go with my little gray-green jersey," she said.

"All these fabulous jewels on little jersey dresses," he exclaimed, "and de Beaumont cutting out pictures from seed catalogs to paste on an eighteenth-century screen. It goes with the way we talk about love and life and all the rest of it, in the vocabulary of defective children. Won't just all that — the incredible surplus and the incredible timidity — be the special, private tone of our society? The mysterious, silly something of a combination, that people who write about us a hundred years from now will never be able to catch?"

Olivier gave them a table in the *corridor*, by common consent the best place to sit. He gave it to them because he liked them and because they were decorative and whoever came in would either know them or think he did.

"What will you eat?" Simon said. "Expense no object. How about pigeons and a nice little Pouilly *fumé?*"

"Excellent."

Françoise remembered this haltingly. She thought, It is like recovering, word by word, a language I spoke in childhood and then forgot. Or rather, it is trying to recover the tone, the atmosphere, of a language. The words are the same words. But they created their meaning then partly from what we were, with our special, personal eccentricities, partly from what that time was. Or what we still believed it was. That time was already lost but we didn't know it. We were still able to say, "I am happy. That is, I am content, I am whole, I am living." That was the basis of everything we said, and its limitation as well. Because even when we said — as we sometimes did — "But we may be defeated, enslaved, we may be separated forever," those words were really meaningless to us. The basis of them still seemed to be "But I am happy, that is, I live in a certain time." Knowledge in its only true form is revelation, not words. That's why all we said strikes me now as extraordinarily frivolous. The words were spoken out of their true place in time.

"How is the hospital going?" she had asked him. "What are you doing there now?"

"Nothing much. Since I took that load down to the Alsatians in Périgueux there's been no driving to do. So I go to lectures. Today I went to a lecture on gas poisoning. Not at the American hospital — at the Hôpital Necker."

"What did you learn?"

"I learned that French medicine must be extraordinarily different. I don't mean that I have any idea whether it's more or less effective than ours. But it seems to me to be in a stage where theory is still in one compartment and practice in another. Take the Hôpital Necker for instance. It's positively picturesque. It's got a half-tropical look. You think the patients must all have yellow fever. The theater has dusty seats and the funny, wondering look of a nineteenth-century medical picture."

"Who gave the lecture?"

"Doctor Binet, I think. He was superb, too. He gave such a realistic dramatization of the three types of gas that if twenty years later I see a man begin to clutch at himself, to water at the eyes, to cough in a certain way, I shall say, 'I've seen all this before, old man. You are simply suffering from yperite poisoning.'"

Françoise laughed. "Poor Doctor Binet! How could he know he had you in his audience? But it's very nice of you to do this work, Simon. It really is."

"Is it? Why? To tell the truth, all the time I'm out at our hospital I get bored with all that wash of benevolence we swim around in. It's not that I'd rather be fighting or even that I would actually rather be painting. But it's that I have a feeling of being completely phony, more phony than when I did nothing at all. I feel the way I did when I got a dog once — the dog the best friend of man! I don't like dogs but I succumbed to the idea that to have a dog would make me sound and give me some sort of exemption. I gave the damned thing to Adrian at the end of a month. Now I've told you all about me. What about you?"

"I don't think I'm very effective either at the moment. I take my turn at the station two days a week and I serve warm wine and coffee and sandwiches. Sometimes I have charming conversations with soldiers. Imagine — yesterday a hairdresser from Toulouse and I had a long discussion about the Albigenses and the poetry of Bernard de Ventadour! I don't feel that that sort of thing represents much effort on my part. I also roll bandages and make dressings, and I collect books for soldiers. And I do some secretarial work for my father. And I go to dinners and parties as usual."

He said, "Would you mind taking off your hat?"

She took it off and dropped it on the floor beside

her. She took out a small mirror and gave a touch to the burnished curls, not quite red, which made a halo for her sharp, exquisite face and slightly slanting, intelligent eyes.

"The Angel of Chartres," he said, "dressed by Alix. I envy those soldiers. But you look out of sorts. What's happened?"

"I thought I had an impassive face. Yes, I am out of sorts."

"The ominous news, I suppose. Norway looks pretty bad."

"It's finished. They've lost. They'll be evacuating it shortly."

"Haven't they practically got Narvik?"

"Oh, Narvik. You'll see that's not important."

"Perhaps." He took on the look of a man who knows that it is time to be worried. Then his face lightened. "It may not be so bad. How do we know what they have in mind?"

"I'm afraid we know."

"Oh, come now, Fanny." He called her that to tease her and because he said the name didn't fit her any more than the pictures from the seed catalogs fitted de Beaumont's eighteenth-century screens. "I'm afraid you're often the victim of too much inside information. This business of being brought up on the laps of Cabinet Ministers! Sometimes it's no good knowing what So-and-So said to Such-and-Such as they left the Chamber. That has a way of suddenly not adding up. Something quite simple and logical but entirely unforeseen may happen."

"Yes," she said, "the amateur always likes to think that."

But, she thought, it is possible that I know too much of intrigue, too much of the restricted political world set in the midst of a much larger human one that I scarcely know at all?

She looked out the window at the blue May sky, at the damp garden where the ivy was putting out tender, pale leaves. In another week or so they would be eating outdoors.

The dining room was becoming crowded with people she knew. On the other side of Simon she heard the famous doctor say, "They have a system of youth training that produces the most magnificent physical specimens the world has ever seen."

And the American fashion editor stopped at their table to say, "Have you seen those new little black suits of Schiaparelli? They are really good, very, very good."

And a man looking like an intelligent turtle bowed to her as he passed. "That's Mandel," she said. "One minister on whose lap I never sat."

How pleasant to be lunching with no one but Simon!

"I wish you'd come down to Rusquec again," she

said suddenly. "Could you get away from the hospital?"

His face took on a childish look from sheer eagerness. "Of course I could. For a week end anyway. You mean next week end?"

"The one after. We are going down on the seventeenth for three days. Come the eighteenth, unless something awful happens to prevent it."

"Nothing will."

"I want you to talk to Blaise," she said.

"What's happened to Blaise? If you want me to give him advice it's no good. He despises me."

"He despises almost everybody."

"If you'll forgive my saying so, darling, you with your terrific family solidarity, I think at the moment Blaise is awful."

"So do I. But he's only sixteen. And besides, he's had a great experience."

"No! You mean the German thing?"

"Yes. It's partly that trip he made there just before the war. He stayed with friends of Father. Some of the youngsters went on a walking tour. The truth is, he fell in love with them."

"I don't believe it."

"Oh, I don't mean in a perverse way. But lots of people do fall in love with them, older and presumably wiser than Blaise. You heard that man behind you just now. *He* fell in love with them."

"Oh, that doctor! He's a fake anyway."

"I think he is. What I mean to say is that I'm afraid there can be a very unpleasant preparation for defeat. It consists of the victim falling in love with the victor — before the battle. It's very complicated. When it happens it requires a lot of remarkable coincidences."

"Such as the Aztecs expecting a fair god and along comes a Spaniard with a blond beard?"

"Exactly. Take Blaise for instance. Remember he's been brought up in this same political milieu that I have. He's seen and heard a great deal too much for his age, too much of the government, the press, and society. He's seen the corruption of the classical order, if you want to call it that, before he was old enough to know its true spirit and architecture. And because he's really an idealistic boy, on the pattern of Father, he has been horribly disillusioned. And can you wonder? Haven't we spent the last twenty years apologizing for our victories and boasting of our decadence? There hasn't been much health here either, and that includes literal, physical health. That's where men like the doctor come in. And there's nothing more to join, nothing obvious to be a part of. Boys want that, as you know."

"But surely he has also heard enough unpleasant truths about *them*?"

"He has. But we've acquired a sort of tolerance, in the medical sense. Then, the Germans have posed as being the true victims. Those people invented self-pity."

"Surely the Jews invented it."

"I don't think the Jews ever pitied themselves more than the circumstances warranted. When they were reduced to slavery they hung up their harps on the willow trees and wept. You couldn't expect them to sing hymns of joy. Now they are being hounded from country to country and I'd not be surprised if they are sorry for themselves again. They have a deep sense of the tragedy of human destiny but they never invented heroes. That shows their self-pity was at least fierce and resistant."

"What about the Greeks?"

"Would you really say they invented heroes? They invented some heroic men. But even their demigods were human. Try comparing Achilles and Siegfried. But the Germans have never been enslaved. They have never been hounded from country to country. They simply pity themselves whenever they do not get the best there is, whenever they don't get *all* there is, the great and the simple. They pity themselves when they lose a war or a colony, and they pity themselves when the boy who polishes their boots doesn't love them, and the family across the street does not invite them to the party. They pity themselves tenderly and heroically."

"I hope you've said all this to Blaise."

"Oh, I have, but he thinks it is pure prejudice. He is deceived by their size, their air of strength. I'm convinced that if they looked weak their self-pity would turn his stomach. Besides, Blaise is in the exact state now to succumb to the romantic. The romantic is another German invention. The romantic is no more than disgust for this same classical order. And it's related closely to self-pity, too. Surely you remember the terrific impact of the German romantic after the Napoleonic wars? Byron, Chateaubriand — all of those swallowed him without a struggle. Romanticism isn't really new. It has erupted out of Germany before. But now it has another advantage: it represents discipline and a new national order — or at least they insist that it does. Why, it's even become something to join. You join it as definitely as you do Masonry or the Mohammedan faith or the Boy Scouts."

"But my darling Fanny," he protested, "Blaise is too clever to fall for it, at least for any length of time. In the end all German ideas are tolerable only when they are set to music. He is sure to get over it."

"Yes, but it's now I'm worried about. We are engaged in fighting them. Don't forget that. Every one of us is important to the struggle."

"Of course," he admitted, "but there must be many people you know — For instance — well, all sorts of people who would have more influence than I."

He grew slightly red and she knew it had been on the tip of his tongue to suggest her father. But he had remembered out of his dim knowledge of politics that André was known as a "pacifist."

Suddenly she wanted to talk to Simon about André, too. She wanted to tell him that she saw in him the disorder of a heresy infinitely graver than Blaise's, infinitely more tragic. The real trouble, she wanted to say, isn't Blaise but André. But it was too soon to talk of this.

She and Simon had talked a great deal of themselves and their problems, but only to a point. They would always stop short and think, No — later; this will come later. They had known each other four weeks, and after the first shock of discovery and pleasure they moved toward each other with caution, partly because they were a little afraid of understanding each other fully and partly because they wanted to enjoy the special quality of what they felt was unique and not retraceable.

Simon had his elbows on the table and was looking at her intently. "Forgive me for being no good about Blaise," he said, "but it's because I haven't enough convictions of that sort of my own. Except for painting and a few general conceptions I absorbed without knowing how, I am nil. What I love about you is that you have such authority. And besides, you are intricate and even cluttered with the debris of the fabulous and commanding order. I know you're in many ways a sweet and simple girl, but you're also the European. And I love you partly for that."

"The Western European," she said. She spoke thoughtfully because it was the first time he had said he loved her, and he had said it lightly, in the midst of something else.

"But the European part," he said, "is the lesser part of loving you because actually I distrust this European world, even the Western, the classical part. I distrust it more than I love it. I'm certain that it's spring has dried up."

"You little outlanders have been believing that for a long time."

"Perhaps for us outlanders it can only flow for just so long. And perhaps I know if I loved it too much, I'd simply never grow up. What I learn here, beyond a certain point, becomes only fairy gold — to me, dry leaves. I can't go on painting the Place Vendôme forever."

Françoise covered her dismay with a teasing voice. "Then you'll get over me. And I'll get over you. Because I equally distrust your order. Only it isn't an order, is it? It's just a world. Lots of us, you know, are as fascinated by you as you are by us. I'm not. I hate cocktails, the hot jazz, things in series, the advertisement. And as for golf courses — I consider

them a degradation of landscape. I like our films better than yours — " She stopped, knowing that in
spite of herself her voice showed hurt and anxiety.
She took a swallow of wine and said, "If I love you
it's only because you're not part of an order. You
haven't got one to be part of. You make me think of
an attractive, amenable savage who has learned every
form of civilized life, in some ways even better than
the ones who taught him, but who when he is at
home worships a tree or a mountain. If I love you,
Simon, it's because you're an accomplished innocent.
You know what we mean by an innocent?"

"You mean a simpleton," he said.

They both laughed a little. And then they looked
at each other closely and their faces grew graver
again.

"I do love you, Françoise," he said, "but I don't
know yet whether it is fantasy or truth."

Françoise thought, It was between the two.

In the four weeks we knew each other we made
an imaginary world for ourselves, because it was the
only one we could meet in. It was the kind of world
two precocious children would make. In that world
everything is decided by them, the décor, the image
each is to have, the events that are to occur. They
decide on the rules. You must be beautiful and I must
be brave and this must be our house and this a dark

forest and this and this must happen. Everything is by consent.

But at this moment Simon and I saw further. We saw that change was implicit in the agreement. We accepted the magical half dimension we had made and we agreed that it was possible to go beyond it, to pass finally into a real world, where we would suffer with real suffering and be happy with full happiness.

We said, "This is only a short love but if we have courage we can make it a long love."

We were mistaken. We never made it last beyond this first shimmering evanescence. It was even more fragile than we dreamed. It was a *tour de force*, a nothing. It did not survive the first impact from outside, much less the destruction of the whole world.

A man stopped at their table and kissed Françoise's hand lingeringly on the wrist. She murmured his name to Simon.

"My dear Françoise," he said, "I was just saying things can't be going too badly because the mistress of one of the Ministers is still in town." He glanced significantly behind him. Neither Françoise nor Simon followed his glance. He leaned toward her and said roguishly, "And I see Edouard lunching with her *en tête-à-tête*. It's strange not to see him at your table."

After he had gone on she saw Simon's face darken.

This was the first time a mention of Edouard had seemed to affect him. Simon had known him for some time, much longer than he had known her, though as he and Edouard disliked each other they seldom met. Still, they had spoken of him before and he must have heard a lot of talk about Edouard and herself. People were always idly speculating as to why they had never married and whether they had ever been lovers. This was bound to have hurt Simon but he had never mentioned it, never given a sign. Why was he disturbed now?

Suddenly she knew that it was because he had just said he loved her and she had said she loved him. That meant that already their feet had taken the last step in the fairy tale and the first step toward the reality. They were both half-frightened.

"What an awful man," she said, looking at her wrist that had been kissed. "I must say I think sometimes that Father overestimates the value of the human race."

Simon was silent. He picked up his glass and looked into it, then he said bluntly, "I suppose you're very fond of Edouard."

"Edouard," she said, trying to be reasonable, "is forty-five years old. He is twenty years older than I. He has been a sort of uncle to me for longer than I can remember."

"Uncle!" he exclaimed. Then she saw him make an

effort to be reasonable too. He said, "Well, I'll remember the rôles uncles usually play. Tell me how he came to be your uncle."

"Don't you know Edouard's story? He was once Father's secretary. It was shortly after he came out of law school."

"Edouard a lawyer?"

"Certainly. But he was terribly poor. He had what you call worked his way. At the *lycée,* for instance, he took charge of the younger boarders to pay for his own schooling. And do you know what the standard fee for a young lawyer was at that time? Thirty francs for Paris, imagine that."

"Well, he's rich now. How did he manage it?"

"That's not only Edouard's story but the story of lots of other people. I can tell you briefly, however, that it consisted mostly of Edouard's ability to snatch at every opportunity a little more quickly, a little more ably, than the man next to him."

"He owns newspapers, doesn't he?"

"Yes. Several. When Father was Undersecretary of State to the President of the Council he was in charge of press relations. Then Edouard, too, came in contact with the press and he discovered it was made for him and he for it. He made a lot of money once on the devaluation of the franc (the inside information you despise) and he bought an *Eclaireur* or a *Moniteur* or something or other."

Simon listened so attentively she saw he didn't want to miss one word that might give him some clue to Edouard.

"He's done pretty rough things, hasn't he?" he asked. "I mean, of course, after he left your father."

"Yes, he has."

"Well, don't imagine we haven't rough characters, too."

"I'm sure you have. And not so different from Edouard, perhaps."

He said, "I do think Edouard benefits by a special grace, though. I think it's the French language. It's such a miracle of logic and elegance that it gives respectability to all sorts of queer states of being."

She smiled and so did he. They seemed to be handling Edouard very well after all.

Simon was even a little carried away by the ease with which they were doing it. He said, "Perhaps I'd really like him better myself if he didn't always eat with such furious *gourmandise*. He doesn't tuck a napkin under his chin but you feel as though he did it spiritually. And the way he tears a piece of bread has such an air of superiority — 'Now, boys, I'll show you how really to enjoy your food.' "

Françoise said laughing, "He puts that on a little. I mean, it's natural but he exaggerates, or rather he allows himself to be more natural than usual. It's partly political. It's the good old Jacques Bonhomme, the man of the people."

"Political?"

"Well, don't imagine that he's not an able politician — more so than most men in office. And he has great intuition in small things, especially very simple things. You should have seen him last summer. We were all at a dinner in Le Puy to celebrate the fourteenth of July. All the mayors of Auvergne and Velay were there. Father was there to speak — and Edouard. Some of the mayors had come in late because of getting in their hay while the weather was so fine. The whole hall smelled of hay and manure. Edouard presided over the speeches and though we were in a hurry to get to Chavagnac, where we were visiting, he kept delaying. Finally he whispered to me that we must wait till they'd had time to eat their cheese. Most of them made and understood cheese. It was the most interesting part of the meal to them. He wouldn't think of trying to get their full attention till they'd eaten it, savored it, and criticized it."

"Very amusing of Edouard. Where does he come from? He's Alsatian, isn't he?"

"Yes, by origin. But he was born in Paris."

Then unexpectedly the naturalness of talking about Edouard suddenly became strained again. All these questions were not what he really wanted to know.

He came back to the essential one but this time less directly.

"How does the terrible Blaise like him?" he asked.

"Oh, Blaise — He's suddenly decided Edouard is ridiculous. He has decided to throw him out like an old piece of disreputable furniture. Blaise says Edouard is a 'pear.' "

But she saw Simon hadn't meant to ask this. She said, "You really want me to say again just what he is to me, don't you? Well, I'll tell you. There's nothing dark and mysterious. It's just this: I've known Edouard for so long he has no outline for me as a man but he has got the power to make his affection visible and always believable. He is an old, old friend who has always been indulgent and generous and kind. He's got only one fault: I cannot trust him."

"But do you try to trust him?" he exclaimed. "What's the hold he has on you that you must try to trust him?"

"No hold on me. It's Father," she said slowly. "It's on Father that he has the hold, and just now more than ever."

Simon looked confused. "I don't understand."

"No, you couldn't, and I can't tell you, at least not now — oh, here he comes."

He was making a stately progress among the tables behind a woman in black. A great many people greeted them. The woman turned to speak to a group standing by the door, while Edouard came on and stopped behind Simon and put his hand lightly on his shoulder.

"Good morning, Françoise, good morning, Astley."

Simon stiffened and without turning around said flatly, "Hello."

"How goes everything?" Edouard asked. He smiled at Françoise but he was addressing Simon because he didn't know him as well.

"I don't know how everything goes," Simon said. "Aren't you the one to tell us?"

"I'm not asking you about the course of the war," Edouard said good-naturedly. "I'm asking you how the hospital goes."

"Since the Army took it over nothing happens. Nothing has happened, in other words, since the beginning of the war."

Edouard said, "It's the phony war. And you're the little boy with a first-aid kit. But they won't even have a nosebleed for you."

Simon winced and Edouard spoke directly to Françoise. "How is André?"

"Better," she said.

"When do you go down?"

"On the seventeenth."

"You ought to go earlier. You look tired. Try to persuade her to go earlier, Astley. She works too hard."

Edouard looked down at her and it was perfectly clear that if he had been alone with her he would have gently touched her cheek or hair. But because he did not make the gesture, but only indicated it, its character was ambiguous, and to Simon more hateful than if it had been made.

"Well, good-by, my dear," Edouard said. "I'll be down week after next. Good-by, Astley."

He joined the lady in black and they moved on.

Françoise saw that Simon's eyes followed his broad shoulders toward the door. She saw also that Simon's general fear and dislike of Edouard had suddenly crystallized into hate. For no more reason than the surprise of finding that Edouard also was coming to Rusquec, and because of the gesture he had not even made, Simon hated him.

This made a barrier over which they couldn't talk.

She might have said, "I see you hate him, but believe me, it's for the wrong reason. He is no danger to us. His danger lies elsewhere, and that I can't tell you about. Not yet."

But they sat in silence, each disturbed, each already less happy.

She wondered now that they could have been so wasteful. They were indulging themselves because they thought they had endless time. They were sulking on the threshold of the long love that they thought awaited them.

But it was only to be a short love.

Françoise couldn't remember what else they had said that day.

Suddenly she fell asleep.

Chapter V

THE CRUNCHING of the carriage wakened her. She heard the wheels squeak as it turned and stopped before the door. Then voices, Edouard's stronger and fuller than the rest. How many times had Edouard come to Rusquec! Long before Simon and long afterward. Edouard would always be with them.

They hadn't seen him though for a long time. They had parted over a year ago in the Hôtel du Parc, when for the first time in their lives their voices had been uncontrollable. They had shouted at each other, furious, beside themselves.

But she had assumed, as André had, that if he had been angry in Vichy he had got over it and had forgotten the terrible things they had said. What they had heard of him since, disturbing as it was, didn't much affect them. He was Edouard. He had answered André's telegram and here he was. Besides, he had long since done his worst.

She heard his voice from below. "Attention there, that's heavy! Don't drop it!" He sounded very dis-

turbed. For a moment she even thought he sounded
alarmed. But that could not possibly be.

Edouard would now have a bath and then he would
be ready to see them. And the sauce still had to be
made. Nevertheless she was in no hurry to go down.
She dressed slowly, hesitating first over two dresses,
both old, one, the gray-green, a favorite of Edouard's.
But because it would have gone with the ruby clip,
which Simon never gave her, she chose the dim-
orange instead. As she brushed her hair she wondered again how Edouard would be and felt at the
moment a paralyzing indifference as to whether he
would be difficult or easy. Only a few hours before
she had been filled with nervous terrors because of all
those wretched people — Madame Simmonet and her
son, Jeanne Peguinot and her husband, the brother
of Yves, even Costard, and even Bouchaix. Because
such a responsibility lay on André to save them.
Because of Maurice, who must not arouse any sus-
picions. Because of Blaise. But now she was only half-
awake.

She sat down on the edge of the bed. I hope he's
brought us some food, she thought. He lives well up
there, and while we don't do so badly in the country
it would be pleasant to be able to give some presents
of food. Perhaps he remembered to do that. That
would be like him. She reached out to the drawer
of the chest for a pair of stockings and saw the let-

ter. And the letter at once tempted her, as the piece of chocolate had done.

I know that letter nearly by heart, she thought. To read it again would be worse than silly. I wouldn't discover anything new in it.

"Whatever became of that young man?" Edouard had said once, pretending to have forgotten all about him. "Wasn't his name Simon? What a *farceur* he turned out to be."

So he had. But still, the letter was there and it was the only one Simon had ever written her. He hadn't realized that it would be the only one or perhaps he would have tried to make it more significant. But if he had tried there was nothing more Simon could have said. In that letter he gave all he had in him to give. It had been written hastily, over several days. It was a series of notes really.

She picked it out of the drawer. She would take only a moment to glance over it. It began: —

11 May, 1940

Darling Fanny: —

So you went to Rusquec ahead of time! I'm sorry your father has been ill. I hope it isn't serious and that the country will fix him up.

I think I'd better send you a telegram to find out whether you really want me on the eighteenth after all. The invasion of the Low Countries is an awful jolt, and no one seems to know yet whether it is

good or bad news, whether it means Hitler has
made the mistake of his life or that he'll be in Paris
next week. Certainly he's started with his usual rush
but no doubt the Allies have expected this and are
prepared. The papers here seem cheerful. Only de
Kerillis strikes a sour note. Still, there is a curious
feeling, almost a curious smell, not of disaster but of
confusion. It's like nothing I know, so I can't describe
it, but I suppose it's the normal confusion of war —
of behind the war. Rumors, doubts, anxieties, sur-
mises, and so on trickling through everything like a
leak of escaping gas.

My house has no hot water any more — the "system" has broken down — and at Adrian's the lift
doesn't work. I met Adrian, our old school-tie boy,
last night at Fouquet's for coffee. He'd been working
late at his Embassy. He's bought two of my "Place
Vendômes," 16 and 18. A queer old girl came and
sat next to us. She had a silk knitted suit that had
stretched down to her ankles and a hat with roses
that looked rained on. Underneath it her face was
one of those extraordinary gentle, rabbit faces that
made you feel she'd lived all her life among green
lettuces. She began to talk to us in a flustered, worried way. You knew she didn't usually speak to
strange men. She was English, of course, and it seems
she'd come from Italy. She was that mysterious
thing "the neutral traveler returning from So-and-So."
You know those paragraphs papers print in the midst
of wars — "a neutral traveler returning from Af-
ghanistan reports Russian infiltration," or "a traveler
coming from Holland reports good spirit among
the troops." What the hell are these travelers?

Where did they get their sangfroid, their sinister attention to the butter-and-egg business? I've always wanted to meet one. Here was one. We asked her what was really happening in Italy, was Italy mobilizing, were there many Germans there, did the people want war?

The following is what she told us. She had been to Florence on a holiday and the consul had insisted that she go home. The man in Cook's was most unhelpful. But the Italians were very sweet people and one couldn't help but love them in spite of their faults. Civilization, however, was breaking down. She had seen it cracking for some time but the certainty came to her when she wrote this letter to Hugh Walpole. It seems that Hugh Walpole had written this book about this author who didn't really exist but he had written about him exactly as though he did exist and were a live person. So she had written to Walpole to ask for a list of the nonexistent works of this nonexistent author. And then Walpole had written her that he didn't exist and had said "There's realism for you," or something like that. What a sell! What an outrage! Fancy a *gentleman* doing a thing like that! Fancy *Thackeray* doing a thing like that!

There's our returning traveler. She was like a scrap of paper with a few unintelligible words on it fluttering out of a burning chimney.

Adrian says the fall of Maestricht and Liége are diplomatic defeats for the Reich. He is very calm. He's one of those Englishmen who like Germany. He has a brother in the R.A.F. He told me how his brother was flying very low over Germany in the

days of the leaflets and the German troops on the
ground didn't even fire on them. "What do you
think happened?" Adrian's brother said. "Their
chaps just waved at our chaps." Adrian still tells this
story. He told it again last night. He still believes
(somewhat as I do and for the same reason — sheer
laziness) that no one is quite as bad as he is painted.
The jerries are going a bit beyond themselves, of
course. They're jerries now — not quite "chaps."
These ghastly English diminutives! The jerries, the
Aussies, and the Bolshies! The Bolshies, of course,
are a different matter. They're rotters, as everyone
always knew, but for the rest Adrian feels that the
world is still in the hands of the right people, even
though they're having a quarrel of sorts among
themselves.

Edouard called me up today and said he'd like to
drive with me out to Rusquec because the train service is so bad and his car is out of order, and that it
would be better to go Wednesday. He said you'd
wired him we'd better come then. So we will be
there a few days sooner. I was beginning to be
afraid it would be called off. Besides, the hospital
is sending out some of our drivers and the rest are
more or less standing by.

I had a long talk with old Winnie in the Crillon
bar. She specializes in the inside dope and she told
me quite mysteriously that Edouard had gone to
Switzerland! I said he'd called me up this very morning and she was surprised. She said, "Then he only
stayed a few days." She also told me he used to be a
sort of unofficial liaison man for the German Embassy. What a very peculiar job that must have been!

She said she'd known Edouard for years, that she adored him and he her and that he had named a horse for her. She has known him since he was a big brown-faced boy in a stiff collar, your father's secretary in fact, but even then she adored him because she picked him for a winner, and besides, he was the only man she'd ever known who was incapable of self-deception.

She told me a story about him. It was when he first began to be *lié* with the press. You know Winnie: she talks half French, half English. It seems he was very *lié* with the director of the journalistic enterprises of Madame Hanau and also very *lié* with the *Journal*, which was conducting a campaign against Madame Hanau. Later, Madame H., after her arrest, complained that she had to pay a cool million to the *Journal* to buy their silence. Edouard had, according to Winnie, been conducting the delicate negotiations, but he claimed he knew nothing of it. And he would have got away with it easily but for a visiting card that a waiter picked up at a restaurant called Kilomètre Cent Quatre, a place where Edouard sometimes lunched with Madame Hanau. On it were a few lines scrawled to Madame Hanau. So, to buy this card from the waiter Edouard had to pay out a good part of his commission on the affair. It's the one time, Winnie says, that Edouard ever took his finger off his number, and that was a long time ago. She laughed over it rather somberly. It consoled her, in spite of the fact that she adored him, to remember that once, at least, he wasn't quite bright.

I must say this about Winnie, in defense of Edouard and in case you don't know her as well as

I do, that she is entirely unreliable because she always has to be astonishing and she has to be right. You get into an argument with her and it degenerates immediately into a free-for-all, she hits you below the belt, and in a moment you're swinging on the ropes. She has lately told me also the following: that the Russians had four divisions in Spain, four divisions — General Georges told her himself, and Weygand is Maximilian's son — didn't you know? The King of Sweden told her. Why, even the Jews didn't write the Bible. I forget who told her that one. I only remember shouting lamely, "But listen, I read somewhere — I mean everybody knows, I mean — by God, the Pope told me!"

Still, I shouldn't have repeated this about Edouard. It's not sporting of me. Adrian would never have done it. What I really want to ask you again is why, this being Edouard, he still manages to seem more respectable than I. He can somehow make me feel that he stands with an honorable offer and that I am the unhealthy type who accosts you after midnight in the Place Pigalle.

And now he's driving with me to Rusquec. Do you imagine I like that? He told me also, most agreeably, that I'd better take my pictures with me. He said, "You know, old fellow, I don't know anything about your own pictures. Maybe they're very good. But Françoise says you've got some things you bought for your uncle's shop. He is a picture dealer, isn't he, a *small* one? And you've got a Renoir drawing and an Utrillo and one or two other things. Well, you'd better leave them with her."

But is the news really so bad? Does he expect

Paris to be occupied shortly? He never mentioned
Switzerland. Anyway, I'll be driving to Rusquec.

I first went there five weeks ago. I'd met you a
week before that at the de Puyblancs' dinner. The
Daladier Ministry had fallen. The Roumanian prin-
cess with the outsize emeralds kept going importantly
to the telephone to hear the latest developments,
and it surprised me at first that you weren't more
interested in what she said. You wore the gray-
green Alix dress and you looked like a smiling
Gothic angel, but fantastically delicate and break-
able. Your smile had a bright edge and when you
spoke your voice, high like a flute and sour-sweet,
dragged downward at the corners of a sentence. I
spent two days after that in a spell. People say that
very easily. I realize as I write it that it's too easily
said, but it was just that, a spell. It had no relation to anything I knew before. I didn't know even
if it was important, if it was durable, if it meant anything other than a supreme momentary heighten-
ing. But when I went first to see you, down the
Rue de la Faisandérie — really a rather dreary street,
much too Bois de Boulognish — a sort of panic came
over me. I had tea with you and you invited me to
Rusquec. If you hadn't, if you had made one of those
vague good-bys, that are really dismissals, I think
I'd have suffered some permanent, irreparable dam-
age, perhaps some slight touch of madness, for the
rest of my life. (*What a queer old fellow he is.
Whatever happened to him?*) But you asked me to
Rusquec and as I came from your house down the
Rue de la Faisandérie that Bois de Boulognish street
entered into a change, the solid shape of every house

was saturated in light. I'll paint the Rue de la Faisandérie, and as I saw it that day.

And then came Brittany. When I drove there I felt like Thomas the Rhymer — I was never coming back. But of course these spells have their lapses, there are intervals when one finds oneself unexplainably sitting at a solid table eating a solid, badly cooked omelette, and the truth is Brittany disappointed me at first (and the truth also is that contrary to expectation I even drove back again, on a chilly day, wearing a coat not quite warm enough).

But my trip to Rusquec was my first look at Brittany. It was beyond Fougères that the country grew rough and poor and sad, the lovely sky of France vanished, the lovely tree shapes, the exquisite order — and the Arthurian magic (or did I only mean Tennysonian magic?) did not at once take its place. Instead I saw a country that repelled me because it did not seem to be your country at all. And so for a brief period you didn't quite seem to be you. It was cold and shaggy with ancientness and a Druidical silence hung over it. I had the terrible omelette that would never have been cooked in the true France. You told me once that someone, Michelet I think, said of Brittany, "*Peu française tant elle est gauloise.*" But I had been thinking of you in another way and here was something that hadn't been overlaid but was stubborn and primal. It had a sort of terror of origin about it.

Well, by six o'clock I had come to the hill that looks down on Rusquec and there was the gray *manoir* with its *colombier*, the orchard, the farm buildings, and an avenue of the finest elms I had ever

seen, even in New England. Then the magic came
again, came without effort from the thing itself,
which after all turned out to be simpler and stronger
than I thought and not cooked up somehow by me.
It was the true magic, and it was yours.

There isn't much use sending this as I will probably see you before you ever get it, the train service
being what it is today. The strange thing is I began
it because I wanted to write you a certain kind of
letter — a love letter — and somehow it didn't turn
out to be one. Why not, I wonder? I should have
thought that even if one had never written a love
letter before — and I never have, though I won't
pretend I haven't made a little love now and then —
the fact that I wanted it to be a love letter should
make it that. But it turns out to be all about travelers
and Edouard and what I thought about Brittany.
And all the time I was writing about them I was
thinking, "Just a minute till I get through this and
then I'll tell her what I really mean, I'll say, 'Françoise, I love you,' in some way that she'll be bound
to believe." But I find it's very hard to say the
whole and honest truth and I don't know why that
is. I am afraid that the truth cannot be said until it
has become completely a part of one. In that case
I have now told you that I don't completely love
you yet. Perhaps that is so, too. I have known you
only six weeks, seen you perhaps ten times. But that
isn't — I believe — what keeps it from being complete. I'm afraid it is that I'm not complete yet. I
have never lived in any full sense until I met you.
I am sure most people never live like that, fully.
I don't know whether it would be a thing consciously worked for, or a sort of divine grace, com-

ing from no one knows where. I don't know yet. But I *will* know. If it can be worked for I'll work for it. But if it is a grace I'll pray for it. And when it comes, if it does, it must be true, not a thing I've read about, not a poem I remember, a picture I've seen, not a longing that's just part of a vague longing for living, not even a spell, a Breton spell, a Françoise spell . . ."

Françoise dropped the letter. There were only a few words more but she couldn't read them. It was too much to be borne. She should have remembered that she would feel like this. It had all come to nothing. Simon had failed her. He had made himself a part of the darkness that had fallen on them. He had added himself to their darkness, hastening it, anticipating it even. It was no solace but only a more bitter grief to think of him.

Someone knocked at the door. She turned her head but could not find voice to answer. The knock came again.

"Mademoiselle?"

"Yes, Maurice."

"Colette wants to know if you are going to make the sauce. Also Monsieur Edouard has brought some food and she wants to know if we are to use any of it."

"I'm coming."

She put the letter back in the drawer and went downstairs.

Chapter VI

WHEN she saw Edouard standing in the library, warming his hands before the stove, she remembered a funny thing about him. It was that his shoes always squeaked. When he was younger and poorer she was sorry for him because of that pathetic squeak. Aunt Albertine had said, "You mustn't laugh. It means his shoes are cheap." But when he got rich they still squeaked. It was almost like a physical defect he couldn't overcome.

His attitude seemed quite natural, but it was after looking at André and Blaise that she realized what a change had come about in their relations. André was silent, with a look already troubled, and Blaise was smoldering with resentment that showed brightly in his eyes.

She couldn't guess what they had been saying but Edouard turned quickly as she came in and went toward her — and yes, his shoes still squeaked. He held her hand a moment and looked at her searchingly.

"Are you well?" he asked.

"Quite. And you?"

"Excellent."

There was gray hair on his temples but she couldn't tell whether he had really changed or not because at first glance what she thought was simply that he was himself.

"How was the trip down?"

"Bad. Every possible delay."

"It was kind of you to bring those things. We'll have some of the pâté, the cheese, and the wine for dinner. But you'll have to be indulgent. We're short of servants, some of them have gone and Marie is sick and Colette cooks now in her place. I gave you the yellow room. Did you find everything all right?"

"Perfect."

Maurice came in to put more wood in the stove and she saw Edouard look curiously at him as though surprised to see him.

"Good evening, Maurice," he said.

"Good evening, Monsieur."

When Maurice had gone Françoise said, "But haven't you seen him before? He was at the station, wasn't he?"

"No, Yves met me."

André said quickly, "Sometimes Yves drives for us. I imagine that tonight he wanted to take in some message or hear some word from his brother."

It was obvious to Françoise that André made an effort to say this inconsequentially.

"No, it was Yves," Edouard repeated. "Your farmer, isn't he?"

"Yes," she said. "In winter there's not much for him to do. He often drives for us."

"I prefer him to Maurice," Edouard said. "Maurice was never a favorite of mine. But perhaps his manners have improved lately."

"Not much," said Blaise.

There was such an edge of impertinence in his voice that Edouard looked at him. "That's a pity," he said thoughtfully.

Maurice came back and said, "Mademoiselle is served."

A bad beginning, she thought. And her apprehension for Blaise began to come back. It isn't that it's possible he is guilty, she thought. It's just that he is determined to act badly. At the least he'll give the impression of being insolent, rebellious, and entirely out of hand. But Edouard could not possibly suspect him in any way. There is absolutely no connection. It's fantastic. Still, it would be better if we could get rid of Blaise until Edouard leaves. As they sat down she threw a beseeching look at Blaise but he pretended not to see it. His jaw was set obstinately.

In spite of this as soon as they began the meal the dinner promised to be a success. There was, thanks to Edouard, more and richer food than they had expected, and the Riesling he had brought was excellent. With the first glass of wine the effect of a gay occasion was suddenly produced. Even Blaise's jaw relaxed and he became less sullen and seemed to be enjoying his food. He did not listen, apparently, to Edouard's talk about Paris.

Edouard told them about a young man they all knew who had put up one of the French war posters in his studio. It was the one that said: *"On Les Aura."* Under it he had written *"Nous les avons."* He told about a dinner some of the Polignacs had given for the German Ambassador, and a performance of "Tristan" at the Opera, where the French mistress of Abetz had sat in a box wearing her virginal stare and pout and very new magnificent diamonds. He told about honors given a famous scholar and writer who had been made head of the Bibliothèque Nationale. He even told about a proposed periodical to be got out under German auspices which would be contributed to by such men as Cocteau, Bérard, and possibly others. These things, to which they made no answer, gradually produced a thickish silence, and it was as though dust were settling on everything.

It was not like Edouard to be so flagrantly tactless. She wondered whether, because of the strain under which he must live, he had lost a bit of his intuitive skill, or perhaps was so deeply preoccupied with something else that he was careless, using a manner and speech left over from another occasion, as though he had worn a traveling overcoat in to dinner. She could not believe it was the affair of the murder and the hostages that weighed so heavily on his mind. Still, she wondered whether he had had time to talk to anyone in town on his way out and whether they had said anything to make him suspicious of them. That seemed quite impossible but she asked, "Did you stop off in town at all?"

"Certainly not," he said.

After dinner they went to the library again and gathered around the stove. They drank their coffee, of chicory and ground beans with a very little coffee in it in honor of the occasion, and Maurice even produced a Grand Marnier. Edouard fell silent for a bit. He was tired from his trip and suddenly they were all spent. The Galles weren't accustomed to so much food and wine and they would have liked to go to sleep. Edouard sat back in his chair, his hands clasped on his stomach, and looked at them dreamily from half-closed eyes.

Françoise picked up her knitting and began work on the stocking but she kept glancing at Edouard. Even though he might doze off she felt she must keep her attention on him because he was the one with power to help them. Looking at him as he sat, drowsy, heavy, she saw that he relished this power and, as usual with abstract things, he was able to give it an almost physical shape. He had always been able to do this, and in doing so, curiously enough, he deceived people without even trying. He made such a direct contact with the thing he desired, never filtering it through any intellectual or moral process, that one actually watched in him the explosion of the meeting. And this gave him a startling air of ingenuousness and honesty.

He had always wanted power. He had gone after it in many ways. Now at last he had it. But as she looked at him she saw that he had not found it what he expected. Perhaps only with them, here and now, did it turn out to have substance. This was what made its charm lie on him now, to be seen by whoever looked.

André with a sigh put down his cup and said, "And now, Edouard, we must talk about the hostages."

Edouard opened his eyes wide and sat up, feeling in his pocket for a cigarette. "All right," he said, "let's get on with it. But I warn you to begin with that the situation is delicate."

"Delicate!" André exclaimed. "That's scarcely the word for it."

"I think it is. Obviously we can't let these things pass without a protest. They make a bad impression on the people. On the other hand, we can't plead for every criminal who chooses to commit a murder."

"We're not pleading for the criminal."

"No? Well, at any rate, it appears to them that we are. We are trying to have no one punished because we can't find the right one. What they are doing is to punish us for having such a state of disorder that the act can be committed and the criminal escape."

André looked at him with contempt. "And what produced the state of disorder?" he asked. "Really, Edouard, I hope you did not come here to talk like a fool."

Edouard lighted his cigarette and went on with an air of patience, "The shooting of hostages is not entirely without precedent. In certain conditions reprisals are the only recourse left. If we're at a disadvantage in being unable to produce the criminal, they are at the disadvantage you suggest of being in a country they hold by military power. Yes, you think I'm talking like a fool but just let me tell you this: it won't do any good to attack them on a moral basis. Either they could see it as you do, in which case they wouldn't be doing it, or they're incapable of seeing it as you do, and you waste your breath explaining."

"In other words," said André, "they are stronger than we are and they do not have to consider morality. Well then, we must remind them that they are still obliged to take into consideration the opinions and feelings of the people, whether they wish to or not, for the strictest reasons of expediency. Because it's easier for them if there is at least a semblance of willingness in those they control. We must make them see that these executions so far have accomplished absolutely nothing. Sabotage and murder go on."

"It's my opinion," Edouard said, "that they go on not because of the shooting of hostages but because the criminal is never caught."

André looked at him steadily. "You see, in spite of yourself you shift back to a moral basis. But every effort is being made to find the criminal," he said. "The local police and the Germans are collaborating. So far he has not been found. But whether he is found or whether he is not found has no real relation to the hostages. What I want of you now is to have the executions not only postponed, which I have been able to do myself, but abandoned, as an ineffective and obscene means of terrorizing the population."

Blaise, sitting on the edge of his chair, started to speak but stopped. Let him keep quiet, Françoise said to herself, let him decide to leave the room. She tried to think of an errand to send him on, but where at this hour of the night?

"As to that," Edouard said, "I've been promised that nothing will happen until I have consulted with the authorities. My only hope, however, is that they will give us a little more time. They will not abandon the idea of reprisal and I want to impress on you all that the only solution is to produce a criminal." He looked at each of them in turn as he spoke.

"Why don't you stop talking about criminals, Edouard?" Blaise's voice was high and sharp. "Don't you think it's a silly word to use among ourselves? The poor devil who shot him can't help that he's so outnumbered and outarmed he had to do what he could." He stopped abruptly, seeing the concern on Françoise's face and the white, forbidding eyes of André. He got up, looked around at them, and said, "Oh, you all make me sick," and stamped out of the room.

Edouard looked after him gravely. They heard him in the next room knocking the billiard balls furiously around on the mutilated billiard table from which some of the felt had been cut.

André said finally, "There you see the effect of tyranny and injustice. It is useless to expect that savagery will ever produce anything but rebellion."

"Ineffective rebellion," said Edouard, "which leaves us still at a disadvantage. We must look at this calmly, André, as calmly as we can. We are in their hands. That, I agree, is a pity. But you know how that came about."

"Yes, I know," André said briefly. He had his report on his knee and he carefully shifted the papers into perfect line. "Let us start from the point where we find ourselves," he said. "Let us abandon the morality of the case. To put it in another form, let us abandon what we have got of civilization. Reason is useless. We are in the hands of neolithic men. What shall we do now?"

"Let us abandon big words first of all," Edouard said. He sank back in his chair and clasped his hands over his stomach. He looked across at André and smiled. "As a lawyer and a politician, André, I'm afraid you've abused words all your life. Not in the usual way, not through carelessness or incompetence, but because of the Sublime, which happens to be your occupational disease, like tuberculosis among miners. Guilty or not guilty! The voice of the people is the voice of God! And so on."

"I think I try to use words honestly," André said.

Edouard laughed gently. "A good thing you qualify that. A man who is hungry has a chance of stating it so that the relation between the words and the fact is fairly exact (though gestures will do the same for him) but from that point on up to your affirmation of faith in reason, everything conspires against perfect honesty, and words most of all."

Now they will begin to argue, Françoise thought. They always used to argue and they will now. That's all right. That's good. That gives the appearance of normality, the natural friction between two opposing personalities. We've sat here in this dark house, Blaise, André, and I, for a long time. The dark is not normal. One is silent in the dark. Our personalities have flattened out in the long silences between us. But tonight we have food, a warm fire, all the lights are on. We're all talking as usual. Just as though nothing had happened. Edouard will not see how queer we've all grown, how changed. He'll never see what has really happened to us. And that's the only way he will ever help us. By feeling our old hold on him. But if he sees beyond that Edouard would be frightened of us. He'd abandon us. And that would mean abandoning old Peguinot and young Simmonet and Jacques, who are sitting now in their cells, thinking about us and what we are doing for them, seeing us — in what strange manner — as powerful creatures holding their lives in our hands. If it were indeed only like that! But at least it's three friends about to enter into a familiar and slight discussion of something or other, in the course of which it will finally turn out that the affair of young Simmonet and Peguinot and Jacques will have been settled.

She saw that André must have felt something of this too. He made an effort to throw off the weight of his concern, he even appeared to make an effort to get a little pleasure out of Edouard's company.

"Admit," Edouard said, "that our lives have now resolved themselves into a pure problem of survival.

Survival, I am afraid, has no connection with reason
or the moral law. It is concerned only with the business of being weak or being strong."

"You are saying that we must be strong to survive?
Or that we must manage to survive in spite of being
weak?"

"That we must manage to survive in spite of being,
for the time, weak."

"Sometimes, Edouard, I've suspected you of believing that weakness has the greatest power of survival. Well, the laws of survival are very mysterious
and it's possible that you are right. The sponge survived while the dinosaur is extinct."

"It survived then because, though it was defense-
less, it had the power to adapt itself. That's my point.
Adaptability is the only course when you happen
to be weak."

"Perhaps. But if you're still thinking of sponges,
they are no good to us as an example, because we
don't know enough. How do we know, for instance,
whether this biological adaptability may not have
been the infinitely remote seed of human reason, that
reason which when it has passed through all its developments finally conceives of a moral law?"

Edouard ran his hand under his collar and sat up
straighter in his chair. He looked hot. "Let's drop all
this," he said. "You know exactly what I am talking
about. I mean we've got to adapt ourselves. We've

got to compromise. This should be no news to you. But you speak as though in suggesting that it's going to be necessary to outwit these fellows I were telling you to strangle your own mother. You've got another weakness, André. You love the heroic. You are always swinging like a pendulum between the heroic and good sense. That's a national failing, by the way." He was pleased at having thought of this and he smiled at Françoise, inviting her approval. Then he grew suddenly more serious. "I wonder if you realize," he said, "how many times I've got you out of hot water of one sort or another."

"It looks as though you were going to tell me," André said drily.

"Well, why not? I always admired you in a way for getting into it. That didn't prevent me from trying to get you out. I'm thinking for instance of the time you and I first met. It was December 1919, wasn't it? You and forty-nine of your Socialist colleagues of the minority had just distinguished yourselves by refusing to ratify the peace. And this struck some people as exceedingly peculiar, since you had wished to make peace as early as 1916. But you said that the peace you had worked for via Kienthal, Zimmerwald, and Stockholm was not the peace of Versailles. So you opposed Clemenceau, and in the general elections that followed the ratifying of the treaty you were defeated by the candidate of the

National Block. Yes, André, when I met you, you were certainly in hot water. You were a man without a visible political future, a poor man with a family, a very poor man. No doubt about it, you were a man who had given himself the luxury of meeting defeat because of a faith. Well, that was a long time ago."

"It was indeed," André said sadly. "I was full of hope in those days. I believed in a great many things."

There's no use trying to stop Edouard, Françoise thought. He is not at all abashed by saying what he knows we expect him to say. He is not in the least afraid of boring us. Edouard has never yet conceived of boredom, his or other people's. Those who go in for common sense are never bored.

Edouard said amiably, "You have made me think of quite a chain of causes and events that I'd like to follow a little way. From a poor man, the man I first saw in 1919, politically dead, you became, in five short years, fairly well-to-do and a deputy once more. After that you made more money, though you never made nearly as much as you could have. But you became Minister and a powerful man. How did all that happen?"

André didn't answer. He appeared to be thinking of something else.

Edouard had not expected an answer, for he was going to make it himself. He sank back comfortably in the chair and his chin fell into a satisfied crease.

"I can remember very well that office you had in the Rue des Tournelles," he said. "You lived above it with your wife and daughter. At first you didn't even have a cook, only a queer man of all work, our Maurice in fact. I didn't see though with the eyes I have now. I was only twenty-five when I came to you with my letter of introduction and I was struck with admiration and wonder. I was impressed by your office, always crowded with clients, all of the working class naturally, all Syndicalists, the Union of the Furniture Movers being the noisiest as I recall it. I was impressed much more than I can tell you by the life you lived in your family. I knew that you had been even poorer than this, almost as poor as myself, but you came of fine intellectual stock, the son of a professor at Rennes, wasn't that so? And your sister Albertine who afterwards came to live with you was a teacher of Latin. The atmosphere of those rooms you lived in, in spite of the smell of the tripe shop across the street, had a charm I'd never dreamed possible. I won't say I began by admiring you. I began instantly by loving you, all of you, you André, Madame Galle, Françoise, and even the tiniest bit, Aunt Albertine. It was absolutely true, absolutely without calculation. For a long time it excluded everything else. It was the happiest time of my life. I needn't tell you how it became less exclusive and how by degrees its meaning changed. But it's true that my first ambitions were actually only ambitions for you."

André stirred restlessly in his chair. "Do remember," he said, "that confessions are always pretentious and very hard to listen to."

"It won't be long," Edouard said. He frowned, not in annoyance but in an effort to choose what he would say next. Finally he said, "I wonder if you remember the case of the explosion in the factory at Asnières?"

"Yes," said André reluctantly. "I do. You mean the injured workers against Le Blanc?"

"Exactly. That worked out very well for us. And I wonder if you know why. Because without your knowledge I played both sides. You were very preoccupied at the time. Madame Galle was very ill. I was afraid you would lose a case which would mean a lot of prestige for you if you won it. So I had a private talk with the representatives of the workers. I assured them that if they pushed Le Blanc too far he was capable of closing that factory and throwing thousands out of work, that he was a man with powerful friends whom it would be dangerous to antagonize, and that the best we could hope for was a compromise settlement out of court. And to Le Blanc I said that we were prepared to go the limit, because you would count on the case to bring you prestige, that public opinion would be on our side,

and that once you appeared in court you were irresistible. I told him he'd be lucky to make a compromise settlement out of court.

"So it was agreed to everyone's satisfaction, and
perhaps to your surprise. And the best part of it was
that Le Blanc was very impressed, and shortly after
a friend of his came in saying he had heard you
were the most brilliant young lawyer in Paris. He
begged you to take a case involving a very large sum,
a case that fortunately did not conflict with any of
your famous principles. Do you remember that part?"

André nodded. In spite of himself he was beginning
to listen, half-repelled and half-fascinated as always
by Edouard's ability to remember detail, something
he could never do, by his way of seeing facts as
though they were purely visual, like round, ripe
fruit, and by his glittering naturalness.

Edouard said, "I found a little house for you in
Passy, a house with a garden. Your wife was much
worse. You needed money to buy the house. You
did buy it. You needed more money, and you got
that. From then on you were seen occasionally in the
antechambers of the Financial Section. Your office was
a new one, well furnished. The Syndicate of the
Furniture Movers found it a long way to go and they
felt awkward when they got there. Also, I notified
them that the fees had gone up. I am explaining to
you how you ceased to be a ruined man."

"You are trying to explain to me how you corrupted me," André said. "I believe you have begun
to fancy yourself as my evil genius. But be sure that if
you corrupted me it was because in certain ways I
was corruptible."

Edouard sat up straighter and said, "But I tell you
I'm not talking of corruption. I'm talking of good
sense. I'm talking of the ability to compromise, perhaps not with the whole but certainly with a part
of one's faith, to change some of the meaning of it
from time to time as necessity forces us. But you
have done this — why talk about it? You have com-
promised. I shan't go over your whole career. After
the clients of the Rue des Tournelles came others, the
naval-construction workshops, the international cartel
of iodine. You made investments in Rio Tinto and
Royal Dutch and Snio Viscosa. You changed parties
and you changed leaders. Against the weakening
National Block you were of the block of the Left, of
the Cartelist majority. You have been Republican,
Socialist, Unified Socialist, and so on. And the leaders?
Herriot for the *rapprochement* with Russia, Briand in
the endless conferences. But why go on? You knew
it was necessary and you did it."

"Yes," André interrupted him. "You have shown
me your contempt for me. And I deserve it. The
sharp decline of the last twenty years may just as
well be due to men like me as to the Hitlers. It was

we who were entrusted with civilization. Under us
Socialism shrank to complete impotence. Hatred
sprang up on every side, and war came and put out
all our lights. From Herriot and Briand I came finally
to support Pétain. I thought I believed in reason but
I must have behaved with unparalleled stupidity.
And a part of my stupidity was in letting myself be
used and in being willing to use others. I don't
wonder you despise me."

"That's not true," Edouard protested. "You know
I've never despised you."

"What, not even when you used me?" André
exclaimed bitterly.

"Not even when we used each other," Edouard
said. "And," he added, "not even now, when you
want to use me again."

The door opened suddenly and Blaise came back.
He stood there looking to see on their faces what
had been going on in his absence. His hair was
ruffled as though he had been running his hands
through it. Françoise made a restraining gesture toward him, telling him to sit down, to be quiet, to say
nothing. He went over to the table and stood turning again the pages of the old *Illustration*.

Edouard did not give him a glance. He seemed not
to have noticed his return. He said, "Yes, you want
to use me again. I don't suppose you look on sending for me in that light. You were looking toward

the end and not considering the means very much. Just as you've always done. Well, here I am." He spread out his hands as though he offered himself entire. "It is curious, seeing you again like this. You remind me of the poor young man in the Rue des Tournelles, the one who had no political future and almost no money and who allowed himself to be in that state almost as a luxury. Why did you really leave Vichy, by the way? I never have understood that and perhaps I never will. They'd made the peace, hadn't they? The peace we had to have. You admitted that at the time. But that doesn't matter now because here you are again, and here I am. The question at hand has shrunk. Now it's a case of a little murder on a country road. It has no conceivable importance any way you look at it. But because you seem the same to me — unchanged — it's a great temptation to help you." He leaned forward and clasped his hands on his knees. "For some time now," he said deliberately, "it is old Edouard who has been protecting you all."

Neither Françoise nor Edouard saw Blaise get up. He took a few steps toward Edouard, spreading out his arms. "Our savior!" he cried in a falsetto voice. He looked as though he were about to embrace him.

Edouard turned and his eyes hardened. "Sit down," he said peremptorily.

Blaise waved his arm before his eyes, brushing away some imaginary web. Then he took two steps backward and sat down.

"Yes, I've done a lot of dirty work for you," Edouard said in a sulky voice. "Whether you want to believe it or not, though you must believe it or you wouldn't have sent for me. You sent for me because you needed some more done, and as usual you didn't want to do it yourself."

"You call this dirty work?" André exclaimed.

Edouard leaned back. He felt for another cigarette and lighted it. Then he blew the smoke out and stared through it.

"The truth is," he said deliberately, "it may turn out to be."

André looked at him and said nothing. Perhaps he had not listened. Perhaps he was confused because no basis for understanding each other seemed to exist any more. He was used to the limitations presented by Edouard's realistic logic, which seemed to him usually to consist in seeing only the benefit that was immediately at hand, but everything that Edouard had said about the hostages was such a debasement of logic that it destroyed the actual form and meaning of each word he used. Perhaps that was why he saw no special significance in this last remark.

But Françoise, without understanding, felt its implication and knew this must not go on. "Father, you're tired," she exclaimed.

André nodded, and Edouard said, "All right. Perhaps we had better talk it over tomorrow."

Françoise thought, this is all wrong. We should not have sent for him. He has come, but the hostages to him seem to be an excuse for something. Perhaps we've lived on the brink of ruin for too long. Perhaps our time is nearly up. It may be Edouard who will finish us off. Because he's sick of us? But even so, can he do it? That we left Vichy is an old story. It needs a pretext, a new crisis. The hostages may not be enough. The murder perhaps. *But if none of us did it?*

Her mother's diamond on her finger caught the light and showered tiny sparks into a corner of the ceiling. The reflections danced there, moved down the wall and vanished. A vagrant life seemed to have flickered for an instant in the corner of the room and the wall seemed transparent and open onto the dark night outside. She felt the fear again, the warning of some extreme limit that had been reached. She looked to see if any of them had changed. André had closed his eyes and Edouard was looking at him, coldly and reflectively. Blaise stared at his book.

"We must all go to bed," she said. "We are all tired to death." Her voice was a pleading wail.

Simmonet and Peguinot and the rest must wait. Lying in their cells they would not know what was happening. They would not know that nothing more could be done. It was necessary for the Galles to take refuge in the darkness again, for a time anyway. The Galles could not keep up the illusion of light and warmth and normal living any longer and they could not placate Edouard nor move him any further tonight. Edouard remained a living creature but the Galles had become shades. Perhaps tomorrow it would be different.

After they had gone upstairs she stayed to straighten the room a bit. Then she, too, went upstairs.

Chapter VII

IN THE upstairs hall a light burned under a blue frill. The doors of all the rooms were closed. Françoise hesitated before Blaise's door. She often stopped for a short talk with him at night about the affairs of the farm, about food and how to get it, about help for the political prisoners at the near-by camp. Since the murder they had talked of that. Tonight there was plenty to talk about. But Blaise had gone upstairs and shut his door without a word.

She stood there trying to think of what to say to him. She could ask him if he had already known about Maurice, or if he felt that Edouard had come with some suspicion of them, or if he knew anything about the murder that he had not told. It would be quite natural to ask all this. But what she really wanted to ask was: "Did you do it yourself, or you and Maurice together?"

If he refused to answer, if he was even evasive, she knew him so well that a single word or look might give her the truth.

She didn't feel that she could face the truth tonight. Edouard's presence, always so large and comforting, had frightened her in a special way. They had been surrounded by fear, for months and months, but now she felt that the fear had alighted like a bird on the roof of their own house.

And yet surely, she thought, going to her own room and beginning slowly to undress, surely Edouard can't mean any harm. I am hysterical when I think that. Edouard is our friend. He said he has been protecting us and it must be true. I must remember him as I used to know him. He can't really have changed so much.

She got into bed and drew up her knees to get warm. Gradually the bed grew warm from her body and because of the wine and the food and the tension of the evening she felt drowsy. Suddenly it was like lying in bed on some other night, on a night of the happy past.

In the darkness the past began slowly to take form around her. What could she see in it? Something a long way off and as yet unspoiled, innocent of the ugliness of disaster.

The beautiful, slow days. The little flat in the Rue des Tournelles. Her mother used to take her to the Place des Vosges to play. She and another little girl made chalk marks on the ground and hopped in and out of them. Once in a while they took a bus to the Tuileries. She remembered going with Maurice, and the delight of the Guignol, and the sailboat in the great fountain shuddering under the perpetual spray.

The rooms in the Rue des Tournelles merged into those of the little house in Passy. There they had a garden with lilac bushes and a seat under a tree, a tiny summerhouse. In the Bois there was a miniature railroad that ran to the Jardin d'Acclimation. There was a *pâtisserie*, warm and smelling of sticky sugar, a candy box tucked away in a wet, gray street.

The children had played *cache-cache* all afternoon, running up and down the lower part of the little, clean house, in and out among the lilacs in the garden, and Maurice had brought them a *goûter* of little cakes made by Jeanne Peguinot. Her mother called down from upstairs and Maurice went up quickly. He came back. "All of you clear out now," he said, "quick! The doctor is coming."

Then Blaise had been born, and her mother died.

Aunt Albertine from Rennes was afraid of Maurice and a little afraid of the children. Françoise loved her below the white rabbits in the garden. She used to say to Blaise, "Do you know who I love best? Mother first, then Father, then you, then Edouard, then the rabbits, then Maurice, then Aunt Albertine."

If Blaise was naughty she told him that she put him below the rabbits, and he would try not to cry from hurt and jealousy. He was nine years younger than she and he was something exquisite and funny, precious and tiresome. "Do we really have to take Blaise? He always wants a drink and to go to the toilet and he asks questions all the time and he cries when he gets tired." When he had scarlet fever she made a desperate, private pact with God: "If You'll make Blaise well You can do anything You want to me, anything at all."

There was the first book, *Les Malheurs de Sophie*, read to her by Aunt Albertine. Oh, that first book! It came even before the fairy tales. And others came later: *Mon Oncle et Mon Curé*, the poetry of Sully Prudhomme and Victor Hugo.

There was the first play at the Comédie, "Cyrano," which made her wake up afterward and cry at night. The first matinee at the Opéra, *"Le Jongleur de Notre Dame,"* and the first "piece" she learned to play by heart, *"Für Elisa."* Many things followed but never quite the same. Not even Racine and Stendhal, not Gide and Rimbaud, not Mozart and Vivaldi, ever gave the immaculate, fresh excitement of *Les Malheurs de Sophie*.

Even the first trifles were best: Parma violets, tight, cool-smelling, in a white-and-gold box. At the bottom a card in an envelope: *Best wishes for the birthday* — EDOUARD. Even the first kid gloves, very silky, with buttons like real pearls. They had to be a little too tight because she remembered her mother's

plump hands in tight-fitting gloves as she was going
out to the theater, holding opera glasses of mother-
of-pearl.

There was the first trip to Switzerland, and the
sudden snowy newness of the Alps. The big hotel
and a feeling of carnival, of holiday, of a strange
country.

Holidays, too, at Rusquec. Not this dark domain
where she was lying now, but a sunlit Rusquec with
bees droning over the flowering broom, the smell of
sea near by, the vast light reflected on the bright
clouds, and she and Blaise plunging into the sea on
hot summer days, themselves all tingling with life.

There were the deep excitements of study, the
pressure, the tension, of so much to know. The
baccalaureat. And meeting her father in the corridors
of the Senate, seeing this and that great man, hearing
a word here or there that gave an impression of
something tremendously important just about to
happen.

Except for André and for Blaise, the world of men
was a pageant of vague figures. Some of them flashed
on her dazzlingly, but their reality was always fleet-
ing or else it was quickly weakened by a distance
in age or circumstance: a professor of literature,
Louis Jouvet, a young Italian in Geneva, the rugged,
cultivated Herriot, the great Briand.

And of course there was always Edouard. In her

intimate hierarchy he ranked just before Maurice, not as close as André or Blaise, and not brilliant with strangeness. He was simply always there.

But at a certain moment he took another place reserved for him alone, and equivocal from its beginning. It was one day in the Jardin d'Acclimation, where the great elephant, monstrous and crafty-eyed, rolled up and down an enclosure with a little rickety seat for children on his back. Blaise already sat there, looking down in triumph, and Françoise had a half-frightened desire to ride herself. "Am I too big?" she asked Edouard. "I'm fourteen." "Yes, you're too big!" Blaise shouted. "Where will you put your legs?" She knew that for her to ride would diminish it for Blaise, making the pleasure and the terror less unique. But Edouard, laughing, caught her under the arms to lift her up. Pretending that he found her heavier even than he expected, he staggered backward and Françoise, laughing too, caught him around the neck and put her cheek against his.

Then Edouard did not move but held her tight and Françoise drew back quickly. She looked at Edouard's face, still close to hers. The beautiful, hardy color of his skin suddenly coarsened and the texture of his eyes was glistening and vulnerable. He looked at her with these monstrously exposed eyes and panic seized her. It was the first time she had felt what the eyes are capable of seeing. Her panic merged with a fear of the great beast behind him. "No, no. I don't want to. Let me down!" she cried, twisting and pushing at his arms. Edouard, as though angry, held her tighter, and Blaise kicked at the footrest with his small feet, catching her fear and shouting, "Let her down. Let her down. She doesn't want to." She felt Edouard's heart beating heavily and more slowly than her own, and after he had given her a little angry shake and set her down her heart went on throbbing for many moments. She was awkward with Edouard for a whole day.

And there was another moment at the races a few years later — the Prix de Diane. Françoise wore a hat covered with violets and Edouard had sent her violets which she held in her hand. It was a delicious day, with sun, and all of Chantilly seemed to smell of cut grass. A man came up and joined them, a lawyer she knew. He bowed to her and then began to talk to Edouard. She was accustomed to the man who joined them on occasion, who bowed to her in a preoccupied way, who murmured to Edouard or to her father, and then went away. It always seemed to be the same man.

There were many things they might have been talking of this day. It was a time of hope and of some sadness. Briand had died in March; President Doumer had been assassinated. In the general elections the Left had a majority in the Chamber. The great

European conferences were in full swing: Lausanne, Geneva, Locarno. Everyone talked of reduction of armaments.

And Edouard was speaking of the cross of the Legion of Honor. André disposed of three but Edouard naturally disposed of none. He was promising one, however. He was explaining how a man who was chief engineer of the Department of Oise had been accused of misappropriation of funds. The brother of this man owned a paper that Françoise knew was a strong supporter of her father.

"Old fellow," Edouard said, "we expect you to handle the case. It won't go badly. I've talked to the judge myself. I've consulted the experts. The man is unquestionably innocent. As to the rosette — well, I needn't tell you it doesn't grow on every bush." He said this in purposely slipshod, casual phrases, not looking at the man but smiling toward the course. As for the man, Françoise saw in his face the literal image of temptation. His jaw was locked, every muscle taut, but already his eyes were sad with the certainty of surrender. She looked again at Edouard and he made her think of a gipsy who knows he has won in a horse trade. In a moment, with glowing eyes he will snatch your hand and foretell a brilliant future for you.

The man said, "I'll write you my decision. I'm terribly busy just now. I'll write."

"Don't write!" Edouard exclaimed, the sly gipsy laugh breaking all over his face. "Never put anything on paper. Telephone."

The man left.

Françoise had never seen Edouard like this. With her father he was good-humored but with an air of sense and sobriety. Here he hadn't even found that necessary. He had again exposed something, and she had seen it. He turned toward her, still smiling, and she looked at him aghast. The smile did not fade from his face. He seemed to say, "Yes, you see me as I am, the bad mixed with the good. I offer no explanation or excuse. I'm not meant for that kind of thing. That's for you to worry about if you must. As for me, I am the entirely and unashamedly natural animal. And besides —" his eyes sparkled with pleasure — "perhaps I do it all for you."

Yes, that moment was the real pattern of her relation with Edouard. At that moment she had consented to accept him as he was. She had agreed that he need make no change, no concession to her sense of righteousness. Moreover, she would go on giving him her affection and indulgence. Even more than that, she would take from him whatever he chose to give. She did not entirely realize what she was doing. She was seventeen years old and her long familiarity with Edouard dimmed her realization. But afterward she knew that her frightened, answering smile had turned into one of amusement, with just a touch of fatuous and possessive pleasure.

Edouard never asked her to marry him. Even now Françoise wondered why. Until the day in the orchard he never even spoke of love. Even when she was very young she knew that he had mistresses. One was a woman with a title, later there was an actress who had made a name for herself in French films. But as though his good sense told him that this sort of thing was too much expense for what was mostly prestige, he took next and kept for years an agreeable little woman of no importance, the widow of an unsuccessful newspaperman. And Françoise was sure that during all this he loved her. Only of the character of that love was she not sure. Perhaps it was so interwoven with love for the three of them, André and even Blaise, that he couldn't entirely separate her. Perhaps their intimacy was so long and so close that his healthy sexual instinct told him there would be something almost incestuous in it. Perhaps he was afraid of her. Perhaps he simply knew that she did not love him.

Once or twice she had met a man who stirred and interested her, but the first time she saw him with Edouard the virtue seemed to run out of him. This was apparently through nothing that Edouard consciously did. Simply he seemed more real than the others. She did not know whether she loved Edouard or not but until she met Simon she had never loved anyone else.

There were a few years when she didn't see much of Edouard. He had quarreled with André over the Franco-Soviet Pact; aside from that they had already grown apart. Edouard no longer needed André; he was extremely rich now and had other friends. He was always making trips to Italy, where he was entertained by Mussolini, or to Germany, where he organized a society for the improvement of Franco-German relations. But as the storm gathered, war in China, war in Spain, *Anschluss,* he sought them out again.

It was when he came back that she began to realize what they would have to pay for having once accepted him. Though he was now closely agreed with André that war must be avoided, by always insisting that it was a matter of stratagems, of being smarter than the others, he managed bit by bit to destroy André's hope. His influence strengthened in proportion to what he destroyed. While André grew always more uncertain, more fumbling, Edouard grew more sure, more dogmatic, with his damnable common sense and his realistic logic. André was ruined already. France was about to be ruined. And Edouard throve.

Yes, Françoise thought, we paid dearly for Edouard. And we are still paying. Even tonight he managed to bring us the final crushing realization of what has become of us. What has become of us is now exactly this, that we are dependent entirely on his whim and his skill, to save, not only the twenty innocent men, but ourselves. Everything has narrowed to this sad, constricted moment. They are finished, the bright lovely days, the small things remembered, all drained into the deep, black gulf.

Around her the dark country lay desolate, betrayed by its own, and prostrate under enemies. As though it were the voice of that country, a dog on some distant farm barked its animal hunger and despair.

Chapter VIII

FRANÇOISE got up suddenly and went to the window, threw it open onto the night. The moors shone through a veil of mist and the tree shapes floated in whiteness.

There was a step on the gravel. She held her breath but heard no more. She knelt there, growing slowly cold but afraid to move. Then it came again, stealthily, almost inaudible. Around the angle of the terrace a dark figure appeared. It stopped, and from it came a faint sound. A less acute ear might not have heard it, or hearing might not have recognized it. It was Blaise, gently and nervously clearing his throat.

She saw him look around, then run quickly along the terrace, where he jumped over the low wall without waiting to go down the steps.

She went back to bed but couldn't sleep.

Where is Blaise going? What is he doing? I should have called to him so that no one else could hear. He might have come back. He might have given me some natural explanation.

Her blood pounded and she asked herself the same questions over and over: Where is he going, what is he doing?

Then she had one of those seeming moments of clairvoyance. He is going to the Relais Fleuri. It is he and not Maurice who goes to see that wretched girl.

But that's impossible. The girl is only fourteen and Blaise is barely eighteen.

But he's seen such a lot, he's lived through so much. First he was so spoiled and now he's had to suffer all these things with feeling still raw and young and at their most vulnerable.

And perhaps the girl has a certain charm for him just because she is a pale, sexless little thing with terrified eyes. That they're both so young might draw them together. She might make a boy like Blaise feel a desperate sort of tenderness for her, or even perhaps a contemptuous tenderness.

The whole story began to form in her mind, to take on color and truth.

And then if the girl were afraid of the sergeant — if she had told Blaise about him —

Perhaps Blaise went there that night. Certainly the sergeant must have gone there. There was no doubt of that. There would be nothing Blaise could do. He would be quite helpless. There would be nothing he could do but follow the sergeant out on the road and shoot him.

It might still be Maurice, though, who had done it. Maurice, who was a murderer already. He also had been out late at night. Blaise said Maurice had a girl. But one simply couldn't believe that Maurice had a girl. And then, why was Blaise out now?

Perhaps he was going to join Maurice.

She got up and went to the door again, opened it and listened. The hall was dark and without sound. A few feet away the stairs led up to the rooms under the roof where the servants slept. She went to the foot of the stairs and called softly, "Maurice! Maurice!"

She heard his bed creak as he turned over. Then his door opened. He listened.

"Maurice!"

"Mademoiselle?" He limped to the head of the stairs, making a little muffled, hopping sound with the crutch he kept beside his bed for emergencies.

"Maurice, I thought I saw a light from an upstairs window. Is anything left on?"

"A light!" he grumbled. "There's no light. Everyone's asleep."

There was a silence.

"I must have dreamed it," she said at last in a low voice.

Maurice didn't speak. She could imagine him standing in the dark, leaning on his crutch. Finally he said quietly, "Try to sleep, Mademoiselle."

Françoise said, "I'm sorry I waked you." She went back to her room.

Then Blaise *had* gone to the Relais Fleuri.

She got back into bed. He doesn't dare go in the daytime now, she thought. He shouldn't go even at night. But then how could he resist it now? He has killed a man for her.

This is frightful, she thought. Frightful that I am able to imagine all this about Blaise. It's nonsense. It's absolutely without foundation.

She lay there listening in the dark, dozed a little. The night passed slowly.

Then suddenly she woke completely, saying to herself: It's all right, he has come back.

She sat up in bed and listened. In the absolute stillness of the house she heard his door close gently. She went back to sleep and slept heavily.

Chapter IX

COLETTE came with the coffee and Françoise saw by her clock that she was much earlier than usual. She drew back the curtains and opened the wooden shutters. "It rained early this morning," she said. "It will rain again."

"Is there anything new?"

"Nothing new, Mademoiselle." But she lingered a bit, evidently anxious to talk.

"What is it?" Françoise asked listlessly.

"I think," Colette said, "that Mademoiselle should speak to Yves."

"What's he done?"

"Last night he came into the kitchen to get some food to take to Marie. And he made various insinuations of such a sort that he and Maurice nearly came to blows."

"What sort of insinuations?"

Colette compressed her lips exaggeratedly and looked grave.

"I asked you what sort of insinuations."

"Insinuations that it would be very serious for him to make outside of this house."

"Well, what were they?"

"It would be offensive for me to repeat them to Mademoiselle."

"Well then, don't repeat them." Françoise swallowed her coffee, not looking at Colette. But Colette, after starting toward the door, turned back.

She blurted out, her face suddenly red from excitement, "He said that if Monsieur le Ministre really wanted to save the hostages he had only to look around his own house. And he said that if he didn't look around it soon, others would do it for him."

"Where is Yves now?"

"He drove the carriage into town."

"Then Maurice didn't speak of this to Monsieur le Ministre?"

"Evidently not."

Françoise saw that Colette was genuinely frightened, on the verge of hysterical tears again. She said as calmly as she could, "Yves is very naturally upset, because his brother is one of the hostages. You know that his wife is sick. And because he had a bad wound in the war. Oh, because of a great many things. So what he says in his present state is better forgotten."

Colette's face puckered. She managed to say, "Yes, Mademoiselle," and went out.

Françoise looked at the gray sky through the

window. A wind was tormenting the garden. She
heard the branches creak. The last chrysanthemums
would be spattered with mud.

As she finished her coffee Blaise came in. By the
color in his face, his blown hair, she saw that early as
it was, he had already been out. He kissed her cheeks
and sat on the foot of the bed.

"You look sick this morning," he said cheerfully.
"Are you?"

Françoise again tried to think of what she must say
to him and again didn't know where to begin.

He said, "I suppose you're going to scold me for
last night. I wasn't very tactful with Edouard, was
I?" He spoke as though it were a trifling thing.

"You were about as foolish as it is possible to be.
After all, we want him to help us."

"Yes. But I get a little tired of having Edouard
help us. It's only common decency to keep those
fellows from being shot. It's not really us he's helping."

"I don't know about that," Françoise said. "We
might get mixed up in it before it's over. He hinted
at that. Didn't you notice?"

Blaise raised his eyebrows. "Why?" he asked. "Because Maurice had a gun? And because he was out
that night? Well, I'm the one who dug the gun up.
I'm the one who shot the silly little hare. He didn't
even want to use it then. He said if we used it once

it would be hard to stop. So I buried it again. As for his being out that night — well, so was I."

"You!" Françoise sat up straight in bed. "Blaise, where were you?"

He shrugged and made no answer but his face grew more flushed and his eyes grew brighter with self-consciousness.

How difficult it is to analyze a look, she thought. The embarrassment and defiance in Blaise's face might mean a number of things. They might mean he was startled at finding he had said too much. They might mean he was lying, or at least not telling the whole truth. They might even mean that he was trying to make himself suspected rather than Maurice. But there was nothing to show why he would have done any of these things.

"I may as well tell you," she said, "that Yves knows something about someone in this house. He's already begun to talk about it. Colette just told me that he hinted all sorts of things last night in the kitchen to Maurice. They were about to have a fight but I suppose Colette's imminent hysterics must have stopped them. Anyway, he'll talk next in town, when he gets a chance. Maybe he'll try to talk to Edouard. You and Maurice seem to have gone in for several imprudences. What do you think we had better do now?"

Blaise's embarrassment had passed. "There's noth-

ing we can do now," he said, "unless someone wants
to drop Yves in a pond with a weight tied to his
feet. It's a bit awkward at this time to have an in-
cipient madman around. He's been building up a
persecution complex for a long time. The war and
the occupation and Marie's sickness are all personal
grievances. Now this business of his brother's comes
along and the world crawls with his private enemies."

"You haven't told me what you were doing that
night," Françoise said.

"No, and I don't intend to," Blaise said coldly.

"You may have to explain it later. It's evident that
Yves saw you either coming or going. Do you think
he saw Maurice too?"

"I don't know about Maurice. I can't be entirely
sure whether he saw me or not. But I doubt if he saw
either of us. Yves goes to bed with the chickens.
He's tired out."

"What makes him suspect you then?"

"How should I know? Unless it was the business
of the gun. He knew about the gun. He knew the
hare was shot."

"You didn't tell him?"

"No. As a matter of fact, he'd gone into town
early with the cart. Maurice and I thought no one
was around because Marie and Colette were going
with him. It was Sunday and they were going to the
earliest mass. But Marie was sick that morning,

though we didn't know it then. She stayed at home and probably heard the shot and told Yves. Then Yves may have remembered the gun. He knew Maurice used to hunt with it and guessed one of us had used it."

"Would that be enough to make him think one of you had killed the German with it?"

"It might. Firearms are rare."

"He wouldn't have any other reason, would he?"

"I simply don't know."

"You've never either of you said anything in front of him in the way of threats, what you'd like to do to the Germans, or anything like that?"

Blaise smiled scornfully. "We don't talk of what we're going to do," he said. "You know us better than that. We're not that kind, either of us. Whatever we are going to do, we shut up about it."

Françoise leaned back on her pillow. She thought over the last year and a half and the changes that had come over Blaise. And it struck her that Blaise was different now from herself and André because he acted as though things still moved and as though they might therefore change. He is not lost, she thought, because he can still hope, hope being an expectation of change.

"Blaise," she said, "you really must tell me about that night. Don't you know that if Yves goes on talking, or even if someone else talks (perhaps some-

one else saw you — you can't be sure), sooner or
later you'll be questioned? What are you going to
say?"

"Say? Well, I suppose I'll give the classic excuse,
too. I'll say I was with a girl."

"You and Maurice both?"

"Not the same girl," he said impudently.

"I don't think this is something for joking about,
is it? You won't be believed, I'm afraid."

"Why not? Because of my tender years? Don't
be silly."

"You'll have to prove it, anyway."

"Certainly I will, if it comes to it. Though I shall
hold off for as long as I can. 'Gentlemen, you understand — a woman's honor.'"

"Blaise, stop it. You horrify me with your stupid
frivolity, not because it's vulgar but because it's
dangerous. Someone might believe Maurice was out
that night with some woman or other, though women
willing to take Maurice as a lover don't exactly bloom
all over the countryside. Who is it, when it comes
down to it? Why can't you tell her name? But to
make them believe that by a strange coincidence, on
the same night, you also found a girl among the
population of farmers' wives and daughters and servants in the neighborhood is simply going too far."

"It's not impossible," Blaise said. He smiled at her
defiantly. Then he felt about in the pockets of his

reefer. "After all," he said, "in these times no one is too particular. I can't have my first excursions into sex with a high-priced cocotte or with the blond American Eve at the Bal Tabarin. I have to take what I can get. That's war."

He drew out a curious object and dangled it in front of her. It was a black-cotton stocking.

Françoise stared at it in horror.

Then Blaise, seeing her face, seemed suddenly to feel uncertain. He stuffed it back in his pocket and got up with an effort at nonchalance.

"Get rid of that," she managed to say. "Throw it away. And somewhere far from the house. Bury it or burn it, but get rid of it."

"Why?"

"Because yesterday Costard told me a black-cotton stocking had been found in the German's pocket."

"What!" He looked incredulous. Then he thought about it and strangely he began to look pleased. He smiled and said, "I'm a fool not to have thought of it."

He turned toward the door.

"Where are you going?"

"I've got something to do."

"You're going to walk?"

"I want to take the bicycle. Are you going to use it?"

"Not this morning."

"All right." He held the door half-open. "I may

be late for lunch. Will Father and Edouard be here?"

"No. They are lunching with the Kommandant at the Mairie."

"Well, don't wait for me."

He seemed suddenly very young and not quite certain of himself. He came quickly back, leaned down, and kissed her, the quick, cool, little-boy kiss.

She threw her arms around his neck. "Oh, Blaise, darling, be careful," she said.

"Don't worry," he murmured. He gave her shoulders a squeeze and straightened up. Then he made his customary salute, the quick flick of a finger, attempted a final confident smile, and went out.

Chapter X

SHE THOUGHT, what does that mean? The stocking. The smile. What has Blaise really done? What has Blaise become?

When they had first spoken of the murder of the German and of the hostages, how did he behave? What was his expression? What did he say? He had just come into the room. He stood still and looked very surprised. He whistled. Then he said, "What a mess — Well, that's one German less anyway."

At that time she had not had the slightest reason to find this exceptional. It seemed the natural way for him to take it. Now it struck her as strange that he had not said more. Now that she thought of it closely, she remembered that he had looked a little superior, as though being now a man and younger than they, he was more competent to accept these things.

But then a look of slow horror had come into his face. "Will they shoot them?" he had whispered.

That also was surely natural. But how did she

know what was "natural" and what was not? Perhaps his horror was of a guilty, intimate character, more than just the shock of realizing that every outward event is made up of the fabric of human personality. She thought: If I only knew Blaise better! If in all this terrible time we had grown closer instead of growing apart.

And yet *before*, though we disagreed so violently we were close — or I thought we were close.

She thought: If Simon were only here! And then suddenly she laughed. Her laugh was forced and angry. Simon! Really it was too stupid to have thought of that. She had had one complete demonstration of the kind of help Simon was capable of. One such demonstration should be enough. It was so ghastly that one never learned anything for oneself but went on accepting certain fixed conceptions made up out of the experiences of so many others that they were only broadly true.

She remembered the little *palazzo* in Venice. It turned out to be always dark, the sheets were damp, she burnt herself trying to light the water heater, the cook was incompetent, the mosquitoes monstrous, and finally the old countess cheated them. But she'd always wanted to go back. Yes even to that *palazzo*. Because the idea of Venice, built up by so many other people, still meant quite a different thing to her. So the idea of the young lover, the young rescuer, remained, even though he turned out to be — well, what he had turned out to be.

Yes, when she asked him to Rusquec she said it was because he might help with Blaise. But that was only partly true. She wasn't greatly worried about Blaise then. Blaise and his romantic Germans! It was all of them who were in peril. André most of all. Because Edouard was with them. And she knew that the peril came from within as well as from without. Germany was their peril, and Edouard was their peril. She wanted Simon to save them from Edouard! The folly and ignominy of such a hope were immeasurable.

They had come together, Simon and Edouard, in Simon's little car. They both looked as though they hadn't spoken all the way down. Perhaps the bad news had subdued them. Simon got out of his car before the door, and his face was sober. It was when he saw Françoise that it lightened a little. And then again when the beauty of the library struck him. The late sun was shining on the rusty-golden backs of old books and the big brownish-golden globes, and everywhere were lilacs, mauve and white, in bowls of old glass. The fireplace was not marred then by the iron stove; a little wood fire burned in it to take off the mild chill of the spring evening. Over it hung the portrait Simon liked, Jean du Rusquec in his

eighteenth-century coat with a red sash around his
waist. A young man, as Simon said, like a sword: Jean
du Rusquec, Grand Nabob des Indes. "He was a
great adventurer," she had told him. "Yes, in those
days we had our Indian kingdoms. My mother
was du Rusquec. That's one reason we bought this
place."

They had been listening to the radio when Simon
and Edouard came. They never left the radio in those
days. As soon as they came in André told him that
Antwerp had fallen and the Belgian government had
moved to Ostend. Françoise remembered the look
everyone used to have when these things were said.
A moment's complete blankness, absolute incredulity,
then a visible struggle to believe.

Maurice, bringing Simon one of the cocktails Simon
had taught him to make, paused a moment. "Pardon,
Monsieur, but may I ask a question?"

"Certainly."

Maurice had two ways of behaving: one was gruff
and slovenly, completely his own; the other was his
public manner. For the public manner he listened with
exaggerated attention, cocked his head to one side,
and nodded solemnly. He used long, formal words
and enunciated them so distinctly that he made them
crisp as radishes. They never knew whether this was
simply his idea of good behavior or a conscious parody
of good behavior.

"How long did it take Monsieur to drive here?" he asked.

"Nine hours," Simon told him.

"Nine hours! Weren't the roads congested?"

"Yes, for a while. Not much after Alençon."

Maurice's lips formed a soundless whistle. "And you had no accident?"

"No accident."

"In ordinary times it takes Monsieur Edouard ten hours. Mademoiselle takes twelve hours. Both have had accidents. How do you explain it?"

"It's safer to drive fast," Simon said. "I have two to three hours less in which to have an accident. I reduce the possibility of accident by from two to three tenths."

Maurice considered this. He suspected the joke. "It sounds logical," he said at last.

When he had gone Simon said to her, "You see — the French language. It *does* sound logical."

This made her smile faintly, though just then the fluting voice of Radio Paris announced that the French line had been broken south of Sedan. They were listening to the news when Edouard, who had gone upstairs, came back. Simon watched him come into the room. He saw Edouard go straight to a chair he seemed to know was waiting for him and put his cigarette down in an ashtray without looking.

At dinner they talked of nothing but the war,

though Simon had made an attempt to have a few words with Blaise.

"Do you do any sailing?" he asked.

"Yes, a little," Blaise said. His face lightened as though in spite of himself. "I've got a yawl," he said.

"Where do you keep it?"

"At Douarnenez."

"It's rather far, isn't it?"

"Not in a car."

They couldn't keep up interest in the yawl, or in each other. Edouard was talking about the new Reynaud Cabinet. He said Madame de Portes was the one who got Léger out. She didn't like him and had stirred up trouble between him and Reynaud. He added that Reynaud had dismissed Palewski for the same reason. Pétain, he said, would be a fine choice for the War portfolio. Everyone, he said, would approve of him.

Françoise asked, "Why?"

Edouard looked at her with alarm. "The hero of Verdun?" he exclaimed.

"You're usually the first to deflate a hero," she said. "In spite of Verdun he was a defeatist all through the last war, and ever since the last war. Also, he's a Fascist at heart."

"What right have you to say that?" André asked.

"Didn't the Croix de Feu recognize him as such and try to organize a plebiscite to make him President in '39?"

"A man can choose his enemies but not his supporters," Edouard said.

"That's just why they give him away!" Françoise exclaimed. "And hero or not, the Fascists have already chosen him and the defeatists have chosen him. He is their *image d'Epinal*."

"Doesn't it seem a little strange that the defeatists should choose a hero?" Edouard said.

"Why not choose a hero when they can?" Françoise answered. "It excuses them right away from an imputation of cowardice."

"The hero and the mistress," Blaise said sarcastically. "Specialty of the house!"

"Don't say that!" Françoise said sharply. "We produce just what most countries produce, all kinds and conditions of human being. And don't get the habit of making easy clichés. I can tell you, for instance, that the clear and logical French can be just as muddle-headed as anyone."

"Don't I know that!" Blaise muttered.

Françoise saw Simon looking curiously from one to the other. Perhaps he thought it very healthy that they should argue so freely. He smiled as he watched them, recognizing a familiar, almost an intra-family, state of affairs.

Edouard began to talk about how well the French soldier was standing up to the new German methods of warfare. "You'll see he'll invent some new methods of his own," he said. "It turns out that the seventy-five is excellent against tanks. The German methods may be new but the French soldier will more than meet them. He has a genius for improvisation." He spoke modestly, as though the French soldier were something he'd thought up himself.

"Improvisation!" André exclaimed. "Are you really putting any hope in that?"

Certainly not, Françoise thought. He is telling us that we're fools.

André went on, "Do you remember once when we visited some of those small, scattered factories near Lyons, where special work was done? For Boulanger and Company, I think. Each man had his own loom. They started out as standard affairs but each man made adjustments of his own, so that in the end no two were alike. On his loom he could play variations — improvisations — as though it were a violin. In consequence, each piece of weaving was varied and imaginative and beautiful. But while I admired it, I could see its end. Boulanger and Company now turns out workingmen's velveteen trousers in series. I simply mean that in some circumstances even certain of our virtues are no good to us."

When they had gone to the library for coffee Edouard came back to this.

"Shall I tell you why we haven't got any planes and guns and tanks in series," he said, "why we still have

to depend on our native talents? It's the fault, curiously enough, of the very people who howled for
war. Who wanted to defend the Czechs, the Poles,
and the British Empire? The same ones who wanted
to ally us with the Communists. They were the ones
who chose Communist Russia, and it happens they
chose a traitor. It serves them right. They also wanted
to make capital with the workers. They wanted to
build up class hatred, so that they could divide and
rule. They exacted nothing and nothing was done.
They made war with nothing to make war with. It's
almost unique in history."

"Do you know what I saw today?" Blaise said suddenly. He had been listening with a somber, scornful
face. "I went into town," he said, "and at the Epée I
saw a fellow I know. He's older than I. He was in
uniform and he was pretty badly battered. His arms
were bandaged and his face burned and his eardrums
cracked. He'd been at Longwy. There was a big tank
battle there. He said our tanks were good. They
chased the Germans out of the town. Afterwards the
Germans came back with their own tanks and we
drove them back again. Then what happened? We
had no more fuel. No more oil. Also, no support, no
infantry, nothing. We gave up Longwy. I wish you
could have seen the faces of the people who listened
to him tell this."

Edouard's eye fell on Maurice standing by the door.

"Maurice, come here," he said.

"Yes, Monsieur."

"I want you to tell us what you think of all this."

Maurice expressed exaggerated surprise. "Me, Monsieur? Am I permitted to have an opinion?"

"Yes, certainly. Tell us."

Maurice appeared to consider the matter. He began to gather the empty coffee cups, squinting horribly at them as he picked them up one by one. "I made the last war," he said finally, "and in consequence I lost a foot."

"Yes, yes, we know the story of the foot. Tell us your opinion of this one."

"Well, in this one it's certain that more feet will be lost. And they'll be lost by poor devils like me. Not by those gentlemen up there." He crooked a finger in the direction of Paris.

"But," Françoise said, "Maurice, don't you want to be free?"

"Free?" he said. "I don't know what Mademoiselle means by 'free.' I've been the slave of capitalists all my life."

He gave Edouard a sour, mocking look such as he had sometimes given Françoise when she was a little girl and was impudent to him.

Edouard flushed angrily.

When Maurice had gone Françoise said, "That serves you right, my dear, for trying to use Maurice as an example to us. You have just heard a Communist who does not want to fight for anyone."

Edouard said, "He is the perfect example of what I mean. Maurice and his kind have been coddled for years. They will not fight, now that war has come, because Russia is against us, but they will seize the opportunity to make a revolution."

"Oh, a revolution!" she cried. "To you that is always good for a scare. He fell on his nose — it's the fault of Voltaire."

"But it *is* a revolution," Blaise cried. "Can't you all see that? It's been going on for years. It didn't start here so we refuse to recognize it. But it will come here. No one minds dying in a revolution, not even through lack of oil, infantry, or whatever it is. But they won't die for what we've got here. You can't make masses of men die for a rotten world. Edouard, we're all sick of your world, didn't you know that? Six per cent on investments, sauces with the best cream and butter, and the workingman in his place. And we're sick of yours too, Françoise. All your clever, obstinate, selfish individualism. You're just like the weavers Father spoke of, each with his independent loom. Even what is good in you isn't good enough."

"Does Germany represent your revolution?" Simon asked him.

"It's part of the revolt against capitalism," Blaise said. He answered Simon sulkily, as though a child had interrupted him with a silly question. He didn't look at him.

"Then you don't want to fight either?" Simon insisted. "The queer thing is no one seems to want to fight, but all for different reasons."

André said, "Peace is so fundamental that each one justifies it in his own way."

"It's a sort of apathy," Françoise said.

"Call it that then. Apathy is one stage in the rejection of war." André's eyes were bright, as though he had a touch of fever. But he looked more wasted, smaller and frailer than ever. "It's a strange thing," he said, "that now as never before in history, great masses of people have come to realize what it means to destroy skilled hands and fertile brains and the complicated, delicate structures they have made. Whatever evil remains in our defective systems, our incomplete sense of brotherhood, peace is the only condition in which they can be cured. Then why," he cried, "why do we fight?"

Maurice, who had gone out and come in again, stopping to listen, to nod or to disapprove, suddenly turned on the radio with a sardonic flourish and the voice of the Service of Information came again, fluting, precise, and slightly singsong. It seemed that the Germans claimed the capture of St. Quentin, but the claim was not confirmed. The situation remained confused.

How tolerant we were, Françoise thought. It was not perfect tolerance because we were angry, but we were never again to talk like that. We were to lose many virtues, and we were to gain many also. Some of them were to be forced on us. Poverty and humility, two of the most Christian virtues, were to be forced on us. But tolerance differs from these in one particular. It cannot be forced.

Chapter XI

SHE REMEMBERED the rest of the evening. Simon had sat looking at her steadily, evidently hoping she would make some opportunity to see him alone. But she felt a reluctance to leave the others and find a private pleasure in the midst of so much anxiety common to them all. But finally she got up and said, "Let's take a little walk, Simon."

Simon jumped up and followed her out. She put a cape around her shoulders and they went into the spring night. The moon was coming up behind the hill. It had not reached the crest but the garden, the whole countryside, swarmed with a vague brightness. It was windless and the still air was full of fresh, cool smells. They walked up and down the terrace. The night seemed to be so completely made for them that for a moment she forgot the war. It made her feel that life, since it could produce this spring night, must also keep in reserve something good for them. They walked in silence. Simon held her hand in his.

Finally Simon said, "I don't feel that I should talk to you. Partly because it's so good just to be with you, and partly because of all this mess going on."

"It does hang over us, doesn't it? And I feel a little guilty when I forget it even for a minute."

"Somehow I feel sorriest for your father," Simon said.

"Yes, I suppose it is worse for him."

"I didn't realize what a complete hater of war he is. It must be a terrible dilemma."

"Yes, in more ways than you know. It's such a delicate balance he has to keep."

"What do you mean?"

"I mean certain things, just because they're fine, degenerate more quickly. But let's not talk about that now. What did you think of Blaise?"

He looked down at her and she saw him smiling. "Frankly, he's terrible. He knows too much."

"No, he doesn't know enough, really. But he is intelligent. The truth is he's had no experience. Even if a few things have happened to him, it's still not experience because it hasn't happened over and over."

Simon sighed. "And the truth is also that adolescence is a sort of underworld we have to live through. Everything is in us, even vice and crime. At the same time we discover free will. I wonder that it doesn't tear us off our bases for good and all."

"Were you a nice boy, Simon?" she asked.

"Fairly nice. But I'd hate to have to tell you everything I thought and did. I wasn't *too* nice, certainly."

"What did you want most?"

"Do you mean what did I want for me?"

"Yes."

Simon pressed her hand under his arm. "I suppose I wanted to be happy. Doesn't everyone?"

"I've always been told that all Americans expect to be happy."

"I suppose we do. You speak as though it were an extraordinary idiosyncrasy."

"It's extraordinary luck."

"Well," he said, "if it's not too complacent, let me say that I don't see why it couldn't be a normal expectation here. You've been happy, haven't you?"

"I've had luck, too. Individual luck. But I'm not at all sure it'll go on. Let's don't speak of happiness till this is over, not personal happiness anyway."

They stopped by the wall of the terrace. The moon came over the top of the hill. The whole world was bathed in benign, soft brightness.

"Can't we talk of it a little?" he asked.

She didn't answer.

He said, "Françoise, just tell me one thing and I won't go any further tonight. It's about Edouard." His voice changed on the name. "I didn't put the right question the other day." He waited a moment. "You don't love Edouard, do you?"

She waited so long to answer that he drew away from her, letting her hand slip from his. Finally she said, "Simon, I've had my adolescence, too, and at that time he fascinated me more than anyone else. It's important that we be honest with each other, isn't it?"

"Yes," he said shortly. He stood still, with his hands on the stone wall.

"Have you heard people talk about us?" she asked. He didn't answer.

"I'm sure you must have. But they didn't know anything about us. Edouard wasn't my lover. You have seen yourself, though, that he has an extraordinary capacity for corrupting. Just now, when he talked about our brave soldiers, he really wanted to make us afraid, and some other time I'll tell you why he did that."

She stopped, and wished sadly that it were not necessary to go on. Then she said, "He has corrupted us all, Father, Blaise, and me, to some degree. But for me that's over. There is nothing he can do now. He has no part of me. He never did have any part that you would ever want. He is just a sort of relic, not a creditable one. I'd like to think that I need never see him again."

Simon turned and looked down into her eyes and she looked back. She felt as though they were swimmers in the moonlight, swimming in the light itself, side by side.

She thought Simon had understood her perfectly and that she had understood herself perfectly. He leaned over and kissed her on the forehead and then on the mouth. And they said not a word of Edouard and in a moment they heard his voice calling from the door.

"You missed the ten-o'clock news. Weygand has been sent for. He arrived today. He replaces Gamelin."

He walked up and joined them. He began to explain what Weygand's ideas were. He had already heard them talked about in Paris. They confirmed his belief in French ingenuity to meet unforeseen obstacles.

"A flexible, mobile front," he said, forming the front before them with round gestures. He seemed to breathe confidence.

But it wasn't that that made her happy. She distrusted his confidence. It was Simon who made her happy in spite of herself.

Chapter XII

SHE REMEMBERED very well, too, that she had even awakened the next morning with this astonishing lightness of heart.

How was it possible, with things as they were, that the mere presence of Simon, the outsider, the onlooker, could bring any happiness? It seemed shameful.

But it was shameful only because she knew now what had happened.

She had promised to show Simon the chapel. On his first visit it had been under repair. It was one of the gems of the district and they were proud of it and kept it in excellent condition. So she drank her coffee and hurried downstairs. Simon was not down yet. Blaise had gone into town. Her father was in his study, trying to telephone to Paris, and Edouard was with him.

She switched on the radio for a moment. "The Germans have annexed the districts of Eupen and Malmédy from Belgium. The Germans have reached Péronne and claim Laon. This has not been confirmed. The situation remains confused. . . ."

She walked out on the terrace and after taking a few turns there went down to the flower garden. It was a fair morning. The sun touched her face and a fresh, tonic breeze blew softly from the sea. There had been a heavy dew, not quite dry yet, and the grass and plants were filmed with silver. The iris was in bloom, celestial blue, and many-colored tulips, and little rosy English daisies and dark pansies set out from the greenhouse. The lilac bushes at the edge of the garden were flowering. The peony stalks were red, one could almost see them grow. Columbine waved fragilely. On the other side of an arbor lay the kitchen garden. Below was the orchard. It seemed suddenly a miracle: every fortunate chance, soil, rain, sun and dew, the bulbs, the roots, even the earthworms, had all mysteriously combined to produce this delicious freshness, this immaculate, bright beauty, this promise of an order so contrary to what was happening.

The Germans will be at the Channel in a few days, she thought. But at least now we have Weygand. His idea of the flexible, moving front may be exactly the defense necessary. It may be one of those last-minute inspirations of a great soldier.

Then a wave of resolution went through her: We must all back him up in our hearts, we must stiffen each of our individual wills, we must be strong and brave and clean to support him.

It is such a terrible thing we face, she thought,

looking at the garden, that it will take the last particle of our faith. But we have everything valuable in life to protect; the test comes when life has never before been so precious.

She saw Edouard standing on the terrace smoking a cigarette. He looked down and saw her, threw away the cigarette, and waved his hand. He came down the steps to join her and his walk was heavy and slow. When he came near she saw his face was quite changed. He was sallow, with the paleness of a dark, ruddy-skinned man who has been ill. His eyes wavered as though he had just been struck a hard physical blow.

She was so shocked that she spoke in a whisper. "Is it so very bad?"

He nodded. He took her arm and she felt that it was she who led him rather than he her. They walked toward the orchard. Perhaps she had an instinct to give him shelter, to put the trees between them and whoever might look at him. They walked for a moment in silence. Then she said again, "Is it really so bad?" And when he still didn't answer she said, "But what about Weygand? He'll be able to do something, won't he?"

"No," he said in a leaden voice. "What's the use of an eleventh-hour strategy? And he has nothing to work with, no planes, not enough tanks, or men."

"But surely — " she began.

He turned, still holding her arm, and said with sullen, low fury, "Now, perhaps, you are satisfied. You, with your ridiculous illusion."

"What illusion?" she whispered.

"That we had only to unsheathe our sword," he said, "and the powers of darkness would vanish."

"Oh, no!" she protested. "I knew what we'd have to sacrifice."

"You knew what we'd have to sacrifice! And you were prepared to do it? How very noble of you! But you don't know what it means. You don't know what you're saying."

"Edouard, for God's sake!" she exclaimed. She put her free hand on his arm. The color was coming back to his face. He breathed heavily and blinked from the returning rush of blood.

He shook off her arm. "No, you don't know what you're saying. You think it's enough to stand there and offer to die for something. Who's going to ask you to die? No one. You'll be put in a car, hustled off somewhere. Well, what if you do die? Does it matter to those others? Have you got any right to say what they shall do? Have you?"

There was no answer. She looked dumbly at him.

"I tell you," he cried, "that at this minute thousands of Frenchmen are dying. Do you know what it is to die? To fall in a burning plane, to be torn to bits by a shell, to be drenched with gasoline in a tank and set afire? No, you don't."

He began to pace up and down, sometimes stopping to hurl a word directly at her. "Do you know the sort of men who have to do these things? Decent fellows, young, some of them mama's boys like Blaise. Some not young, men who have fought before and worked hard and earned a little rest. Workers, tough, industrious, honest. What good is their death? What does it get us? We need them in fields and factories, eating solid food and sleeping with their wives. We need *them,* I tell you — not their death."

"Yes," she whispered, and tears came to her eyes. "I know we need them."

He waited a moment, looking at her. "Do you know what the roads of France are today?" he said. "I'll tell you. Whole villages have been turned into little puffs of dust and the people who could still crawl out of them are moving along the roads, carrying the iron pot and the sewing machine and the mattress, pushing each other like a crowd coming from the races. The village they've come from is dead and the village they go to is dead. The little French village, the church, the Mairie, the shop, the café where the old men play dominoes and settle the world, the school with the kids in their black aprons. What's worth the death of those villages — of one village? You're the one who knows. Tell me."

She stood with her head bent. Her few tears had dried quickly.

Edouard repeated, "Well, what have you got to say? Out with it. Let's have it."

"I have no right to say anything," she said, "except that I would be willing to die myself."

"That's fine," he said, "that's splendid! The only thing is you won't have to do it."

She thought he would walk away from her. But instead he stopped and, with hands that still shook, took out another cigarette and lighted it. He inhaled the smoke deeply, throwing his head back.

"You know absolutely nothing," he said at last. "Once it was a pleasure to me, that unique, that all-embracing ignorance of yours. And learned, too — a regular bluestocking with it all. It came from living with a man like André. I suppose you never knew where children come from, did you? A regular 'Miss' in an English novel. We all had to guard you. Me too. Wasn't I damned careful of you? Well, I'll still be careful of you. I'll tell you nothing to spoil it. Thank me for it someday, will you?"

His face became a grimace and she thought he would spit on the ground. "Hang onto your ignorance," he said. "It won't be so easy from now on."

He leaned back against an apple tree, exhausted. He smoked his cigarette angrily for a moment, then he threw it away. He took a large, fine handkerchief out of his pocket and wiped his face and under his collar. Then he shook the handkerchief out with a curious, frivolous flip of the wrist. He folded it carefully and put it back in his pocket.

Suddenly she saw something in that gesture, coming so close to his passionate words, and those words rearranged themselves and their meaning changed.

She saw what he meant to do. She saw also what he meant André to do. This was the trap that had been laid. Everything had come together at once: Edouard's realism, his common sense, his passion, his drive and sureness, and André's luminous humanity, the best of it and the weaknesses of it as well. And over both of them the plane hovering, the smoke of the village, the smell of death.

"You think we're lost, don't you?" she said.

"I know the war is lost."

"But then *we* are lost."

"Not necessarily."

To look at him was like seeing a door close. But she could see what was behind the door. She saw again the phrase in Simon's letter: *Winnie said Edouard had gone to Switzerland.*

"Why did you come to see Father?" she asked.

"What a question! I planned to come two weeks ago." All the heat had gone out of his voice. He leaned on the tree, looking at her insolently and warily. "Do you mean you didn't want me?"

"I mean that you came for a special reason. I think I know what it is. I wish I were wrong."

"In any case, I am leaving in an hour for Paris."

"Oh, you are — and will Father go with you?"

"I imagine you will both follow me shortly."

Françoise looked past the trunk of the apple tree, past Edouard, toward the flower garden. It was more vivid against the grass of the terrace slope and the worn gray stone of the house. It looked tiny and bright, like a garden in an old illumination.

"Didn't you go to Switzerland last week?" she asked.

This surprised him. His face closed tighter.

"Yes. Who told you that?"

"I heard it indirectly. An old gossip in Paris, actually, told Simon. He didn't think it had any importance and he mentioned it. I know it is important."

"What makes you think so?"

"Edouard, there's no use our talking like this, is there? I know that if you went to Switzerland it meant something."

"Naturally it did. I went on business."

"You have business in Switzerland?"

He nodded. He looked up at the sky as though she bored him with her questions.

"Or is it business with Germany?"

"My dear," he said, and how reasonable his voice had become, how different from the choking voice

with which he spoke of the dying men and villages,
"it can hardly shock you to know that a great many
French, and a great many English too, still have
money invested in Germany. Naturally we don't want
to lose it! I, for instance, have, through an intermedi-
ary, a block of I. G. Farben."

"What!"

"Come, come. I've had it a long time. It was not
treason to own stock in operations outside the country. We were not at war then. Now, to tell the truth,
there's a war economy order in Germany that affects
the interests of the investors. It concerns a fifty per
cent increase in payable income tax on excess profits,
and at the same time a stabilization of wages. I fancy
that in the end they'll get around it, but I went to con-
sult with some of the other stockholders."

As he spoke a faint glint of the gipsy horse trader
came into his eyes, the look of the man who has been
smart, though no one but himself knows it yet.

"I don't believe you went to Switzerland for that,"
she said. "I believe you went to see someone, a group
probably, and no doubt others went with you, to hear
what terms they might be willing to give us."

He gave a sharp, awkward laugh. "Your father in
1915 sent a man on exactly that errand," he said.
"Merrheim, of the Metal Federation, was at that time
a close friend of his. He and several others met the
Germans of the Socialist minority at Zimmerwald.

There were Italians there also, and others. Lenin represented the Russians! They wished to make peace. Yes, I see already what you think. You think that André's effort was nobler than any I might make."

"But wasn't it?" she cried. "He had no money invested in the Farbenindustrie. As to what you said just now about all that death, it's absolutely exact, I know. It is an exact statement of the most awful tragedy of our time. But somehow it's not honest. That is, from *you* it is not honest. Because I know you too well. I know that to you peace means a good bargain. You think it's madness to oppose Germany, not because we couldn't win our freedom, but because our freedom isn't worth it. It would cost too much. You think no one should pay too much for anything."

She stopped, suddenly thinking that it would do no good, mean nothing, just to be angry. That was not the kind of courage she had imagined a while ago. She looked up into the apple boughs. The rosettes of green leaves were still glistening with freshness. A few white flowers clung like little stars to the branches. She tried to summon all her force. But when she spoke it was with a bitterness that had become more personal and intimate.

"You're too economical, Edouard," she said. "Even a bit miserly. Also, you think you're cleverer than they, that in the end you'll get the best of them. Isn't that so? You want to buy us off cheap."

"Well, you're wrong again," he said. And with him also personal injury was beginning to crowd out the rest. "Because we couldn't win even at the highest price asked of us. We haven't got the actual physical means. Forget about righteousness for a moment. I tell you we'd be completely destroyed. England knows that, that's why she'll be clearing out shortly. The United States knows it, and that's why in spite of all the flattering of officials, all this Lafayette, this Jeanne d'Arc, this flame that will never die, and so on, she won't give us so much as a company of men or one destroyer. We know it ourselves! But it will take a special kind of courage to admit it and to do what is necessary."

"If that's true it's because men like you, without faith, made it so."

He gave an exclamation of disgust and again he looked as though he would spit on the ground. Her voice rose and became a little hysterical.

"I know your special kind of courage. The worst is you think Father has it, too. You dare to think you are alike in this. And again you're going to make use of him. Everyone — your friends, your countrymen, the enemy, the world — is just something to be manipulated by you. You know you can make Father join a peace movement. That thousands would listen to him who would turn away from you in disgust. In the end he'll be your victim. He won't know it till it's too late, and once this peace comes he'll be without hope, and the country will be without hope. You can't do that, Edouard."

His anger boiled up in him again. He made a sudden furious movement toward her and gripped her shoulders.

"Keep still," he said, "and listen to me. You're going to be saved, whether you want it or not. I tell you squarely that in a matter of weeks, maybe less, we'll make peace."

"No!" she cried.

"And when it comes," he went on, "you'll want a scapegoat, naturally. The righteous always want a scapegoat. Well, you can take me. Here I am. I've always been your scapegoat, haven't I? It's all I've been good for."

She pushed back from him. But his eyes came nearer, shining and open, exposing all that was in him. It was like that day long ago. She heard again the solid pounding of his heart.

"Make up your mind!" he said between his teeth. "Once and for all. Do you hate me? Have you decided at last to hate me?"

She made an effort to draw away. To forget Edouard and find a larger, deeper strength somewhere in her own faith. But she said in a whisper, "Yes, I hate you."

They stared at each other in silence, because what they had said was irrevocable.

He said, "Then you hate me for the worst reason

in the world. You hate me because you wrong me."

For the first time he kissed her full on the lips. She didn't move but accepted it with a sort of awful relief. Because it was the point that had to be reached before they could draw apart finally and forever. It had been years in coming and when it came it was not only Edouard, all of him in one compass, but it was disaster, treachery, and defeat. In kissing Edouard she tasted the bitter dregs of all he had done to them in the past, and for the first time knew the sharp foretaste of what would come.

It was really no wonder that she did not see Simon standing in the middle of the flower garden, still and rigid as a stone.

Chapter XIII

WHEN Edouard let her go he looked down at her gravely and without ardor. He looked at her questioningly. Then, seeing the answer at once, he turned and walked heavily away.

Françoise sat down on the ground under the tree. Now Edouard has gone, she thought. And for a moment she felt empty and strange. Edouard was right in one thing. He knew that in her way she leaned on him. Just as André did. She depended on him in an ugly, almost sly way, letting him take whatever blame there was. So she was punished for that, because most of her confidence had vanished with him.

Now she was alone and hurt and shaken. There was no one to help in this struggle that was going to come. Not her father, not Blaise.

But how dare I think of it! It is a struggle, but is it my struggle? Who am I to claim a part in it? As Edouard says, it isn't I who will die. It isn't Father and Blaise who will die. I won't even lose Simon. Who am I to presume to make an act of faith for thousands of others, an act of faith that if it were accepted might only offer them up to horrible, useless death?

Are we perhaps really lost? Are we in some way deserving to be lost? Is my lack of faith a sign of that? What shall I do? If I decide the risk must be taken, could I by my secret will touch anyone?

If Father were right — What if peace that all men long for, even if it were only peace to do business, only peace to cheat and oppress each other and be dirty in, were better than destruction? Peace at least binds up and war shatters.

The children in their little black aprons going to school. The young men falling in flames. If the whole unseen order that holds us together should be peace and not resistance, not struggle, then any crime would be better than a crime against that.

Men like my father believe this, not only the Edouards.

But who knows what conditions them, what distorted memories, personal and racial? Even men like Father.

What about Simon, my innocent, my fortunate Simon?

It couldn't be that he might guess better than they —

No. That is nonsense. But still, one has a deep instinct to question the one who is empty of experience. The idiot, the child, the oracle. We distrust experience. Edouard represents experience. We want something purer than that.

What shall I do? I'm not equal to it.

She got up and went back to the house.

Simon was sitting in the library alone, slumped in a chair with his long legs stretched before him, staring at the floor. When she came in he looked up slowly. Then he got to his feet, politely but without a smile.

"Oh, Simon," she said, "I'm so glad you're up. Have you had coffee?"

"Yes, thanks." He pointed to an empty cup on the table. A burning cigarette lay on the edge.

"You don't feel well?" she asked quickly.

"Oh, yes. Quite."

"You look so thoughtful."

"I've just been thinking I ought to go back."

"Now?"

"Yes. The hospital has been sending some of us out. My turn will come any moment now. I shouldn't have come here."

Her disappointment was so great she couldn't speak. But not now, when I need you, she thought. She didn't notice that he would not look directly at her.

"But Simon," she said, "you came all that long way for just one night!"

"It's been worth it," he said stiffly.

They stood in awkward silence.

After a moment she said, "Wouldn't you like to see the chapel before you go?"

"Thanks," he said. "I would like to see it."

As they walked across the terrace she said, "I suppose you'll be driving Edouard back?"

"Yes. He asked just now if I was going."

So it was Edouard coming through the library and Simon asking, "Have you seen Françoise?" And Edouard saying, "Yes, I left her in the orchard" and perhaps the look of Edouard's face, still heated, still disturbed. She had seen how it hurt Simon to watch Edouard sink into his accustomed chair. She had seen how a gesture of Edouard's that was not even made, had roused real hatred in him. And now in this terrible day he found room for his jealousy. She thought wryly, if it was an innocent I wanted I've got him.

As they crossed the garden she put her hand on his arm and they stopped. She did not speak but she thought if he so much as looked, he must share with her the exquisite, tragic sense of her country around them. And he would feel her question: What are you and I in all this? Because you're part of it. If you love me you can't be the mere onlooker forever. What are we? We are nothing unless we understand first what this means, and second what must be done to save it. If we don't succeed in understanding, if we fail this test, then we fail in everything.

And we fail in each other.

They stood looking at the garden.

"You've got very pretty flowers," he said.

They walked down the paths and instead of going

to the orchard, turned to the grassy lane that led
toward the chapel.

Simon asked her stilted questions — when was the
chapel built, was it older than the *manoir*, were the
Rusquecs who had built it direct ancestors of her
mother? She said absently that the chapel was built in
the sixteenth century and dedicated to St. Herbaud;
it was simpler, smaller, and less beautiful than the
famous one at Plovenez-du-Faou but very like it; the
manoir was built a hundred years later; her mother
was a collateral descendant of that Jean du Rusquec
whose portrait hung in the library.

Bedded deep in the earth, with the boughs of ancient
apple trees pressing against it, it had the look of so
many Breton chapels, of being older than it really was.
Indeed, it looked like a strange, battered little ship of
some primitive, forgotten form, encrusted with gray-
ish coral growths.

Françoise had the key in her pocket and she opened
the door. The inside smelled of earth and dampness
like a cave, and was filled with twilight. She showed
him the little chancel screen, richly carved out of oak
in a rustic, Renaissance style. Over it was a group of
Christ on the cross, with two angels receiving the
blood in a chalice, carved with extraordinary poignance and simplicity. Then there was the monolithic
stone table on which the peasants laid offerings of the
tails of cows on the feast day of St. Herbaud, who was

the patron of horned creatures and of stables. There were the tombs, bearing the arms of the Rusquecs, "*d'azur au chef d'or, chargé de trois pommes de pin, de gueules.*" And finally in a niche she showed him a strange little Bodhisattva of gold lacquer, a Buddhist saint, smiling and alien, brought back, according to tradition, by that Grand Nabob des Indes who had put it there as a tribute, or perhaps with the cynicism of a man who has known many religions.

When they had seen the chapel they went out and she locked the door again.

"Shall we sit here a minute?" she said.

She sat on a low stone wall, thick with moss, and Simon sat beside her. The grass under their feet was sprinkled with daisies and they could see the orchard, which had once been much larger, of which these apple trees around the chapel had been a part. Beyond was a low green hill.

"If we climbed the hill we could see Locranon," she said. "You must come again when there's more time. I want to show you everything."

Simon took out a cigarette case and offered her one. She took it, waiting for him to speak. He lighted it and then his own. But still he said nothing. And she couldn't think of words to say what she wanted.

"What's the matter, Simon?" she asked finally. "What's wrong?"

"Why," he spoke with an effort, "isn't everything wrong?"

"Yes. It's so wrong that probably everything has never been so wrong before. But you don't think it's hopeless, do you?"

"I'm no military expert," he said. "But it doesn't look good, does it?"

"Simon," she said, "I'm going to tell you something. If we're really friends, if we're really what we think we are to each other, you ought to know it. And I have no one else I can or want to share it with."

He made a quick, uneasy movement and said, "Are you sure you want to?"

"Yes, I'm sure. You see, the truth is I am depending on you now, more than you know. You told me the other day that I'd been brought up in a political atmosphere of intrigue and involved and false values. I suppose that's true. You also told me that I belonged to something that was going to die, was finished. But I don't want that to be true. I think even for you it mustn't die. But I'm terribly close to it, so close and I love it so much, perhaps I don't see clearly. I was half joking when I said you were an 'innocent,' but in a sense that is true, too. I was thinking just now that you might have a power of seeing that's still unspoiled, if you could be brought to use it."

Simon leaned his elbows on his knees and his face against his hands. He was looking at the earth.

"All right," he said in a muffled voice, "go ahead."

"First it's about us," she said, "about me and Blaise and Father."

"And Edouard?" he asked.

"Yes, Edouard too. You've seen us all here and you know what we are — terribly divided and yet also terribly united. We have all got an ordeal to go through which is going to be worse than anything we can imagine. Things are going so badly that it will take a miracle to save us. But I'm convinced miracles only happen through complete willingness to believe on the part of each creature. And from that must come the complete willingness to sacrifice anything and everything for the miracle. Well, as it is now with us, we haven't all got that belief."

She found it hard to go on. Simon waited stolidly. Then she said hurriedly, "My father is going to try to make a quick peace."

These words shocked him but she could feel he was shocked in a way she hadn't expected. In the silence that followed she felt his shock came mostly from an outer, conventional, self.

Finally he said, "Why would he do that?"

"Because he is all ready to believe that it must be, and because Edouard is here to give the final push."

"Edouard!" he exclaimed.

"Yes. You think it's strange that Edouard could determine it for him. But I'm afraid he will. Oh, I can't tell you now, it's too long, but for years and years he has had a power over us. He has seemed to be a balance for us, a great rich store of good common sense that we dipped into, when our own knowledge grew too thin and too abstract. Now all his arguments have everything on their side. The whole great physical certainty is on their side. Father won't be able to resist. At the last moment there is always something pathetically uncertain about Father. I've seen it so often. He doesn't trust himself. He doesn't entirely trust people. At bottom he's astonished and frightened by them. He has no confidence in them. Oh, Simon, don't make me explain — try to understand. Sometimes one has to beg for an understanding beyond reason."

Simon said slowly, "But I don't see what your father can do. He's a private citizen now. The men in power are the ones to worry about."

"The men in power won't make the peace. Others will do it. I'm afraid Father will be one of them."

Simon dropped his cigarette unsmoked and put his foot on it. "Are you just imagining all this? Or has he told you?"

"He hasn't told me because he hasn't yet made up his mind. And perhaps he won't tell me anyway. But you know what his career has been."

"Yes. I've heard that in the last war he tried to do the same thing."

"He did. But there were powerful men then who had faith to go on. Now I don't know who we have strong enough. You mustn't think," she added, "that Father wants peace from weakness. He has devoted his life to it. And he was right to do so, absolutely right. Now he'd go through martyrdom for it, perhaps. But you see, what I believe is that *now* it would be the wrong kind of martyrdom. It would be sterile. I believe that peace now would be the wrong kind of peace. It would be, quite simply, slavery, unspeakable degradation."

"And just what is it he could do? I don't understand."

"He could join with all those who feel as he does. And there are a great many. Some of them are honest and courageous like himself, others are unscrupulous, cowardly, and self-seeking. It would be easy for them to wreck a complicated machinery like ours, a machinery already under such a fearful strain. There would be plenty for them to do. They could make a disintegration from within to match the pressure from outside, in the army first, in the whole life of the country, in public morale. Then, in the midst of chaos, one man would step in and say, 'It's over. We must have peace at any price.'"

"Who would that be, your father?"

"Oh, no. He's not powerful enough. You can be sure that whoever it will be, is already picked out. But he'll need support of all sorts, even noble, idealistic, support. My father would be one of his supporters."

"And Edouard?" he said.

"Certainly. You told me, you remember, that Edouard had been to Switzerland. Well, I know why he went. He must have gone to see someone there. Perhaps Abetz. It doesn't matter. I know what they said to Edouard. They said, 'See here, the whole thing is madness. We want to be your friends, we'll give moderate terms, exact only a sort of token victory, life will go back to normal, men return to work, factories will produce goods instead of munitions, and we'll buy them.' It's tempting — I can see that. The only trouble is it's false. It wouldn't happen like that."

Simon leaned over and uprooted a daisy. Then he put it back and patted the earth around it with his foot.

"Are you very sure yourself," he said, "that this fight ought to go on, are you sure it isn't hopeless?"

"That's just it, Simon. That's just why I want to talk to you. I am sure, yes. But I've just had a moment of fearful doubt. This morning when I woke up I felt we could do anything. But since then it has changed a little. How can I say that I'm willing that millions of men and women and children should die? I can only say that *I* am willing *I* should die. My belief can't stretch beyond myself. The ones I love don't believe. No, they don't believe. So what shall I do, give up to despair? But if there is a miracle mustn't it be made of many parts, each part vital to the whole? If I give up, who knows? It might be just the one tiny part necessary to turn the balance. Simon, you come from an outside world; anything can happen there. Miracles do happen there. Tell me what you think."

Simon patted the earth around the daisy again.

"That's a question I don't think you want answered," he said. "Because there's only one answer and you know it already. If your father is really willing to make a deal with the enemy, that is, to do it separately, behind the Government's back, behind your Allies' back, too, I suppose, then he's a traitor, technically speaking. And if you believe what you say you do, you ought to inform the authorities."

Françoise sat stunned. Then she said, "I didn't put my question plainly. But I can tell you that in the first place treachery has nothing to do with my father, and second, it would do no good to inform anyone. Because it isn't only he, it isn't only Edouard — it's hundreds, thousands, who feel as they do. Maybe it's millions. I don't know. As to what they actually plan to do, I have no proof and no one would listen to me."

They sat silently while Françoise waited for him

to speak again but he did not, and shame slowly filled her at having said these things, at having exposed all this, to the man who sat stolidly and full of smug disapproval and untried righteousness — a stranger, as she now knew. And she had betrayed her father to this stranger who didn't understand or care. Herself also. Simon no more than Edouard would believe in the miracle.

But he did speak finally. He said, "I think you should do nothing at all, and it's clear you don't intend to. Anyway, I shouldn't have said that about the traitor. It was insufferable. I am sure your father is only a victim of his own good will. As to Edouard," he said with sudden bitterness, "that's different. But you don't want to give *him* up as a traitor, do you?"

"Edouard!" she exclaimed. "If it would do any good, I'd kill him."

She turned to see that he was looking at her at last, with a cruel, silly smile on his face.

"You would? It didn't look like that a little while ago."

Françoise stood up suddenly and Simon stood up too. She looked straight ahead of her down the path she must take back to the house.

Simon, having begun to talk, couldn't stop.

"After all, it's hardly fair or wise to ask *me*. It's not my country, not my father — my friend. To fight or not to fight — it's entirely up to you."

A deep shudder went through her. All she could think of at this moment was that it was horrible to have him stumble on like this. Though she wanted to fly from him, she still couldn't move.

"I appreciate your confidence," he said in a wavering voice, polite, regretful.

"Good-by, Simon," she said.

After a moment he said, "Good-by," and held out his hand. She didn't take it but walked off quickly.

Later she heard him from her window saying good-by to Blaise and André. He spoke in a voice still unnatural with strain. "Don't forget how to make cocktails," he said to Maurice.

The car door banged. The engine started. In a few moments the sound of it died away over the hill.

He had the right to judge me, she thought, because I asked for it. His judgment is correct. No doubt we are lost. No doubt we brought it on ourselves.

Well, even so — we'll go on fighting. For a time anyway.

That afternoon she and André and Blaise started back to Paris. And from then on it was like being in a house that slowly collapsed, dragging down one loved and familiar thing after another in its fall.

The memory of these things tormented her as though they had happened only yesterday. But re-

membering them she thought that whatever was to
happen now was inevitable. In the sun and beauty and
riches of the South, surrounded by friends, gorged
with food and wine, even wearing a foolscap of
power, they had finally made their choice. And now
it no longer mattered who had been wise or who
fatally mistaken. Each in his own way had been part
of a betrayal, she as much as any.

That was why now the tragedy of the hostages was
to prove their own. Not only because they were involved somehow, still mysteriously, in the actual murder, but because they themselves were hostages. In
doing what they had done, willingly or unwillingly,
blindly or in full consciousness, they had given themselves up to another logic, another order. They had
accepted the law which takes vengeance on the innocent as well as the guilty. The law which recog-
nizes no innocent and no guilty, but only the weak.

Chapter XIV

WHEN she came downstairs the house seemed very small and dark. It had begun to rain and the lash of water against the panes gave it a beleaguered look. There was not much for her to do and she sat down presently with her knitting near a window. But it was too cold to sit still. She was full of restlessness, physical restlessness that made her nerves twitch and also mental unease that gave her mind no peace.

She thought, Partly I'm suffering from acidia, the peculiar boredom of those who have had their emotions stretched too far. I couldn't possibly read a book, play the piano, or put flowers in a vase. No, any simple thing, any ordinary action, would be flat and dry as though it were cut out of cardboard. I spend my time in emptiness or a breathless haste to have the next disaster arrive.

I wait for the next disaster because I want to get it over. I am running down a hill toward disaster, toward death. Toward peace perhaps. I want to die because I will not be able to face what must happen to Blaise if he did it. I will not be able to face his being shot.

I am not even able to face his having done it. Not
because I can't understand his doing it but because
of Peguinot and Simmonet and Jacques. I cannot believe he would do it, for whatever reason, and then let
them suffer for him.

But, she thought, perhaps the stocking is not conclusive. Am I to believe that only one girl in the
countryside wears black-cotton stockings? And that
she gives them away as souvenirs? I am acting and
thinking under a horrible inner compulsion toward
death. But I must not, I must certainly not, include
Blaise in it. He must survive even if no one else does.

Suddenly she got up and rang the bell. Presently
Maurice appeared.

"Come in," she said, "I want to speak to you."

He came inside but left the door open to show he
had more important things to do and must get back
to them.

"Mademoiselle wants to scold me," he grumbled.
"The service was bad last night. But with that hysterical hen in the kitchen . . ."

But seeing this was to be a serious conversation he
lapsed into silence.

"Where did Monsieur Blaise go?"

"Has he gone?"

"Yes. You don't know where?"

He looked completely indifferent. "Perhaps to
Douarnenez."

"Why to Douarnenez?"

"How should I know?"

With his gorilla arms hanging and his gloomy ridged brow, there was something frightening about him. There was also something cold and lonely. Why would he never take part in their troubles, never accept their estimate of them? These endless parodies of his. His unwillingness to recognize the true and the tragic. Once he killed a man, and that was the time he made a fool of himself. Never again! If war came it was just a stupid business of those others, who had never learned how to run things. All his complaints were of trivial things, the food, the card to circulate, the extra work. He refused to believe what was behind these things. Or rather, he reduced it all to one thing: he'd never had any gifts or pleasures, he was a poor man, and poor fellows like himself no one really gave a damn about. Everything else that happened was *their* affair, those others, the ones on top, the fortunate. The ones who went around enjoying things, eating the best food, making love, never doing an honest day's work. Those others, who in some mysterious way understood each other, communicated with each other. That was the worst of it. Because he was lonely. His whole life had been an attempt to break out of loneliness.

So he made dirt on them, those others, and they could take that, too.

"Maurice," she said, "you know we're all in trouble here."

"Everyone is in trouble," he said.

"I'm not speaking generally. I'm speaking about what has happened here, among ourselves, in this house."

"Then you mean Monsieur Edouard?" he said.

Françoise was surprised. She said, "Why do you say that?"

"Well, isn't it bad luck that he should turn up just at this moment?"

"Bad luck! But he was asked to come."

"Then it's bad luck that he was asked."

"But he was the only one who could help us."

Maurice shrugged. Then he said, "If Mademoiselle thinks that Monsieur Edouard came to help, she's entirely mistaken."

"I don't think you know what you're talking about, Maurice. He came because he was asked to come. He was asked to come in order to help us save the hostages."

Maurice shook his head and said no more. He had lost interest.

But Françoise persisted. "When we asked him to come, we did it in good faith. We didn't want innocent men to suffer. We didn't ask him to come in order to save those who were guilty."

"Evidently," Maurice said.

"But someone is guilty."

"Evidently," he repeated.

"You don't know who it is?" she asked abruptly.

He said ironically, beginning one of his imitations of correct speech, "I have not as yet been informed."

This will get nowhere, she thought. She said, "Think what a position it would put us in. We got Monsieur Edouard here to help us. Suppose suspicion should fall, by a curious chain of circumstances, on one of us."

"Monsieur Edouard would like that," he said.

"You think he would!" she exclaimed. "What makes you think so?"

"Monsieur Edouard has had enough of this family," Maurice said. "He wouldn't mind a bit if something happened to rid him of the whole lot." Then he added more succinctly, "He's sick of you."

"But then he was sick of us at Vichy, and why did he come here? He had only to stay away."

Maurice shrugged. He wasn't interested in following it further. "You ought to have let him stay away," he said. "I always say, let well enough alone."

Maurice irritated her. For once he had seen a truth but it was a small, personal piece of bitterness affecting, as he appeared to think, someone else, not himself. And it was only a half truth. Edouard might be sick of them, might even want to get rid of them, but if that were entirely true then Edouard had mutilated part of himself, lost part of himself.

She said, "We mustn't let him have any reason to suspect us of anything. Last night it seems Yves made several strange remarks in the kitchen. . . ."

Maurice's face changed. His mocking look disappeared. He carefully closed the door behind him and said, "I know to what Mademoiselle refers. It's the business of that damned gun. I should never have spoken of it to Monsieur Blaise. He's only a kid. The idea of a hidden gun struck him as interesting. I suppose it made him feel we had a good joke on *them*. Anyway, he shot the rabbit. That wasn't criminal, was it? But Marie heard it. We didn't know she was around. But she heard it and told Yves. And Yves, as you know, is crazy." He put his finger to his forehead and suddenly lost interest again. "That's all there is to it."

She had never heard him say so much, except sometimes at a distance, through the kitchen door.

"You and Blaise seem agreed to consider Yves insane," she said. "Maybe he is, a little, but if he talks to other people what will happen?"

"That depends on whom he talks to."

"To Monsieur Edouard for instance?"

"Well, all he could say is that I have kept a gun, and I will deny that, of course. No one can find the gun, so what then?"

"Are you sure they can't find it?"

"It's buried."

"Where?"

Maurice shifted his feet and looked uncomfortable. "It would be better if Mademoiselle didn't know. The less Mademoiselle knows the better."

"No, Maurice, I want you to tell me. I want to be absolutely certain that what you say is true. I'm sure it offends you for me to say this but I have to. Because I am involved in it almost as much as you are. There is no use pretending we aren't all in danger from this. Something is wrong here. I feel it. I have felt it for the last three days. You prowl around here at night — " He made a gesture of protest. "Yes, you do. It's useless to put on a show of innocence. My father has seen you. You seem to have no explanation for that. Monsieur Blaise too." She hesitated. "He has done one or two imprudent things." She thought of the black stocking and it froze all her blood again. She cried, "No, I must be sure the gun is where you say it is."

Maurice looked at her darkly, his whole face full of obstinacy. Suddenly he said, "All right. Come."

He opened the door with a jerk and without waiting for her to go first, he went out into the hall. She could see by his back that he felt, If you're going to make a fuss this serves you right.

Françoise followed him. At the door leading to

the terrace she took her raincoat off the hook and
threw it around her. They went out in the heavy rain,
across the terrace, down through the garden and the
kitchen garden, and through a gate into the farm
court. Maurice looked to be sure no one was around.
In the house occupied by Yves all the windows were
tightly closed, blind from the darkness behind them
and streaming with rain. He seemed satisfied that no
one was looking. He went to the barn and opened
the small door cut in one oaken leaf of the big
one.

Françoise stepped inside. Only a little light came
into the cavernous space. The vaulted stalls stretched
into a thick twilight and over each was written a
name, delicate and pastoral — CHLOÉ, MARGOT, ROSÉE,
DELPHINE, and TULIPE. One would have expected
cows from a *toile de Jouy*, the kind that browse on
buttercups and primroses in an eighteenth-century
Roman ruin of stucco. But there were no cows now
except Tulipe. The others, Chloé, Rosée, Delphine and
Margot, had been requisitioned. Only Tulipe, gaunt
in the flanks and dull of eye, languidly switched her
tail in the stall nearest the door.

The smell of the place was so sharp and stifling
that Françoise felt sick. "Is it really here?" she asked.

"It's really here," Maurice said grimly.

He went over to where a group of implements were
stacked against the wall, some hay forks, an ax, a

spade, a scythe. He took the spade and came back.
"This way," he said.

He went to the stall next to the end, the stall of
Rosée, and pushing his spade into the packed mixture
of dirt, straw, and manure, put his foot on it and
turned up a great clod.

Françoise watched him without a word. Presently
his spade rang on metal.

He gave an exclamation and bent over. It was a
horseshoe he had struck. He picked it up carefully
and hung it on a nail. Then he took off his coat and
threw it over the barrier. He went on digging.

He seemed to tire quickly. He worked more
slowly and still with his sullen, angry look.

"You didn't really bury it in all this muck, did
you?" she asked.

"It was wrapped in oiled rags and paper," he said.
He had torn up half the floor of the stall.

"Are you sure it's this stall?"

"Certainly," he said.

He worked on. But gradually she saw by his face
that he knew it was gone. A look of something like
consternation came into his eyes and sweat began
to pour off his forehead. He turned the last spadeful
next to the wall and a nest of tiny pink field mice
came to light. Maurice pointed to them. "Look,"
he said. Then he raised his spade and plunged it down
on them savagely.

This and the stifling, acrid smell made her feel sick. She turned and walked trembling to the door. She opened it wider to let the cold, fresh, rainy air blow on her.

In a moment Maurice stood beside her.

"It's not here, is it?" she said.

"No," he answered. "Someone has come and got it."

"Who could have done that?"

He waited a moment. She glanced at him and saw he was rigid. She did not know whether it was anger that locked him or fear, but he leaned against the wall hardly able to breathe.

"It was Yves who took it," he said.

"When?" she asked. "Before — or after?"

He began to put on his coat, pulling it into place, buttoning it carefully.

"He must have shown it already to Monsieur Edouard," he said. "Last night when he went to the train. He told me he wanted to take some things for Jacques. He had a big bundle. He must have taken it then."

It was his only answer to her question, but it was enough.

"Couldn't you *see* it was your gun he had?"

"No. It was a big long bundle. It might have been anything. Besides — " his face twisted in a grimace — "part of the barrel had been sawed off. An idea of

Monsieur Blaise's! He got it from the American
films."

"Maurice!" she whispered. "What are we going
to do?"

"Where is Monsieur Blaise now?" he asked.

"He took the bicycle and went off."

"Did he say where he was going?"

"No."

Maurice drew his face into a net of wrinkles and
closed his eyes. He was thinking intently. Finally he
said, "Mademoiselle, I've got to leave. Only Mademoiselle will be here for lunch and Colette can bring it
on a tray. I'll be back in time to serve dinner. There's
something I've got to do."

She accepted this without question. Maurice actually had not admitted that he or the gun had anything to do with the murder. Neither had Blaise. It
was still possible, she thought, suddenly drawing an
easier, fuller breath, that he was only worried because of the appearances. Still, she would accept
whatever he said was necessary to do. She nodded,
gathered her raincoat about her, and stepped outside
the door. "Are you coming?"

"Not yet. I have to get that earth back in place.
Though it really doesn't matter."

"You'll be here tonight?"

"Yes." He stretched out his arms, holding both
sides of the door frame. His simian face was quite

calm. He even raised his bushy eyebrows in his mocking, superior way. "I want to leave a message for Monsieur Blaise in case I don't see him myself. Please tell him — " he hesitated as one might hesitate to give an important message to an inquisitive child — "tell him the excursion is for tomorrow."

She received this in silence. Perhaps he was only trying to mystify, to dramatize. This was so much that ugly, teasing way he had. It made her suddenly angry. "I'll tell him nothing of the kind," she said. "Whatever he's done, if he *has* done anything, he won't run away."

"Ah?" he said.

She would have liked to slap him. She turned and ran off in the rain. When she neared the house the telephone was ringing. Colette had answered it by the time she reached the door.

"What was it?" Françoise asked.

"They're coming back," Colette said.

She could only mean André and Edouard. "Well, what of that? We can get some lunch for them."

"Yes, but that means something has gone wrong!"

"Nonsense. They are coming back for lunch. That simply means they have finished sooner than they expected."

"By the voice of Monsieur le Ministre I know something is wrong."

Françoise pressed her lips tightly together. Then

she said, "Colette, if you persist in enjoying this in your peculiar manner I'll have to send you away."

Colette, whose face had been puckered for tears, suddenly gave her a dignified look. She turned and walked to the kitchen.

Chapter XV

THEY were coming back. But why? They were to
have lunched in town with the Mayor and the Kommandant.

Then Colette was right and something had gone
wrong. But if the authorities had intended to arrest
Blaise or even Maurice they would not have let André
telephone in advance. They would not have let him
plan to return for lunch. No, there must have been
some hitch in the interview with the Kommandant.

It wasn't possible the hostages had been already
shot. André would have said so.

But Françoise couldn't be quite sure of that. She
sat in the dim library where the rain lashed the panes
and wondered if after all some trick, some sly, stupid
trick, had been played on them all. She wanted to
go to town, but André and Edouard had the carriage and Blaise the bicycle. The only way to get
there was to take one of the farm carts, or to walk to
the Douarnenez road and catch a bus that might or
might not come. Or to telephone.

The last was almost impossible. There was always

a supervisor listening in and he might cut the connection at any minute. Sometimes the connection could not even be made.

She went to the telephone, however, and gave Costard's number. The pharmacy seemed a number that would have less interest for whoever listened. She heard the ring but for a long time there was no answer. Then a woman's voice shouted into the phone. "Hallo — Hallo."

"I would like to speak to Monsieur Costard."

"Hallo. Hallo."

Is she deaf, Françoise thought, has she never used a telephone before?

"Here is Mademoiselle Galle," she cried. "I would like to speak to Monsieur Costard."

She heard the woman speak to someone near by. Then she shouted into the phone again. "But Monsieur Costard is dead."

"Ah. But I saw him only yesterday."

"He is dead."

"When did he die?"

"At six this morning." She spoke to someone again and added, "Six-fifteen."

There was a long pause. Then Françoise asked, "He died naturally?"

"Yes. A hemorrhage of the throat."

After another pause Françoise heard the woman hang up.

She sat by the phone and thought of Costard. From the many deaths that they lived with, Costard had been given a "natural" one. In its actual physical aspect, worse than the firing squad beyond a doubt. But death, like any other part of life, is inextricably entangled with what we have built in ourselves. The firing squad would be a violation of what had been built. It would destroy more than flesh and blood; it would destroy human right. Costard's death in spite of the choking, the bloody basin, was gentle, obedient, dignified. Tears slipped down her face for Costard, tears of relief.

But the fate of the hostages was still uncertain. To whom could she telephone now? No one. André and Edouard would be back shortly in any case, and she would know.

But if the hostages had been executed — then what of Blaise? What had he perhaps brought on himself? What would he be from this time on, if the blood of twenty innocent men were on him?

It could not be. The answer to this was that he must be innocent. Her mind took a strong swing away from the circumstances that had made him seem guilty. The gun, the absences at night, the black-cotton stocking, his extraordinary manner, the "excursion" he was to take.

She thought, now in order not to get this idea again of Blaise having shot that man, let me try to see just why I think he has changed so much. All the time she thought of it, reassuring herself, her nerves and instincts went on quaking and stirring with fear. But she went over his conduct carefully, starting from the moment she had first heard him whistling in the house. The whistle had been the beginning of some sudden satisfaction and release. There was no doubt of that. He no longer gave the impression of immobility. No matter how hard he had worked all this last year, he had made them feel that he held his mind and his feelings in a sort of icy suspense. Now the life showed in him once more. It seemed dangerous and strange, but after all it was still in Blaise and a part of him. The kiss on the cheek he had given her, the squeeze of her shoulders, were of the most familiar essence.

But she was interrupted by the splashing clop-clop of the tired horse coming up the drive.

She met the two men in the hall. They were taking off their damp overcoats.

"What happened?" she asked.

"Nothing at all," Edouard said. He was angry, though his white teeth gleamed in a smile.

"But I thought — "

"That we were to have seen the Kommandant. But it seems there was a stupid misunderstanding. He has gone to Rennes. He won't be back till this afternoon.

As he wouldn't be present at the lunch, it was called off."

"And the hostages?"

"Alive," he said grimly.

As she came nearer to him she saw that he was more than angry; he was in a lashing rage. He had been humiliated before them all. This power that he enjoyed so, when he could wear it visibly before them, had been flouted. She felt a sickening throb of fear, and she wondered what could be done to soothe him, what servility, what flattery, would put him in a good temper. But then almost at once tiredness came over her again.

André said, "Is lunch ready?"

He also looked tired and very preoccupied.

"Yes, we'll go right in," she said.

When they sat down André said, "Isn't Blaise here?"

"He went out. He may be late," she said.

Edouard was looking at Blaise's empty place when Colette came in with the omelette. He glanced up at her. "And where is Maurice?" he asked. "Has he also gone out?"

"Yes," Françoise said, "he has. And there's no significance to it. We live under difficult conditions and transportation is a problem. I had to send them both on errands, that's all."

Edouard raised his eyebrows. "I can see you are upset," he said.

It was dangerous to indulge in nerves. That was not what she had meant to say at all.

"Did you know Costard died?" she asked.

"No." André came out of his preoccupation and looked at her sadly. "Costard — " he murmured. "I'm very sorry to hear it. But it had to come."

"I thought we should go to his funeral," she said. "I want very much to go."

"We must. I'll find out when it is."

Then even while he still looked at her she saw his mind return to other things.

"Did you see Jeanne?" she asked him.

"Yes. She came out to the carriage for a moment."

Edouard said, "She was the first to tell us that the Kommandant had gone. Apparently everyone in town knew except ourselves, but it was she who had the pleasure of telling us first."

"You don't think the Kommandant means to be difficult?" Françoise asked.

"Certainly not," Edouard said. "He wouldn't dare to be." He spoke arrogantly and Françoise was surprised. He had always been too adept and too sure of himself to be arrogant. That was usually left to weaker men. Now he was both angry and arrogant. It occurred to her again that he did not get along in this new world as well as he had thought he would, and that a part of why he had come to them was to prove once more his old force and skill and to enjoy it through them.

André said quietly, "It may not matter about the Kommandant, because something very curious seems to have happened."

"What?" she cried.

"This morning they took Bouchaix into custody."

"Bouchaix!" This was so unforeseen that she felt nothing but confusion. "But that's absurd."

"It seems so to me," André said, "but it may not be. As Bouchaix lives near by, they searched his house last night. In his stove they found some charred remains of what appeared to be a woolen coat. He hadn't had enough fuel to burn it completely and they couldn't be sure. He insists it was scraps he'd decided were worthless. But it is hard for a man to convince anyone today that he found scraps worthless."

"But what if he did actually burn a coat? Does it mean he committed the murder?"

"The police believe so," André said.

Edouard interrupted, "The dead German was clutching a button torn from a coat. The supposition is that the German seized his murderer with a dying grip and pulled off a button. The murderer, discovering the loss of the button, does not know what to do with his coat. He dare not be found with a coat from which one button has been torn. He cannot re-place the button except by trying to buy a matching one and so arousing suspicion. If he throws the coat away, or tries to hide it, it may be found, and even if it is not found on his own property it will be recognized by someone as his. So he cuts off the buttons, which will not burn, and throws them away, then he puts the coat in a stove, pours a little kerosene over it, adds some paper or thin kindling or waste of some sort — naturally he has little fuel — and he tries to burn it."

When he had finished Françoise thought, Then we have nothing to worry about. Bouchaix is the one. But it had come too unexpectedly to believe. Instead of relief she felt only flatness.

She thought, Yes, he was frightened. I saw that he was. Frightened enough to have gotten drunk. He told me that he was a coward, too. He knew then that his real crime was the hostages. Once, when he held my bicycle there at the door, there was night-mare in his face. What suffering cowardice is!

But it wasn't Blaise then who was the coward. Thank God for that.

But because André's face showed no relief she could feel none. "Do you think Bouchaix did it?" she asked.

"No," André said dully.

"But isn't it possible?"

"Where did he get the gun?" he said. "And if he got one, where did he hide it?"

She didn't dare say that if Maurice could hide a gun so could anyone. But she said carefully, "Perhaps a great many people have guns hidden."

"It won't be pleasant for them if they're caught." Edouard's voice had snapped like a whip.

And suddenly she remembered what for a moment she had strangely forgotten: that Maurice had said Yves must have shown Edouard the gun.

And again the dull tiredness came over her. She saw without knowing why that the Bouchaix business would not fit, that there was a different pattern to what had happened and that it included them irrevocably. Why struggle against it? Looking across at André she saw the same indifference in his face. She wondered if he had told Edouard that Maurice had hidden a gun, or if Edouard had told him he had seen it. Or if they were both holding back what they knew. All of them uselessly prolonging an ugly thing from cynicism, from cowardice, or from hopeless apathy.

"What will you do now?" she asked.

"I will go later this afternoon to see Bouchaix," André said. "If he is formally accused he has the right to counsel."

"You mean you'll defend him?"

André nodded.

Edouard gave an exclamation of disgust. "It needed only that," he said, "that you should now decide to defend Bouchaix!"

"But will he be allowed a trial?" Françoise asked.

"He has the right," André said.

"Probably there will be no trial," said Edouard. "But if there is, you'll only be allowed to see him once beforehand. And any defense you make will be useless. Actually there will probably be only a brief examination."

"Then I'll insist on being present," André said.

Edouard got up. "André, you're pushing this a little too far. You're acting just out of a sort of routine of heroics. Do you want me really to believe you'd save Bouchaix if you could? What for? To have the hostages to worry about again, to have the criminal still to be caught?"

"Exactly," said André.

Edouard looked at him cynically. Then he said, "You had better think about it. As for me, I've got letters to write. I'll go up to my room if you'll excuse me."

He left them.

Françoise followed André to the hall. She put her arm around him and started to speak but his tired, discouraged eyes stopped her words. They stood a moment together. Finally she said, "What does it mean about Bouchaix?"

"I don't know."

"You still think he didn't do it?"

"I don't know. I think it's unlikely."

"Because of the gun?"

"Yes, because of the gun."

She looked up the stairs where Edouard had gone. Then she said in a low voice, "But does that mean then . . ."

He did not ask her to go on. Finally she said in a whisper, "What are you thinking of?"

He shook his head and she saw that he looked ashamed.

They heard the crunch of a bicycle outside.

"That's Blaise," she said.

He turned abruptly away and without a word walked into his study and closed the door.

Blaise came in sparkling with rain. It dripped from the edges of his hair. He carried a loose white canvas bag. It looked like a sailor's duffel bag.

"You've eaten?" he said.

"Yes, all of us. They came back."

"They did? Why?" He paused on the balls of his feet.

"I'll tell you later."

"Bad news?"

"No."

"Ah — well, I'm soaked. I'll be down in a minute."

He bounded upstairs three at a time. In a few

minutes he came running down again. He had changed his coat and put on felt slippers.

"Has Edouard left anything to eat?" he asked. He went to the dining room and Françoise followed him in and sat by him. He attacked a plate of warmed-over food as though he had never eaten before. "What's up?" he asked. "Did they get the hostages released?"

His calm assumption that this would happen, as easily as that, made her angry.

"No. They didn't even see the Kommandant. He's away."

"Well, well," said Blaise with his mouth full, "quite a little slap for Edouard. When is the Kommandant coming back?"

"I don't know. Anyway, they may be released because they've made an arrest."

"What!" His eyes widened in surprise. He stopped chewing and stared at her. Then after a moment he chewed again and swallowed as though his throat hurt. "Who is it?"

"Bouchaix," she said.

"Bouchaix!" His voice was a shout of anger. It was like an accusation hurled at her.

"Yes. Bouchaix," she said. "They arrested him because of a coat, or some such woolen thing, he tried to burn. They say it was because of a button torn off by the German. It may be there are other reasons for suspecting him that they haven't told yet."

He was not listening. None of this explanation interested him. It seemed to her that the button and the coat were only unimportant details in what he knew. He pushed his plate back, got up from the table, and walked into the library.

Françoise looked for a moment at his half-eaten food, then she followed him. He was standing before the stove, his hands in his pockets, staring at the floor. She sat down and took up her knitting. Her fingers fumbled with the thread, which had a knot in it.

"Did Bouchaix accuse anyone else of the murder?" Blaise spoke in a low voice.

"I don't know. I suppose not."

She heard a sigh, a quick one of relief. Then he said more confidently, "Won't Edouard do something about him? They haven't any real evidence."

"Do something? Do you mean try to have him released? No, of course he won't. He thinks Bouchaix would be a good solution of the difficulty."

"They'll try him?" he asked.

"Try him! Not at all. If they think they have any evidence they'll simply shoot him. Father will try to prevent that. He's going in this afternoon to see him. To try to do something for him."

"They wouldn't shoot him at once, would they? Today, I mean?"

"I don't know. I think not. I think Bouchaix isn't much of a catch for them."

"They mustn't!" he said passionately. "Damn them! Why did they have to snoop around in Bouchaix's stove? Can't a man burn old rags if he wants to?"

He began to walk up and down and his voice grew louder. "See here: Edouard's simply got to prevent their shooting Bouchaix today. He's got to prevent it for today and tonight. Bouchaix didn't do it."

"How do you know Bouchaix didn't do it?"

He stopped close by her and said without bothering to lower his voice, "Because I know who did."

Her knitting fell from her hands. She closed her eyes by instinct, not wishing at the moment to see Blaise's face. What he said was an acknowledgment of guilt. How else could he know?

Her voice sounded very weak and white. "But Blaise," she said, "the hostages — and Bouchaix."

"They won't be shot. And Bouchaix won't be shot. It will be told. But not now. It's impossible to tell it now."

"Why?"

"Oh, I can't tell you!" he cried. He took a few steps, then he looked at her as though a doubt had come to him. He said hesitatingly, "Poor little Françoise. Perhaps I ought to tell you — But, no — Believe me, it's better not. You see, it's hard enough to

keep it to myself. You'd be sure to let it out. And
with Edouard here — No, it can't be done."

She shrugged wearily. "I don't insist."

"Poor Françoise!" he said again. "Poor, darling
little Françoise." He came and put his arms tenderly
around her and kissed her.

She sat slackly and without response. "I think
Edouard knows," she said drearily.

"I suppose he does," Blaise said. He sat on the edge
of her chair, his arm about her.

Why didn't this surprise him? Perhaps he'd seen
Maurice after Maurice left and he had told him.

"Did you know Maurice and I looked for the gun?
It wasn't there. Maurice said Yves must have shown
it to Edouard. I don't know what Edouard would
do about that, do you?"

"I don't think Edouard would do anything. Hold
it over our heads perhaps. It's Yves who would do
something."

"Tell the authorities?"

"Yes. As soon as he's sure Edouard won't. And
perhaps he didn't even show it to Edouard. He might
more likely brood over it for a while, trying to decide what to do. He might blow his own brains out
with it. If he has it, though, he'll do something, and
pretty soon now."

"Maurice said to tell you the excursion is on for
tomorrow. Does that mean you'll be running away?"

"Maurice can keep his trap shut!" He got up abruptly, white in the face, and began to walk up and down.

Françoise got up, too. Her knitting fell to the floor.

"Blaise," she said, in a suddenly broken voice, "I don't want to be ashamed of you."

He shook this off with an angry shrug of the shoulders. "Don't be idiotic!" he said.

"But you can't run away. You can't leave it like this. You needn't tell me anything you don't want to. But you must see that you couldn't go on living with yourself, not if a man were to be shot, or twenty men — and you knew how to save them."

He looked as though he would cry with impatience and exasperation. He came over to her and gripped her arm.

"Try to understand me," he said. "No one will be shot. It's entirely a question of time. Today they are all safe. We've been promised that. As for Bouchaix, Father will go there this afternoon. He'll hold that off for a time. Tomorrow everything will be cleared up."

She leaned her hands against the table behind her.

"Does that mean that by tomorrow you'll have run away? And that then I am free to say you shot the German?"

He stared at her defiantly.

"That's exactly what I mean."

"All right," she said. She went out without another word and upstairs to her own room. She sat down on her bed.

The rain beat at the windows and on the roof.

She heard Blaise come upstairs, go into his room, and close the door.

Chapter XVI

I KNEW this before he told me, she thought. Blaise did it. He expects to get away, somehow, so he took a chance on the hostages.

That was wrong.

I wish Blaise hadn't done it that way.

It seems to be the end but not exactly a complete end, not a logical end. There's an unbelievable element in it. There still is no reason why he would be willing to take such a chance on letting other men die. He's never seemed a coward. Of course he thought he could get away. I'm afraid he can't. Where could he go? They'd be sure to pick him up. At best, if he gets away, we'll never see him again.

Perhaps they will shoot us as accomplices, or just to encourage the others. I wonder if he thought of that? Probably not. He thinks Father's importance would stop it. They haven't shot any ex-ministers yet. But they have imprisoned them. He thinks that Edouard would stop it. He looks on Edouard as a sort of useful lackey we've kept for a long time. He thinks

Edouard is stupid and we can handle him, and all the
time Edouard thinks of himself as guile incarnate
and he believes he can handle us.

I wish Blaise hadn't done this. I can stand his
killing the German but I don't want him to be a
coward.

And it doesn't matter what happens to us.

It only matters what happens to Blaise.

How did we ever get into this! People like ourselves, who lived as we did. What was in us to make
it likely that Blaise would kill a man on a dark road
and fly for his life like a coward, that Father and
I would end our days in prison? (When that lovely
Marie de Puyblanc came out of the Cherche Midi
prison her hair had turned gray. And she'd only
been there six weeks.)

It isn't the suffering I mind. It isn't the death. It's
the disorder, the confusion, the revelation of how
meaningless, and insensate, the struggle is. The revela-
tion that we are not really what we thought we
were, that it's in all of us to turn murderers or cow-
ards or traitors at any moment. As soon as the mold
is broken we can be anything. Our lives are no more
than the protracted struggles of the drowning.

And if Blaise goes there is nothing, nothing to
live for.

Blaise and I are not so close now, but how close
we've been all our lives! How close in those last days

— at the end of everything. If it hadn't been for Blaise I would have died after Simon left — after the defeat.

But we lived through it all together. It didn't matter what he had thought before. It didn't matter that he had said all those parrot words.

We stood in the house and watched it fall on us. It is possible, and even easy, to hate the house and what it has come to stand for — false security, blind, selfish ease, corrupted beauty. But to watch it fall is another matter, to see it destroyed and its pathetic ruins dishonored is another matter. It is another matter to see that the new structure is not the glorious edifice of the future but a primitive makeshift. It is another matter to see that in the great company where all were to work together one is not a trusted comrade but a slave.

They had followed Simon and Edouard into Paris by a matter of a few hours, making their way along roads already beginning to be crowded with refugees. There was a continuous honking. In the darkness the shapes of cars and trucks, grotesque from the things piled on them, mattresses, furniture, and bicycles, passed like great lumbering animals from a strange circus.

In Paris their blue headlights threw a ghostly glow on the walls of houses, that seemed like the walls of old rooms, with torn and peeling paper, violently sad and abandoned.

In the Rue de la Faisandérie a man carrying a hand torch passed. It was as though he were searching for something in a ruin.

No one had changed the flowers for days. In the hall sprays of Japanese plum had turned brown, the water around them stale and smelly. As soon as they came in they turned on the radio and the voice that followed them everywhere chirped out its story of defeat: "In the full tide of battle, King Leopold, abandoning the Allies whom he had begged to come to his aid, has surrendered with the entire Belgian Army —" Then the telephone began to ring sharply in another room.

Françoise and Blaise spent their days at the Gare du Nord serving food to the refugees, taking care of lost babies and sick mothers and trembling old men and women. When they went home she said to Blaise, "Well, good night, old boy," and had a tray in her room and then lay on her bed in a half-awake stupor of fatigue. She knew that André was in the house and all she and Blaise had seen during the day seemed to come to rest on him.

André spent all day shut in his study. She heard the telephone ring there sometimes and his voice but she didn't hear what he said. The work at the station was the excuse for their lack of contact. She wrote no letters for him, though he had no secretary now, since the young man had been mobilized. Visitors came sometimes at night but she was always in bed and did not see them. Edouard came, she knew, because Maurice told her, and once Blaise had dined with him and André, but she never saw him.

One day she felt an irresistible exhaustion, not so much physical as spiritual. She had been invited to lunch in a house in the Place du Palais Bourbon. Blaise went to the station without her and she put on a new dress and hat, took her small car, and went out. As she waited for the light at the far side of the bridge she leaned out to look once more at the perfect harmony of trees, stone, and flowing water. The sirens began. Their alarm made a sudden madness in the sunlight. Françoise drove on and got out before the house.

The nervous guests were already in the drawing room holding glasses of sherry. "Shall we go to the *abri?*" No, they decided. She was worried that she was not at the station. There would be panic there. But she knew that she would not be allowed through the streets during the alert. The antiaircraft in the Tuileries sounded very near and overhead was a curious high, continuous humming like a swarm of monstrous bees. Suddenly other sounds came, heavy crashes, dull and without cadence. This time it was real.

The All Clear came at three o'clock. She went out and got in her car. A press car with a camera man was swinging off the bridge onto the *quai*. There was heavy smoke along the sky. The beauty of trees, stone and water was untouched.

She went to her home and changed her clothes and then to the station, where she spent the rest of the afternoon. Later, when she and Blaise drove home, they went first to see what had happened. In the Rue Poussin a large house had been struck: the entire three top stories were completely demolished. The lower ones had lost one wall. The dead and wounded had been carried away. A man was taking snapshots. She and Blaise looked for some time at the obscenely exposed rooms, the mirror dangling on the hook, the disheveled bed. They looked with the intense, rapt curiosity of those who see the image of their own future.

A low English car drew up and a man got out. It was Adrian. Françoise called to him.

He looked as elegant as ever, ridiculously unperturbed. He came toward her and said, "Hello, Françoise. Bad show, isn't it? They got the Citroën plant and they nearly got the Air Ministry."

She was repelled by his nonchalance. Yes, she thought, your "tone" hasn't changed. But it is not you who are setting the "tone" at this moment.

She said, "Have you seen Simon?"

He said, "No, he's off with his ambulance I think."

"I wonder where."

"Somewhere around the Somme. I really don't know."

After a few more words she drove on. He may be killed, she thought. Someday I may hear Adrian saying, "They got old Simon, had you heard? Rotten luck."

It would be rotten luck. To die in Europe, which he had first wonderingly loved and then loathed. But it didn't matter about Simon. Too many young men would die on the Somme.

On the tenth of June Italy declared war on France and Great Britain. The Germans crossed the Seine at Beauvais. The Government left for Tours.

Paris began to be deserted. There were no busses or taxicabs. The thick leaves of the chestnut trees murmured in an almost country silence. Only the railroad stations were a seething Gehenna of misery, panic and flight.

The Galles stayed on, though the house was silent and the telephone seldom rang now. One night Françoise dined with her father. Blaise was out and the two of them sat at table in the heavily curtained room. She could hardly bear to look at his small, beloved face, sick and desperate and driven. They had nothing to say to each other.

Then came the last night. At six when she got

home Maurice met her at the door. "Well, Mademoiselle," he said, "we're off tonight."

"Off?"

"Yes. Monsieur le Ministre has ordered the place
closed and the big car ready by ten o'clock. We're
going to Tours. Or maybe Bordeaux, if those gentlemen have found Tours too hot for them."

"To Tours?" she repeated stupidly.

"That's what he says."

Maurice never failed, even now, to announce disasters with a brisk, defiant air. They were never his
disasters. Take that, he always seemed to say, and
then see if you can go on being so damned genteel.

"But Maurice," she said, "we're not abandoning
Paris."

"It seems that's exactly what we're doing."

At nine o'clock André telephoned from somewhere that they would leave at midnight.

She and Blaise got in her car and drove slowly up
the Avenue Foch, the Champs Elysées, and into the
Place de la Concorde. She drove along the Tuileries
and into the Rue Castiglione to the Place Vendôme.
Here they got out and stood under the column. The
shopwindows were dark and everything had been
taken away, the Cézanne, the gold chair, even the
jar of cold cream. This side of the Ritz was closed.
A strange black fog of smoke had hung over the
northern sky for days; through it long bluish beams

of searchlights moved like the sticks of a waving fan.

From where they stood the open, classic city stretched around them, the last great democratic city of this continent, the last refuge of this continent for the oppressed and tortured. Tonight it was abandoned by the world and by its own. It was not to be defended. No men were to die for it. It was to exist from now on only in the imagination of its lovers. A city of the spirit, without form or substance. What physically remained was a graveyard for the dream of human freedom, for the most beautiful hope man ever had.

Blaise made a savage gesture toward it, of mingled love and rage. "The dirty past!" he exclaimed. She knew by his voice that he was ready to cry.

He got into the car but she lingered a moment longer.

"Place Vendôme — Number 30," she murmured.

They left Paris at midnight. It was the thirteenth of June.

Chapter XVII

OUTSIDE Paris the moonlight was pure and brilliant and frogs croaked from the low ground. Toward morning they heard more country noises, roosters crowing, a cow, the creaking of a pump.

The roads were crowded with refugees, in wagons, in cars, on bicycles, and on foot. By daybreak they had got just beyond Maintenon.

Here they heard the sirens. Their noise rushed over the tops of the trees like a wild scattering of birds. The cars all along the road stopped. People scrambled out and stood looking upward, uncertain what to do. Just ahead a man began to toss his children, like bundles, out of a wagon; another stood holding the head of a frightened horse.

There were two children standing by the road, a boy and a girl. They wore black aprons and they had been to town on an errand probably, for the boy had a loaded basket and the little girl a long loaf of bread. They jumped into a ditch and lay there on their stomachs, their heads hidden on their arms. Françoise noticed that the little girl had curly hair.

"Better get out," Maurice said.

"But there are no troops on this road," André protested.

Maurice, abandoning the wheel, said without ceremony, "Get out anyway."

They got out, and like the others stood looking up.

The planes came out of a cloud bank, they spread out along the road, and dropped their bombs with deadly precision. Somewhere ahead Françoise saw horses, wagons, and cars dissolve in a muddy geyser.

"Look out!" Maurice yelled. "Under the car!" It was too late for that but he seized Françoise and dropped her against a fender, putting himself between her and the sky. A plane diving on them sprayed the road with machine-gun fire.

When the noise had moved on they heard a faint rattle of antiaircraft from Maintenon and a continuous sound, curiously small and futile, of screams ahead on the road.

They got to their feet and André said, "Those children in the ditch . . ."

One of them was standing there rubbing his hands against his eyes.

It was Blaise who was first into the ditch. He turned the little girl on her back and stood looking down at her small face on which freckles showed with startling clearness. A little trickle of blood oozed slowly from her nose and out the side of her open mouth.

At Chartres they had to get more gasoline from the

airport. Chartres had been badly bombed. The cathedral stood with all its glass taken away, looking
fragile as the skeleton of a leaf.

Before they got to Tours the roads, packed with
refugees, were bombed again.

They spent the night in the Hôtel de l'Univers.
The Government had gone on to Bordeaux.

That night Tours was bombed.

Next morning they passed two regiments moving
north to defend the Loire. These were the first troops
they had seen. Françoise leaned out to look at them.
They were all very young, they didn't seem much
older than Blaise, and they seemed to be mostly
country boys, with fresh color and raw, reddish wrists
and hands. But each face was different, full of wit, of
stoicism, of desperate determination or of thought.
There was no pattern, no sameness about them. One
of them, looking impudently at Françoise, drew his
mouth into a kiss. Blaise watched them intently as
they passed.

Just before they reached the great suspension bridge
over the Garonne they saw English soldiers camped
by the road with their trucks spread all over the
near-by fields. One of them waved a tin cup in salute.

"What are they doing here?" Blaise asked.

"Getting ready to clear out," Maurice said in his
briskest manner.

In the open space by the Splendide the little painted

pavilions of a local fair looked as though at any moment they expected to be the center of a gay crowd
and the music of hurdy-gurdies. In the sunlight the
shopwindows of the Cours de l'Intendance were full
of wine, chocolate, perfumes, and ladies' bags of
crocodile.

The sun shone hotly and the terrace of the Splendide was crowded all day.

"*Garçon, un pernod, une demi.*"

"The Germans will come down here in parachutes."

"What are the English doing?"

"Verdun has fallen and the Maginot Line is
broken."

"No word of the Council of Ministers?"

"Madame de Portes says . . ."

At seven in the evening Edouard came into their
room. The three of them had been sitting by the open
window. Through it came the continuous symphony
of disaster from the terrace below and the air smelled
of dust, of motor exhaust, and of an odor of gerani-
ums and urine, and now that the evening breeze was
blowing, a faint tang from the tepid sea.

Edouard stood before them and said, "It's all over.
Reynaud has resigned. Pétain is Premier."

He sank into a chair and covered his face with his
hand.

After a little while he began to talk in a low mo-
notonous voice. "The Council met three times. First

they discussed Roosevelt's answer — no help from
that quarter. The vote was thirteen to eleven in favor
of resistance.

"Then at the next session they talked of England's
offer of a joint Government, the evacuation of the
French Army, the turning over of the Fleet to England. The vote was still thirteen to eleven to continue."

Edouard raised his head from his hand and looked
directly at André. He hadn't shaved and his cheeks
looked bluish and haggard.

"I met Laurent-Eynac," he said, "as he came from
the Council. He told me what had happened. He said
he had voted to continue the fight, but I looked at
his face and knew he didn't mean to keep it up. As
a matter of fact, he was on his way then to talk to
Pétain. As for Chautemps — well, you can imagine
the rest."

In the silence of the room Françoise heard André
give a long, heavy sigh. Blaise got up and went to the
window, his hands clenched at his sides.

Edouard said, "You can imagine the end. There
was a lot of oratory no doubt, a lot of patriotism."
His voice grew harder. "But they were all in the
soup and they knew it. They got down finally to the
hopeless position of the armies, to England's desertion,
a possible Communist revolt. And can't you see each
one secretly thinking 'But what will happen to *me?*'
Anyway, Chautemps again demanded an armistice.

This time Laurent-Eynac supported him, and Queuille and others. Even old Papa Lebrun put his word in. The vote was taken — fourteen to ten for capitulation."

The *valet de chambre* came in and began to draw the curtains over the windows. The lights in the crystal chandelier sprang on.

The waiter appeared with the dinner menu but, seeing them sitting there in silence, laid it on the table and hurried out to spread word that something grave had certainly been decided.

The telephone in the antechamber gave a tinkling burr.

"Ah," Edouard said, "there it is. I haven't had a chance to tell you. But it must be from the Marshal."

André got up slowly and went to answer it.

Françoise did not even hear what he said.

Finally he came back. He stood under the pale flood from the chandelier, his small head erect, his face full of sharp, black shadows.

"The Marshal has asked me to accept a post in the new ministry," he said. Then he added in a flat, lifeless voice, "Tomorrow we will ask for an armistice."

And after that?

When André left the hotel he did not kiss them good-by. He did not look at them.

Under a clear moon, and after the armistice had already been asked for, Bordeaux was bombed. The planes flew low and even now she shuddered to remember how, after they had passed, all the street lights, by some mistake in the central control, had gone on again. She and Blaise drove through strangely lighted streets to the poorer quarters of the city, which had been made a shambles. There they picked up wounded and carried them to the hospital, an old couple, one of whom died on the way, a boy Blaise's age with a leg blown off, a woman with extraordinarily long hair, holding a dead baby.

The day the Germans came to Bordeaux they were still living at the Splendide. They heard the military band playing in the Place where the Girondin monument stands. Blaise did not go to the window to look out.

Later she and Blaise went to St.-Jean-de-Luz. The beach was crowded with Germans and there he looked his full. The Germans were playing ball games, swimming, and lying in the sun. They were all young, with their strength showing in their muscles and tendons, but their bodies never seemed quite harmonious, and the strange thinness of their skins and something self-conscious in their movements made them look more naked than others. When one looked at them, one saw that they had been humble a long time but that now they had been told they need never be humble again. They had been told they must be gods, and that they must be correct. So here they were, full of merriment and good clean fun, courtly to women and children when the occasion arose. They were putting on their act and they seemed not so much like gods as like jugglers or acrobats. Françoise expected to see one of them wipe his hands and then toss the handkerchief into the air for his assistant to catch.

Suddenly one of them recognized Blaise. He came over at once and introduced himself. He was the older brother of one of Blaise's companions on the walking tour. He clicked his bare heels together before Françoise, then he lay down on the sand by them and talked about mutual acquaintances. He expressed great admiration for André, he spoke to Françoise at length on the poetry of Charles Péguy. He made all the conversation, for Françoise said nothing and Blaise only answered in formal and brief sentences. Blaise did not invite the German to join them at lunch and they never saw him again. They never spoke of him.

After that Blaise's silence grew deeper and deeper. He was studying in Rennes when André and Françoise left Vichy and he made no comment on their return. He asked no questions about Vichy. He never spoke of politics. He behaved as though the world outside their immediate circle did not exist.

During the summer he came back to Rusquec and his only interest seemed to be the farm. He was content to work as hard as a peasant and to be taciturn as a peasant. His only friends seemed to be Maurice and the fishermen at Douarnenez. If he saw some of the boys of his own age and class in the neighborhood it was very seldom and he never spoke of them.

When autumn came again he told André that he could not go on studying because his studies were now entirely useless. They had days of argument behind the closed doors of André's study and it seemed that Blaise won out. Anyway, he stayed at Rusquec. "There is too much work to do here," he explained briefly to Françoise, and that was all he said about it.

Silence became a film on the stagnant water they lived in.

Until now. Until three days ago.

But still she could not bear to lose Blaise. No, if he were to be taken away she did not see how she could live. In some way so mysterious that she could not analyze it, it even seemed to her that to lose Blaise would mean that the last link with Simon, some infinitely obscure, infinitely fragile, unacknowledged link, would be broken.

And if that was the final absurdity, it was also the final horror.

Chapter XVIII

FRANÇOISE lay on her bed and the long afternoon was simply the long afternoon without Blaise.

She began to have a headache. It ached so badly that she slipped away and moved to another space, leaving her aching body there on the bed. First she tried her closet, but the clothes hung there like creatures who had been obscenely murdered and that was no better. It was too quiet in the room. Even the dust could not be seen as it stirred. It could only be seen when it had settled on the table.

Outside was better. There everything was on the move. The gusty, heavy rain poured down and occasionally stopped abruptly and a hole was torn in the sky. She saw blue, like water, shining through; was it looking up or looking down? It was too far to reach, though something hurt again with the effort she made to soar or to plunge, whichever it was.

The closer things were best. Brown leaves blowing across the terrace and huddling in wet drifts under the stone wall. The struggling chrysanthemums, beaten

down, stalks broken, mud on their russet flowers.
All these resisted in companies, not alone. But they
wouldn't recognize her or her trouble.

If one could join the snail, a very large one,
monstrous-large — What had sent him out at such
an unpropitious hour? If one could watch him
closely one might see where he was going and why.
It must be a great secret, a secret of all secrets. But
he too was cruel. He slipped under a loosened pav-
ing of the terrace and drew in his horns and no one
could tell him from a smooth pebble lying there.

The shutter under the roof was the only lonely,
uncertain thing. It banged back and forth, back and
forth. A frenzy had come upon it.

The shutter has gone mad.

How did I get back in the room? I didn't want to
come, because now it has grown so much larger.
That is because there are mirrors on four walls. That's
a trick. A dirty trick. It means that now I can't move
in any direction, not even get to the garden again.
The room, the afternoon, will always be the same.
But it's only done with mirrors. I won't stand for it.

This headache is intolerable. I haven't left it after
all.

She broke out in a drenching sweat and sat up.

Her head felt better. Have I taken aspirin? I can't
remember. No, there is no aspirin any more.

That was a bad one, she thought. That mustn't

happen again. I must seriously begin to plan how to
stop that. There's too much to do.

I have to make sauces and see that the house is
kept clean. I have to see that Blaise gets away. And
that no one is shot until he does.

After that I have to see how we are going to go
on living here, the two of us.

She slipped back on her cool pillow. Almost at
once she fell into a heavy sleep.

When she woke up it was dark. The wind had died
down and the rain fell very gently, like a veil spreading out. Water dripped from all the eaves.

She felt very weak but clean and sound again.

She heard Blaise come out of his room and go
downstairs. Blaise was still here.

He had said he couldn't go till morning.

It must be time for dinner. The sauce.

If the house had no noise in it but Blaise going
calmly downstairs, then everything was still all
right.

I'll wear the best dress I have for Edouard.

When she saw them in the library waiting for her
she saw the long afternoon in their faces, too, André's
and Blaise's, even Edouard's. But he, too, must have
slept because his eyes had the refreshed, slightly
cruel look of a cat's eyes waking from a nap.

"Did you go to town?" she asked André.

"Yes."

"What about Bouchaix?"

"They wouldn't let me see him."

"What will they do then?"

"I don't know."

She tried to see in his impassive tiredness what had really happened.

"Didn't they say anything?"

"They were pleased to be very obscure. The Kommandant was still not there. But the Captain — Hessler is the one I mean — said that everything would be cleared up tomorrow."

"What did he mean?"

"I don't know."

Then that was all right, too. After a second she glanced at Blaise. He was sitting quietly, with a faint smile on his face.

Maurice came to announce dinner. Maurice had slicked his rough hair down with water. He was freshly shaven and a slight cut showed on his chin. This gave him a gala air. Maurice had always just cut his chin when they had guests.

They talked about food. Edouard praised the egg entrée and Françoise told him of an old cookbook she had found in the attic some time ago, written in a precise eighteenth-century hand. "But our cuisine is going to suffer from this," she said. "It used to be based on the produce of the most fruitful country in Europe."

"Not necessarily," Edouard said. "For a long time the English have had the best meat, but they don't know how to cook it."

"I don't agree," Blaise said. He spoke of steaks he'd had at Simpson's in London. It was on a trip he made with André in '38. They talked about this for a while.

Then Edouard said, "You are at least better off here in the country. These eggs, for instance. One can smell the clean straw they were laid in. And then it's impossible to ration eggs. Even if the chickens are rationed their output is variable. A sufficiently enthusiastic hen — " He smiled and made a flourish with his fork. "And I don't doubt you've got hams, too, hidden away. And a few excellent cheeses. The country is a great place for hiding things."

They all chewed more slowly to listen.

"And then birds, rabbits, all that sort of thing," he went on, "provided one has also hidden a gun to shoot them with."

No one's face changed.

Maurice served the next course. Then he took up several plates from the serving table and walked deliberately toward the kitchen.

Well, now they all knew that Edouard knew. And that he had known probably from the moment he arrived. Everything he had said had been based on this knowledge. Whatever his intentions had been in coming, they must have undergone a change when he found out that the Galles were themselves involved. That was why he didn't commit himself that first evening. He was probably deciding whether it was more likely that Blaise had done it or Maurice. If he had decided it was Maurice he would not have hesitated to turn him in. So he must have decided it was Blaise. No doubt he couldn't easily make up his mind what to do. But from the beginning he had obviously been drawn in several directions.

There was his old affection for them, his habit of helping them, and then there was his vanity. He would want to show them that he was a big man, and also that things weren't so bad as they had been so loudly claiming they were. He would want to show that he had not made a mistake in assuming he could get along all right with these people. He had not been made a fool of, not been outwitted. He had a trick or two up his sleeve yet. But to do that they'd have to collaborate. They would have to do their share and be reasonable. They couldn't indulge in being noble or heroic or any such tripe as that. They would just damned well do their share and then they'd all be friends again as before. But with him, Edouard, on top this time. Yes, she could almost see him leaving the room after it was all over, satisfaction shining in him like a light, and his shoes squeaking.

And then there was the other side of it. Perhaps

his original intention had been to help them, but on finding out what he had, he had suddenly realized that it was in his power to finish them. And mixed with his long devotion and service there may have been also a long rancor, a long subconscious hate. She had felt that hate twice already, first at Rusquec, when he told her they would make peace, then at Vichy. After all, sure as he always was, there must have been times when he doubted himself a little. There must have been secret cracks in his certainties. Perhaps he had even been more uncertain after André had been so bitterly ruined. In his ruin it was even more obvious what manner of man he was.

So it probably came to this: Edouard was still undecided. If they were willing at the eleventh hour to give in, he might help them. If they were not, he would certainly push them over the edge.

Françoise saw that all of them had relief showing in their faces. And that Blaise was even smiling. "Edouard," he said, "you are positively comic."

Edouard smiled too. "What a tough boy you've gotten to be," he said. "The roughneck of the neighborhood I hear."

"Have you been gossiping about us?" André asked.

"It's not necessary to gossip. These little local reputations practically announce themselves. Besides, I can see it. Blaise is a changed boy. Can't you see it, André?"

"Yes, I can see it."

"He's not the boy I used to know."

"He's older," Françoise said.

"Yes, of course he is older. But one grows older in different ways. I've got an idea Rusquec isn't the best place for him. There isn't enough activity for him here."

"You think so!" Blaise exclaimed. "How long since you've lived on a farm?"

"Well, it's obvious you have spare time. One wonders what you do with it. You've got the mysterious air of a fellow who thinks he has done something clever behind your back. Perhaps he has just pinned a piece of paper to the tail of your coat. What have you been doing, Blaise?"

Françoise was struck again by the pang of how young Blaise was. Everything about him was young, the shape of his wrists, the fresh color in his cheeks, the cowlick in his hair, even the sharp, instant way he drew himself together to meet the weight of Edouard.

"What have you been doing, Blaise?" Edouard repeated.

"Well," Blaise said, "I've been doing what I can. Sometimes I paint large black V's on walls. Once or twice I've let the air out of the tires on a German car. And I've learned how to play 'The Marseillaise' on a mouth organ."

"Blaise!" André murmured, but Blaise didn't seem to hear him. Edouard went on cleaning his plate of food. He took a piece of bread, broke it expertly, and ran it around in the sauce. Then he sat back like a man with time on his hands.

"Well, well. And what else do you do?"

"You want to know all my activities? Well, once I went out with a flashlight and made signals to some planes going over. They were German planes but I thought it would be nice to confuse them. And once I made a dirty drawing on an official proclamation. The drawing concerned a funny little man with a mustache and his hair hanging over one eye — "

"I see," Edouard said. "And how old are you exactly?"

"Exactly eighteen, three weeks and two days."

Maurice put a plate before Edouard and began with a ceremonious crooking of his arm to pass a compote of stewed dried fruit.

Edouard said, "I'm very much interested just now in the welfare of young fellows like you. The new State we're trying to make will be obviously based on them. There's a lot to be done. I have various organizations in mind for creating a more healthy feeling among them."

"They aren't healthy then?" Blaise asked.

"I am speaking of the moral side."

"Ah! I thought you meant rickets and such things. You haven't thought of any way to get them a few beefsteaks, have you?"

Edouard dropped his elbows on the table and looked at Blaise with steady eyes.

"Young man," he said, "I'll come straight to a little plan I have for you, for your personal health, and you'd better listen carefully."

"We'll all listen carefully," André said. "There are no plans for Blaise that don't concern us."

"Well, I've got a plan for you, too, André, but I'll come to that later. But first to Blaise. Here he is a big strong boy of eighteen. Active, too, by his own admission. Much too active. Don't protest or explain, André. I know what's the matter. He's in the same boat with all our young people. No obvious direction. It's the curse of this period of half peace. We can't be allowed normal activities because the State itself is in the position of a boatload of people being held up at a pier. Well, that won't go on forever but meantime, here we are. Blaise must find something to do."

"I've got plenty to do," Blaise said.

"You find time to indulge in activities that may end in trouble," Edouard said. He still spoke mildly.

Françoise thought, Before he gets down to the point he will manage to put us all through the hoops. It will be a miracle, too, if he doesn't make some reference to the past or to what he's done for us and how much he loves us.

"Understand," he said, "that I'm trying to keep Blaise out of trouble, grave trouble. I'm trying to keep you, all of you, out of trouble. That's what you sent for me for, isn't it — though you weren't as frank with me as you should have been. I could be hurt about that, if I were sensitive. After all, we're old friends, aren't we? But instead of being hurt I've been thinking things over. I've come to a conclusion, I've decided what Blaise must do."

He leaned on the table and pointed his finger at Blaise.

"Well, what is it?" Blaise said.

"There are volunteers being sent to Russia," Edouard said. "Several companies have already been organized. In the end there may be forty or fifty thousand. You had better enlist."

"No!" André cried. He pushed his plate away from him. "No. I won't permit it."

Edouard leaned back and turned toward him. "I expected you to say that. But it's no use."

"But, I repeat, I won't permit it," André said. "Those volunteers are not volunteers at all. They will be dying for something they don't believe in. Blaise isn't going to be one of them."

It was amazing to hear the firmness of André's voice. All his tiredness and his shame had gone.

"Don't get things confused," Edouard said. "It doesn't matter what they die for. Maybe they won't die, maybe Blaise will survive. He's not likely to survive here."

Now he had said that, too. Now they looked at each other, the three of them, and saw what was before them. Blaise for a moment grew white with excitement, almost with pleasure. It seemed to Françoise that he was like a violin string that had been slack and mute, and now had been tightened, struck by a harsh hand, and had answered with a bold, vibrant note.

Edouard gave them no chance for thought. He said, "As for you, André, let's get things quite clear. First I must tell you that I am willing to believe you didn't know yourself what had happened when you sent for me. I believe you probably began to realize it about the time I did. It couldn't have been pleasant for you. I know you, and I know how repugnant an act of violence would be to you. But in any case, I came and I knew almost at once. I couldn't think what to do at first. I wanted to keep you all out of it but I knew that I couldn't do everything alone, that you'd have to help yourselves too. I knew you'd be delicate about that. So first I tried to remind you that it wasn't altogether unthinkable that you should take a little trouble. You hadn't really been plaster saints all your lives, not one of you, though you all have an irritating way of acting as though, because your conception of man was noble, that made you noble too. Noble all together, complete and invariable! So I reminded you of one or two things, the sort of things you did once and might do again."

Françoise saw that Maurice had come back and was getting the coffee ready. She motioned to him to serve it at the table. He put the silver coffee pot before her and she began to pour.

"Very well," André said, "then we will be clear: what do you want me to do?"

"I want you to go back to the Vichy Government," Edouard said. "That's no great hardship, surely. They wouldn't mind having you, though they wouldn't offer you anything very important. Perhaps the Ministry of Youth and Education, perhaps something even less important. There are going to be changes there shortly. I tell you this confidentially. You might as well be in on it."

"Don't bother to tell me," André said. "I will not accept any post and I will not leave Rusquec."

Edouard took his cup and stirred, though there was no sugar in it to stir.

"Why not?" he said.

"Because I left the Government of Vichy once for a good reason. I had lost confidence in it. Nothing has happened since to change my opinion."

"Surely," Edouard said, "you can only agree that they were doing the best they could."

"But they were not doing the best they could."

"Aren't you overly critical?"

"I don't think so."

"When you consented to become part of that Government, you certainly knew what they would have to do."

"I thought I did. Let me explain. What you say about nobility is nonsense. I never had any pretensions to being anything but a man like other men. I have made the concessions and the blunders you point out. They weakened my power to see clearly and they undermined my courage. When the crisis came I found myself in a dilemma. It was the dilemma of every man in our country. The dilemma was whether to submit to overwhelming physical force or to oppose it. Each man made his decision. I made mine, but I also took the responsibility of representing others beside myself."

Now André too had grown taut with excitement. His eyes blazed. "You've asked me, so now you can listen. I thought that to submit to overwhelming physical force was the first stage of the solution. That to brute force we would simply surrender our own brute force. But I knew that there is not only one kind of force. There is spiritual force, there is intellectual force, and our spiritual force and our intellectual force we would keep intact. They would remain unconquerable, exactly in proportion to the faith we had in them and to the loyalty we gave them."

Edouard moved restlessly. "Oh, you didn't get along with them down there," he said. "You never could get along with anyone. Then you were in such a state of nerves — "

"You want more specific reasons," André said, "you want them categorically? You never understand things, Edouard, unless they are translated into the simplest terms. Well, do you remember Paragraph 19 of the armistice? We talked about it, you and I. You said it was a matter of form, and I thought that we'd never really be required to turn over our helpless political refugees, who had come here trusting in our law of asylum. But we did turn them over. It was the first time I saw that we were going to surrender what no man has a right to surrender."

"What of it? Most of them were Jews and Communists. And if the Boche had a million and a half of our soldiers, what did that riffraff matter?"

André did not listen to his answer. He went on. "You remember when the Socialist deputy Spinasse said in the Petit Casino that man's independence and individual liberty were an illusion beyond our reach? You and I said that this was only temporary hysteria and cowardice. Not two days later the French Parliament voted itself out of existence. And think, Edouard, that among all those men, freely elected representatives of the most civilized and intelligent race of Europe, descendants of the men who formulated the rights of man, children of our revolution, only one man, only one, the brave de Chambrun, stood up and cast his vote against it! When we permitted that, we threw all our true force into the refuse heap. And there was more: shall we go over it all? It is shameful even to have to speak of it. There were our vulgar anti-Jewish laws and the weak pretense that we were in a position to pass just judgment on the men who had been selected for Government by a still free people. No, I will not go on. But I say we were willing to surrender what men cannot surrender and live."

"Parliamentary government has gone out of fashion," Edouard said, "and that's its own fault. It had a long trial. The truth is its record was bad. Mostly, the politicians were a lot of second-rate and venal incompetents. The Jewish laws were very mild. As for the scapegoat trials, why shouldn't a politician be tried, no matter how he got there, if he commits fatal errors that amount, in their results, to crimes?"

"But by whom?" André said. "By the politicians who shared in the crimes?"

"Well, it doesn't matter, because the trials haven't come off yet. As for the Vichy Government, I repeat, it has done the best it could."

André said, "It has obviously tried to ameliorate certain conditions. It has tried to feed the hungry. It has even tried to hold back a few things to bargain with. While it was willing to surrender its spiritual and intellectual forces, it wasn't ready entirely to surrender its physical force. It was willing to set up a little force of its own, a sickly parody, in every way contemptible, because it represented nothing. But it has not solved any dilemma, it has only brought it closer, made it more intricate, more frightful, more hopeless of solution. The hostages are an example of what we have come to. And even here you pretend that we should go on surrendering."

"But the dilemma never changes!" Edouard cried. "I'm trying to tell you that. And it's only high-flown words to pretend we could go on being intellectually and spiritually strong with a rope around our necks. The dilemma is insoluble because you want impossible solutions."

André said, "And now you have become such a part of this new 'force' of ours that in order, presumably, to help me, you feel obliged to threaten me, to blackmail me. Come over to us, give up everything, you say, wear a fetish around your neck, join the crocodile clan. Do this, you say, or one of two

things will happen: innocent men will be shot in reprisal or your son will be accused of murder."

Edouard gave one of his enormous shrugs. "The
Sublime!" he exclaimed in an exasperated voice.
"Always the Sublime."

Then he put his elbows on the table again and
clasped his hands tightly together. His expression
and voice entirely changed. He looked good-tempered
again and slightly sly, like a man at last getting down
to business.

"I must tell you," he said, "that Yves has the gun,
and that he saw Blaise go out with it the night of
the murder and come back and bury it. But — " he
held his hand out arrestingly — "even that is not
hopeless. I have been thinking pretty hard, and I'll
tell you what we can do. In the first place, André,
this business of yours is easily settled. Before I came
down here it had been suggested to me that you might
care to come back to the fold and I took the liberty
of saying I thought you very likely might, and in any
case I would try to persuade you. So they expect
an answer, and we could send them a telegram tonight if you want. And anyway, this afternoon I
called up Hessler and I told him incidentally that
you were about to return and accept an important
post. As to Blaise, his change of heart would look
better coming a week or so later. There's no hurry
there."

"You dared to tell Hessler that!" André said.

"I did, and I also told him another thing. I told him I thought we had the murderer here."

He looked around at them to enjoy their consternation. Then he laughed. "Who is the murderer? Yves, of course. It's so simple. *He* has the gun now. I told him to keep it. I made him promise to say no more until I had done what I could to straighten things out. He won't wait, though, beyond tomorrow. But it doesn't matter because tomorrow we can accuse *him*. He will deny it, of course, but he will be the only one to say he saw Blaise and there will be two of you against him, three if necessary. And I might even add that he confessed to me, or some such thing. Not only are we more important than he is, more to be believed, but everyone knows he is a bit touched. His brother was in the camp for an insult to a German, wasn't he? Really, there's no use going into it — it tells itself."

Blaise got to his feet. He took his wineglass in his hand as though he were going to make a toast.

"But that — that — " he stammered. Then he shouted suddenly, "But that's obscene!" And he dashed the wine in Edouard's face. Then he turned and ran out of the room.

The silence made a circle around Edouard, and Françoise watched him fascinated as he took his napkin and slowly and carefully wiped his face and

collar. He smoothed his hair back, and then he looked
at them with eyes hard as stones.

"That's how it is," he said. "Do as you please."

André said, "You didn't come to see justice done.
You came to enjoy a mediocre triumph and to win a
little approbation from those who rule you. If I have
shrunk, so have you. My God, Edouard, how little
we have become! But it doesn't matter. You knew
we'd never accept your proposition. Perhaps you're
glad. It will be a more substantial triumph to get rid
of us than to humiliate us. Because whatever Blaise
has done, we will take the consequences."

Edouard got up. "I think I'll go back to Paris in
the morning," he said. "It wouldn't be dignified for
me to be here when all this happens. And it would
be useless. Unless — you should change your minds."

"We won't do that!"

"Then I think I'll have a smoke in the library. Will
you come?"

André shook his head.

"Françoise?"

"Yes." She got up.

"Only one thing," Edouard added. "You're a man
who reads books. Well, here's a maxim for you to
ponder over. I saw it this afternoon in a book by
my bed. La Rouchefoucauld. He says, 'The weak
are never capable of being sincere.' Think it over."

Françoise stood behind André's chair and put her

hands on his shoulders. He reached up and held her hands.

"Do you want me to stay with you?"

"No," he said. "Go with Edouard. I want to be alone for a bit."

"Will you let me come later?"

"I'll call you. I'd rather be alone now."

She kissed his head and went out. As she walked with Edouard she saw he was not as tall as she had thought. Broad-shouldered but not really tall. He had always seemed bigger than he was. He walked heavily and she saw he had lost many things, robustness, color, earthy glow. His common sense had become only weakness and cunning. Lacking vitality he was a vulgar man.

His squeaking shoes made an accompaniment as they moved towards the library.

Chapter XIX

She took up her knitting and sat in her accustomed chair. Edouard sat in his.

They didn't talk. Edouard smoked and looked at the ceiling and sometimes crossed or recrossed his legs.

Maurice came in with a few pieces of wood in his apron. His hair was ruffled again and he looked quite natural.

"Has Monsieur le Ministre gone to his study?" she asked.

"Yes, Mademoiselle."

"And Monsieur Blaise?"

He looked up to the ceiling to indicate he had gone upstairs.

Then he went quietly out.

She couldn't bear to think of going upstairs to her own room. She could not bear to be left alone. Sitting here with Edouard she felt herself, as well as him, to be flat and without dimension, without taste or color or mystery. But it was better to feel that than to see too much, to have the barrier that shielded her grow thin and transparent. Better to see Edouard as a simple lump of flesh than to see the anguish and terror and struggle of every particle of life about her. Edouard, by his sheer blindness, kept visions away.

Finally he said to her, "You're very quiet, Françoise. You don't rail at me the way you used to. You've changed, too."

"I suppose I have."

"Haven't you anything to say to me?"

"Nothing that would matter."

"Say it though," he insisted.

"You want to know what I think of you?"

"Yes."

"You really care? Why should you?"

"You know why," he said.

"Oh, come, we've decided on common sense. You gave me beautiful violets once. The first flowers I ever had given me. Don't pretend, though, that you ever gave me hopeless love."

"I know whether it was love or not. And whether it was hopeless." Then he said somberly, "Have you ever heard again from that fellow?"

Françoise held up to the light a woolen strand that was tangled. She said between the steel needles in her teeth, "What fellow?"

"Astley."

"Oh, Simon? No, I've never heard."

"You loved him, didn't you?"

"I did love Simon. But that's all over."

"Is it? Why? Because he's not here? Surely that doesn't matter."

"No, that's not why. It ended long ago and for another reason."

"I can't believe it," he mocked. "The perfect love."

"Don't talk about him, Edouard. In the end, he didn't love me."

"I don't believe that either. You had a quarrel, that's all. Here at Rusquec. I don't know what about, but he drove me back to Paris and he never said a word all the way. He hated me! Could it be he was jealous of me?"

Françoise didn't answer.

"How wrong he was! Because it was he you loved all the time. I nearly told him so when I saw him again."

"Where did you see him?"

"In Vichy. I ran into him one day. Didn't I ever tell you? He was on his way home. I suppose he'd come to Vichy because he thought you'd be there. But he must have found out at the hotel that you weren't with André. I can't imagine why he didn't ask André where you were but he obviously didn't dare."

Edouard spoke slowly and Françoise never took her eyes off his face.

"Yes, I saw him sitting outside a café. He didn't want to speak to me but finally he couldn't resist asking me where you were."

"Did you tell him?"

"I said you were in St. Jean-de-Luz but might leave at any moment. Perhaps he went there to find you. And you may have passed each other on the way."

She dropped her wool and clasped her hands.

"I wish you'd told me before."

"Does it mean so much?" he said bitterly.

"Yes."

Even if he had tried halfheartedly and given it up so easily. Even if it was only one more senseless accident, one more senseless waste, it did mean something. It was a little tenderness, a little remorse, a little bit of Simon coming now at this last hour.

She pushed her wool from her lap into the basket. If there was another ball there she would go on but otherwise not. The thread was tangled and the stocking could go to the devil. She felt in her basket. There was a heap of wool waiting to be untangled and joined and rewound, and a piece of paper, torn from André's new notebook, with a few faint marks on it.

She let the wool and paper drop.

"I had no luck with Simon," she said. "That love never took a real shape. I tried hard to make it come to life but I couldn't do it."

Edouard sat slumped in his chair. "Then it was not meant to live," he said.

"No, I suppose not. But just the same, I feel that even now, if by some miracle I had another chance, I could make it live."

He gave a sound, half groan, half grunt. "You're not made for it," he said. "You were never made for love."

"It was you who spoiled it," she said. "Yes, it was you. He was jealous of you. He knew I depended on you in a shameful way. And you did love me then, didn't you?"

"Yes. For years."

"But not now."

He looked at her and his eyes gleamed for a moment and then grew dead. "One can't love forever without hope."

He got up. He was beginning to suffer and he wanted to go.

But when he left she would be alone. And when she was alone she would be frightened again. He came over and stood by her, looking down. He let his hand rest on her hair.

"What was wrong?" he muttered. "Why was it always hopeless?"

A wave of pity for him went over her, and she saw why Edouard no longer loved her nor any of them, why at last he was only sick and ashamed to be with them.

"You don't understand, do you?" she said. "It was because you always gave your worst to us. And so you spoiled us for yourself, and you can't love us. You can't love anything. Not even your country, which you gave your worst to also. You'll never love anything again."

He drew his hand quickly away but she reached up and caught it and held it. She held it tightly and he let it lie in hers.

Suddenly, because she was so afraid, her fear wiped out the man who stood there and put in his place the old warm, benign image. But her fear was incommunicable. She could not tell him what she was afraid of. She wanted to cry out, Don't go, because when I am alone I'm not myself. I have no support, no hope. I'm mutilated, lost, wandering half in life and half out of it. I'm not afraid of death. It's not that. But I am afraid to be alive and outside the normal law. I'm afraid to be mad and I'm going mad.

She let his hand drop.

"Good-by, Edouard," she said.

He hesitated a second, then he drew a harsh, long breath. And then he walked heavily and slowly to the door and went out.

After she had sat a while she got up and emptied his ashtray into the hot embers in the stove, looked around to see if there was anything else to do.

Tomorrow we'll probably be taken away. It must look neat to whoever comes.

She saw her father's notebook, the one she had bought him at Mademoiselle Marthe's. In it were the last pages of the report on the murder and the hostages. She opened it and saw the close writing. One by one she tore the written pages out and crumpled them. She crushed them together and put them in the stove. She looked around and saw her knitting basket beside her chair. She went over and gathered up the loose ends hanging over the edge.

The paper was there. As she started to crumple it she stopped. There were the faint pencil marks on it.

She sat down and spread it on her knee. It was a drawing.

For a second her tired eyes swam. She could hardly make out what it was. It was so lightly, so hastily done.

There seemed to be classical roof lines and a column with a figure on top. There was a comic intention to this figure; he was pompous, military, godlike, wrapped in a toga, crowned with laurel. And below, two smaller figures walked bravely away from his shadow, resolute but clinging to each other. Something like rays came from a quarter of the sky and would soon envelop them.

"What a queer drawing for Blaise to make."

She got up and the paper fluttered to the floor.

She was riven in two and drawn in separate ways. The room and the house fell away from her. *Oh, my God —*

She fell to her knees and snatched it up, held it close to her eyes under the lamp.

A pencil had scratched below it *Place Vendôme Number 30.*

Chapter XX

THE LIGHT shone in her eyes, the fire smoked a little, and she felt a crick in her neck. The paper lay a few feet from her on the floor. She reached over and picked it up again. Her fingers were so cold she could hardly fold it. She tucked it away in the front of her dress and its sharp edge pricked her skin.

Then, not seeing it, she no longer believed it. The room around her, the absolute silence of the house, denied it. She took it out again, unfolded it, and looked at it. It was a piece of paper with marks on it. It meant so little that anyone might have seen it and never given it a second look.

She thought, Clearly it was done by someone else, it was done most probably by Blaise in a fit of reminiscence. Its hasty lines might either have been made by an expert or by a talented boy. And Blaise knew of that obsession with the Place Vendôme. Wasn't it also the last spot he and she had looked on in Paris?

But the message had Simon's quality, said exactly what he would be sure to say. This is where we were happy and loved each other. This is the world we had. It is true that war hovered over us and we quailed before it and we were right to quail. And yet in some period of yet unknown time, perhaps, with luck, we can go on. You see, the sequence goes on and is irresistible. This is a new one coming up — Number 30.

Well, if it were by Simon — had it come in a letter? A letter to Blaise, perhaps, smuggled in. He might not dare write directly to her. And Blaise would perhaps think this a clever way to please and astonish her.

But the paper was a page torn from the notebook, and she had bought that notebook the day before.

Then the suffocating certainty became too much. She began to sob in quick gulps without tears, almost in a perfunctory way.

She put the paper back in the front of her dress and held her hand to her mouth and drew deep breaths until the sobs, like a fit of hiccoughs, passed away.

Then she carefully turned out the lights and went upstairs.

Under Blaise's door was a crack of light. She knocked softly and heard his steps coming toward it, then his voice, low and close: "Who is it?"

"It's me — Françoise."

The key turned in the lock. He held open the door and she went in.

His room looked as though a wind had blown through it. Everything was in wild disorder, drawers open, papers torn, clothes lying on the bed. In the center of the floor stood his canvas bag, open and half packed.

She looked around and Blaise nodded. "Yes, I'm going," he said.

Then he put his arm around her suddenly. "Françoise, what's the matter? You're sick."

She whispered against his ear, "Simon is here, isn't he?"

He made no answer and held her more tightly with his arm.

"Come and lie down," he said. He led her to his bed, pushed some clothes aside, and propped up pillows. "Yes, he's here," he said. "How did you find out?"

She took the crumpled paper from her dress and held it out to him.

Blaise looked down at it. "The idiot!" he said.

He sat down by her on the bed and held her hands in his. "He's an idiot," he repeated. He said it carelessly and affectionately, exactly as one speaks of a friend in the next room. Not as a judgment passed on someone far away. That manner told her more than anything that it was true. But how was it possible to believe? In the midst of this house, this darkness, this last hour —

"I must see him."

"Of course. I was coming to tell you. But I wanted to wait till they were all in bed. I heard Edouard come up but Father is still downstairs."

"Where is Simon?"

"In the chapel."

"Is it safe?"

He made a grimace. "No. But we're clearing out tomorrow."

"What time?"

"Before daybreak."

"Then I can only see him for a few hours — Why didn't you tell me?"

"Because we were afraid."

He was here, but presently he would be gone. That also made it seem more true. If he could have come in safety, been seen by daylight, if he could have lingered and talked of trifles and had time to spare — No, that could never be believed, that would be too much happiness. She was too shrunken to hold that.

Even this much, even short, whispered words in the dark — If it's true, if I see him, how am I going to stand it?

Blaise said, "We were afraid to have you go back and forth. Father caught Maurice the night Simon came. He nearly caught me, too. I'd stayed to bury the gun. Yves seems to have seen me do it. I suspected it at the time. I thought I heard someone outside the barn. I put out my light but not quickly enough apparently. And too many people knew already about Simon. There was Bouchaix, there were all the ones at Audierne, there were Maurice and me, now the ones at Douarnenez. Besides, look at your face now — you couldn't go around with a face like that! Everyone would guess. Edouard would have guessed."

So many knew? Bouchaix, that day in the shop? He knew? Maurice, when I got up and called to him at night, he knew? The people at Audierne, the ones at Douarnenez, and Blaise when we first spoke of the murder. Only *I* didn't know.

"You think Yves hasn't suspected it?" she asked.

"I'm sure he hasn't. He thinks of nothing but his own troubles. He thinks of nothing but the gun. You know how obstinately a peasant sticks to one thing. That gun is the secret of everything to him. I don't think the possibility of anything else has entered his mind. He just thinks I took the gun, shot the man, came back, and was willing to let them all go to hell for me."

"And you have to leave tomorrow?"

"Yes. No question about that. All the arrangements are made. We're leaving on Pierre's boat from Douarnenez. He's got the Diesel oil saved and hidden and the permission to go three miles out, for fishing. It's got to be tomorrow. If Simon and I aren't there Pierre'll go out anyway, and then we *will* be in the soup."

"You leave about five?"

"Earlier."

She looked at her wrist watch. "It's eleven-thirty now."

She tried to measure the time. One hour. Two hours. Maybe more. But it couldn't be measured. It was like saying to a man who had forgotten what food was, "Now you shall have one, two, three loaves of bread." Until he has eaten again he doesn't know what one means.

André was still downstairs. "See if there's a light under Edouard's door," she said.

Blaise went quietly to the door, opened it, and peered down the hall. "No," he said, "and he seems to have gone to sleep. I even think I hear a snore."

"He's leaving tomorrow morning. I wish he were gone now. If he should find out about Simon — I can't bear to think of their being so close."

"He won't. How could he possibly suspect it? Why is he leaving? Through with us?"

"Entirely. But we can get along. I suppose Father doesn't know, does he?"

"No."

She imagined André under the green reading light in his study, his head sunk on his chest, his beautiful, small hands lying helplessly on his knees. What was he thinking of? He believed Blaise had killed the German. He expected him to be executed. Perhaps tomorrow. If he were told now that Simon was here it would make no difference to him.

"No. It would have been crazy to tell him," Blaise said. "I didn't want either of you in it. And I didn't even know what Father would do. So, of course, I didn't tell him."

She put André's grief aside. She had lived with it and would live with it again. But this moment was Simon's. She hadn't yet asked how he got here. It could only be by a miracle.

I asked for a miracle and it didn't come. Now here is another, a small one, a strange one, only for me. Perhaps I shouldn't take it because it's so exclusively mine. I shouldn't dare be happy in it. But I'm beginning to believe it, to feel happiness. I needed it so terribly. If others need miracles and don't get them I will think about them later. Now I'll simply accept it. To accept is beautiful also.

"How did Simon come?" she asked.

"Simon was on a British motor torpedo boat,"

Blaise said. "About a month ago he took part in a commando raid on Brest. The boats were to bring the air men back — they drop them in parachutes, you know."

"But how was he on a British boat?"

"I'll tell you from the beginning, shall I?"

"Yes, do hurry."

"Well, after all, I can't give it to you like a capsule. It's quite a long story. First, of course, Simon went home."

"To America?"

"Yes. And it seems he hung around there worrying over things all summer. Then in early winter he got sent to England to do some pictures for a periodical, something about blitzed towns. He managed to get into the Naval Reserve."

"Simon!"

"Yes. It's rather comic, I know."

"No, it's not comic!" she cried. "Why shouldn't Simon be a good seaman? Everyone today does something foreign to him."

Blaise smiled mockingly. "I see you still have a *béguin* for him. You still have a mash on him. Well, anyway, to go back to the story — there was a leaky fuel line. The fuel leaked out and ran into the bilges. They make better than seventy knots — just imagine that, seventy knots — and the vibration is so terrific they have to wear rubber between their teeth. He

thinks there was a short circuit in some wiring, torn
loose by the vibration, but anyhow, there was a fire.
A thing as small as that doesn't carry any lifeboats
naturally, only life jackets. The crew went overboard."

And this happened to Simon. What did his face look
like as he went overboard, what did he think of, was
he afraid — I'll never know.

"He was saved," she whispered.
"Of course. Listen to the rest. They floated around
for a long time in icy water. None of their own people
could make more than the briefest effort to pick them
up. They can't, you know. The important thing is
to get the greatest number back. You see, the fire
would attract the Germans. Their patrols would be
after them in no time."
"Blaise, can't you tell it quicker?"
"Not if you want to know exactly what happened."
"Yes, I do. Go on."
"The tidal current runs out from Ushant for six or
seven hours at about six knots. He figured he must
have been carried twenty-five or thirty miles in that
one tide. Well, anyway, he was picked up."
"By one of ours?"
"Yes. A fishing boat out of Audierne."
"Oh, then it must have been Bouchaix's brother."

"That's it exactly. Now you see what happened."

"But I don't really. The murder must have had something to do with it."

"It did. You see, when he was picked up Bouchaix's brother decided to bring him in and turn him over to the authorities. But Simon was pretty sick. I imagine he already had pneumonia. Anyway, he was suffering from shock and exposure. He told them that if they turned him over he'd be put in a prison camp and be dead in a few hours. He's got an ingratiating way. I suppose Bouchaix's brother really wanted to help him. So he gave him some odds and ends of clothes and got him ashore. He was carried off unconscious and they said he was one of their crew who had fallen down a hatch, or some such tale. No one was suspicious, anyway.

"They took him to Bouchaix's brother's house. He was sick a long time and the Bouchaix family began to get worried. They hadn't bargained on having him so long. And if he died, what were they going to do? How were they going to dispose of him? But he got better, though by this time so many people in Audierne knew he was there, that they simply had to get rid of him. Bouchaix's brother had had some talks with him and naturally Simon asked him where he was. And then he mentioned us, told Bouchaix he was a friend of ours. But he insisted he didn't want to make use of us now and Bouchaix himself thought it would be dangerous to tell us. He thought that Father might turn him over at once, turn all of them over. But after a lot of talk this Bouchaix came to see our Bouchaix and told him about it and suggested he speak to Maurice, so Maurice could put out feelers as to our attitude.

"Maurice came to me. We talked it over and decided we'd do what we could but tell no one, not Father, not you. As I said, too many people knew about him already."

It began to fit in, like the lace laid over a design. But it was less a miracle because the means were becoming clear. And less a miracle, too, because it was not ended. He was in terrible danger and so was Blaise, so were they all. It was a miraculous moment that might still end badly.

But Blaise had a confident air. He had seen certain solutions and he naturally expected others.

Even though he said now, "Here comes the bad part — While we were still discussing what to do, Maurice and I, and before we had any definite plan, our Bouchaix came one morning and announced that Simon had been brought to his house. His brother had simply decided that they had to get rid of him and couldn't wait any more. Bouchaix said we'd have to come and get him that night. He was scared stiff.

He's a funny fellow, in a way brave, in a way not, like most people, I suppose. He hasn't given us away and certainly that was brave. But at this time he was scared.

"We decided to keep Simon in the chapel. We took the bicycle that night about eleven o'clock and went to Bouchaix's house. But I insisted on taking the gun too. That was the mistake. Because we might have killed the fellow without it and that would have been better. Maurice was against it. I'd already sawed off part of the barrel. I don't know why I did that. Sheer silliness — an idea that I was secretly doing something pretty desperate. Anyway, I took it. It was loaded and I carried it under my overcoat.

"When we got to Bouchaix's house we found Simon. You don't know how queer that was! Of all the things that have happened seeing Simon there was the queerest. The last time I'd seen him was here. And he'd seemed such a fool, such a clown, so outside everything that went on. And yet he had been out fighting, while I was sitting here.

"Well, he looked very badly — he still does, and the funny thing is he still has something of that almost insane lightheadedness. That drawing, for instance. Last night after everyone was in bed I brought him up here to have a wash in warm water and a shave. We sat in the library and had a cigarette and the last of the Grand Marnier. Imagine it! I knew it was sheer

insanity but he has such a different sense of proportion he made it seem normal. I went out for a few
minutes and he must have made the drawing then."

She thought, How could he help but make it? He
sat in that room, in that room, and I was just above.
But then, he loves me, she thought. Until this moment
I never dared think it.

"But the murder," she said, "how was that?"
"Well, we stayed over two hours at Bouchaix's
house, mostly arguing with Simon. Bouchaix had hidden some brandy, for a special occasion I suppose.
He got it out and gave us all some. None of us was
used to it and it went straight to our heads. We
argued and argued. Simon said he wouldn't come to
us because of you. If he were caught they'd get you.
We told him our place was the safest of all, the place
where no one would hunt for him. And we said we'd
put him in the chapel and not tell you, so if he were
caught you wouldn't have had any knowledge of it.
And he said, 'How do you think I am going to stand
that?' That was what was really worrying him."

Françoise smiled and closed her eyes for a moment, and Blaise went on, "Finally we agreed he'd
speak to you just before he left, when it seemed quite
certain he could get away.

"We started out, all a little drunk I'm afraid, and Bouchaix came with us. Everything went all right until we passed the fork of the road and got to within a hundred meters or so of the Relais Fleuri.

"Then that German sergeant came along. He came along with a funny, soft, hurrying step, half a run. He came so quickly we had no time to jump into a ditch with Simon and the bicycle. Before we knew it he had a flashlight on us. He turned and stopped short and pulled himself up and said, 'Halt!' But we all saw right away he was drunk, too.

"It occurred to all of us at once that we ought to be able to handle him, because he was only one and drunk and we were four and only slightly drunk.

"He began to ask us questions in bad French, rather as though it had to be done but he wasn't interested in it really. He seemed very pleased with himself, too pleased to care about our answers. While we stood there he would chuckle to himself and hum some tune he had in his head.

"I can't tell you what there was about him that began to get into my blood. It would have been easier to have one of the bully boys turn up. This one was soft, almost ready to be friendly, to assume that we would be flattered at being treated well by him, and he looked a little like that rabbit we shot. He kept snapping his torch on and off and the glow came up on his face. I kept thinking of the rabbit and how easy it had been to kill him.

"At first, as I said, he asked us questions. He wasn't in the least afraid; he'd met four of his enemies on a lonely road in the middle of night, but he wasn't afraid. Because he knew he was armed and he thought we weren't, and so he despised us.

"So in this friendly and this soft and nasty way he questioned us: 'Where have you been?'

"'A little party at a friend's house.'

"'You have your permits, your papers?'

"'Certainly.'

"He didn't ask to see them. Instead he said, 'Why does the man ride the bicycle, and why do you hold him on it?'

"'Because, my Captain,' Maurice said, 'he's a little drunk.'

"But the 'my Captain' didn't go over at all. He balanced himself back and forth on the balls of his feet and said very calmly, 'Not Captain — Sergeant. It's not correct to call me Captain.' Then he gave his chuckle again. 'Were there girls at the party,' he said, 'was it a nice party?'

"'Lots and lots of girls,' Simon said, spreading his arms out, 'all ravishingly beautiful.'

"The German looked very sly then. He fumbled around in his tunic and got out the black stocking. He dangled it in front of us. His upper lip curled back and showed all his little white teeth. 'French girls are nice,' he said, and he said it with this almost fraternal air, and we didn't do anything about it. It was not the moment to defend the honor of the girl at the Relais Fleuri, or of all the girls of France. But then with his other fattish hand, holding the torch, he made a gesture I won't describe, very slowly, and before I knew what I was doing I had snatched the stocking out of his hand.

"He stood watching me while I put it in my pocket, and his face got very dreamy and almost sad. He said, 'Show me your papers.' We got out ours and he examined them by the torch. Then he said, 'Let's see yours.' But of course Simon had none.

"'He lost them,' Maurice said, 'left them at the party. He's the drunk one, remember?'

"I suppose it was at about this moment we began to realize we couldn't let him get away. He'd seen us and seen Simon. He'd report us certainly, perhaps he'd try to take us in right now. Bouchaix began to breathe like a steam engine. He knew we were in for something bad. I imagine he wished he'd stayed at home. We all drew closer together, without thinking of it, and suddenly the German took a step back. He snatched out his revolver and held it quite steadily.

"'Halt,' he said again.

"No one moved. Then he said, 'You must all come with me.'

"Well, it was Bouchaix who jumped at him. He's

a powerful man and still quick on his feet. Perhaps he's still something of a sailor. Anyway, he fell on the German and whether his revolver jammed, or whether Bouchaix was too quick, I don't know. The revolver and the flashlight fell on the ground and Bouchaix, who had grabbed him in a sort of hug, suddenly lost his nerve and let him go. Perhaps he felt what a disaster it would be to have to kill him.

"I had taken the gun from under my coat but I didn't do anything either.

"So there we stood, the German looking at us and Bouchaix and the rest of us looking at him, and me holding the gun. Maurice picked up the flashlight and turned it on again. Then the German saw we had a gun and he saw his revolver on the ground, and he stood there frowning. He hadn't thought of anything like that!

"Simon said, 'Better go easy now. We could knock him out and drop him in the ditch.'

"Maurice said, 'And have *them* all hunting for us tomorrow?'

"Bouchaix said, 'He's seen us all. Where could we hide?'

"The German knew what was going to happen to him. If we didn't his face would have told us. His lower lip began to shake so his rabbit teeth showed and his eyes blinked. I don't believe in the last second he saw us at all.

"Maurice handed the flashlight to me. He said,

'Hold this, will you?' Just as though he were going to do some ordinary thing. Then he took the gun from me. I let him. I felt like a small boy. I could see only the reddish pupil of the German's eyes in the light. Maurice moved a little closer and shot him."

"Maurice shot him!"

"Yes. He went over without making any sound, except that for a minute we heard a queer noise like water gurgling.

"It was Bouchaix who felt the worst. He grabbed hold of the bicycle and I thought he would be sick. But he got over it and without stopping to talk about it he ran off down the road to his house. We came on here. We put Simon in the chapel and he's been there ever since."

He was there now. That was what was hard to believe, the exact nearness, the five minutes between them. She could see Simon in the dark tossing sea, though that image was dim. She could see him, more closely, lying sick in the little stone house, in the stone street that smelled always of sardines and tar. She could see him in Bouchaix's kitchen. Here was Bouchaix, tough looking but frightened, Maurice glum and wary, and Blaise full of suppressed excitement and pleasure, being now a man at last. And in their midst Simon, thin from sickness, flushed perhaps from the brandy, being flighty and obstinate, saying absurd things perhaps, and suddenly saying, "How do you think I'm going to stand that?"

She could even see him making the drawing, looking up to her room. But it seemed to end there. There was no other end to it.

After a moment she said, "So Maurice killed him. I thought you did it."

"And you thought I was pretty vile to have done it and then kept so quiet about it. But I did all I could to make you and the rest suspect me, slowly. But you and Father were too quick. And then Yves, the fool! But you all had to believe I'd done it, because I was the one who was going away."

"When did you decide that?"

"We talked about it the next day. The hostages were taken and somebody had to do something. We knew they'd wait a few days to try to catch the murderer — they'd like to catch one at least once. Also, we had to plan to get Simon away. So I thought of my pals at Douarnenez. They're better than the Bouchaix lot, they've got more guts. I knew there were some there who were planning to get away themselves, though they never said much about it to me. So I went there the very next day.

"Pierre was cleaning his engine. I often help him around the boat. While we were working I got thirsty. I went to the water tank for a drink and

found it was full of Diesel oil. I thought, Then he's
saved it to get away with, and it must be fairly soon.
While we were bending over the engine I said,
'Pierre, if I were in trouble would you help me?'
and he said, 'Why not?' "

Blaise was beginning to talk in almost an exalted
way, though he tried to hold it down. He was in
love again. Not as he had been with the Germans, but
in love with danger, in love with loyalty, sacrifice,
and bitter, almost hopeless courage.

He said, "Pierre had heard about the murder of the
German. He went on with his work for a while but
suddenly he stood up and gave me a quick look. He
said, 'Do you want to come along with us?' I saw
he thought I'd killed him, or at least had something
to do with it. And it struck me like lightning that
both Simon and I could go. I said, 'Yes, but I've also
got a pal, an American.' There was no use explaining
all about Simon, but I said, 'He's a sailor, too.'

" 'Ah?' he said.

" 'What about him?' I asked.

" 'You can bring him along,' he said.

"I told him it would have to be pretty soon and
we began to plan it right then."

"What about Maurice?"

"He thought it was a good idea."

"Doesn't he want to go?"

"No. He hates to move, and he thinks England is

all cold and fog and he hates the English. What could he do there?"

"So it's tomorrow morning?"

"Yes. We meant it to be day after tomorrow — tide's better then — the twenty-second. You see, some others are clearing out, too. And they had their arrangements to make. But when Maurice found this morning that the gun was gone he went straight to Douarnenez. He had to wait for a bus. It took him some time. I had already gone on my bicycle but he wasn't sure till he got there that he'd catch me there. He told me about Yves and we agreed it was better we should leave tomorrow. Pierre said it could be managed for tomorrow. He could change his permission for fishing to tomorrow. It's a good thing, because when I came back (I had the bicycle and got here quicker than Maurice, who had to wait for the afternoon bus) you told me about Bouchaix."

"But have you everything arranged? How will you both get there? How will you get aboard?"

"We'll bicycle down. I've borrowed Philippe Contes's bicycle. His permit to circulate, too, for Simon, just in case. We'll go aboard the *Serpente*. It's been tied up for months. It never goes out. But it's alongside another boat that's alongside Pierre's. After they've examined Pierre's boat we'll slip aboard her — if we have luck."

"It sounds as though it might be possible."

"It will be," he said. "I have a conviction it will."

Suddenly she said, "So have I. Because it will be a miracle. And the miracle has already begun. It won't stop."

"Yes, we'll make it," he repeated.

"You and Simon —" she cried. "Oh, God, how I wish I could go!"

Blaise shook his head. He tried to be sorry that he must leave them. Later, sorrow would well up in him, many times, but now he could not feel it. The pleasure of action after imprisonment was too intense. He was lightheaded with pleasure. And Françoise didn't resent his release. She too, was released for the moment.

"You don't mind my going?" he asked.

"No, no. It makes me happy. You must go."

"You'll get along."

"Of course."

"What do you think I'd better do, leave a letter to say I did it?"

"Yes. It would make it safer for Maurice. Just to have me tell them might not be enough."

"I have one written, as a matter of fact. And I thought I'd leave the stocking, too. Just to prove it. It must match the other they found in his pocket. When I leave I'll put them on my table. You can find them during the day. Or they could be mailed, as though I'd mailed them."

"That might be too late."

"Yes, that's right. And I suppose if Edouard leaves, they'll have to shoot someone tomorrow."

He got off the bed and began to put a few more things in his bag, to close drawers, and to tear up a few papers. He stopped every now and then and looked around his room. His eyes shone and he drew a deep breath.

"When I come back," he said, "it will all be different." But he was thinking only of leaving, not of coming back, and excusing himself for his happiness in leaving.

Françoise lay back on the pillow. It was nearly twelve. André would either come upstairs in a few moments or fall asleep in his study. He often dozed half the night in his chair. In a moment she would creep down, slip out the back door, and see Simon. After that, nothing mattered.

"It's Father I'm really worried about," Blaise said, putting a rolled pair of woolen stockings in his duffel bag. "I feel he isn't as strong as you are. You always seem to me to be made of tougher material."

"Do I?" She smiled faintly.

"Yes. I don't know why exactly. I know it's been bad for you, but you're more flexible than he is. He seems frail in some way and he stands or breaks. Do you think he'll worry very much?"

"I don't know."

"What will he think about my joining them, fighting with them?"

"I don't know that. But don't think about it. You have to go. We will think only of what you must do."

He closed his bag and looked anxiously at her. "*You* think I must go?"

"I do," she said. "It's the best you can give."

He looked embarrassed. "Well, then it's settled."

After a moment he said, "Hadn't you better get along, and haven't you some way to fix yourself up? You look so tired."

She laughed this time. "I think I'd better make up a bit. I must look awful."

"You lie there," he said. "I'll get your things. Where are they? On your dressing table?"

"Yes."

His solicitude gave her a sudden pang. But it was funny, too. She got up and went to his mirror. The brushes still lay on his table. She took them and began to brush her hair into place.

"I need lip rouge."

"Where is it? I'll get it."

"On my dressing table. Bring me powder, too."

Blaise slipped off his shoes and opened the door gently and went out. In a moment he came back with powder and rouge. Françoise made up her face slowly.

❋   ❋   ❋

I'm trying to put on my youth, she thought, but it is all worn to a thread and my beauty doesn't exist any more. The only way I'll ever look as I did is if he sees me that way. I remember two old women talking once on a bench in the sun. They were talking about something that had happened to one of them a very long time ago. Suddenly I saw what they had been when they were young. For a moment I saw two young women, two young women who had utterly perished and only existed in each other's memories.

Blaise had been watching her make-up and his face had grown suddenly older with care.

"You'll be all right here?" he asked. He put his cheek against hers. And he said weakly, "It's so awful leaving you."

"Oh, we'll be quite all right. We haven't anything to fear here, except dullness. We'll think of you and even that will pass away."

"You'll tell Father for me, won't you?"

"Yes. I'll explain everything to him."

"I don't dare tell him now. If he didn't want me to go I don't know what I'd do."

"No. I'll tell him."

"You'll explain why I had to, won't you?"

"Yes, I'll tell him you had to have hope. And that hope has to be fought for. We've got no future unless you can make it for us."

"Yes, that's what you must tell him."

He kissed her cheeks. "And kiss him for me," he mumbled.

Then he said, "For God's sake, do go now. Take off your shoes, the heels make too much noise."

Now the moment had come. She went to the door and opened it. The house was silent but they both saw a crack of light under Edouard's door. They looked at each other.

"Never mind," he whispered. "He's turned it on for a minute. He won't hear you."

She hesitated, imagining Edouard's room filled with the curious empty light of the middle of night and Edouard, perhaps sitting on the edge of his bed, slack and hunched forward, staring vacantly at the floor. She reached up and turned off the hall light. Blaise handed her his torch. It made a white circle in which she saw dust between the floor boards and a frayed edge of carpeting.

Blaise squeezed her arm and she left him, and holding her shoes and the torch started toward the back service stairs.

Then they both heard it. In the stillness — the humming sound.

She stopped. She knew at once what it was. A car, a camion perhaps, climbing the hill from the Douarnenez road. And as it came nearer it sounded like two, a car and a camion together.

She slipped back and ran into Blaise at his door.
He threw his arms around her.

"What's that?"

He didn't answer but she felt his heart pounding
like a hammer.

"Cars coming here," she whispered. "Listen!"

They heard the sound change as the cars, the
heavier and the lighter, reached the top of the hill
and one after the other started down. In two minutes
they would be up the drive and at the front door.

"Blaise, run," she gasped.

He didn't move. He listened a second longer.

She put the torch into his hand. "Run, run! Get
Simon! Get to Douarnenez, get on board! Quick!"

As he didn't move she said, "It's Yves. He's told
them. It's your last chance."

Blaise without a word lurched from her. At the
head of the stairs he stopped. He said in a clear voice,
"But Edouard — "

"No use. Perhaps he told them."

Blaise ran down the stairs. As the car came up the
drive she heard the back door bang shut.

Edouard's door opened. He stood against the light,
peering into the black hall.

"What's that?" he said. "Who turned the light
off?"

"I did." She reached up and turned it on.

He stared at her. She was rouged and powdered,

her hair in shining curls. She was transfigured with anguish. She looked like a brilliant apparition of herself. She began to laugh hysterically.

"Your friends have come," she said.

He made a gesture of helplessness, a gesture she had never seen him make before. If he was guilty of this it was only because of absolute failure. He did not fit into this world any better than she did. They had tricked *him*.

He was fully dressed, except that he had on bedroom slippers. He rocked back on the balls of his feet, stupidly, because he knew there was nothing he could do and he knew again what it was he would never have, and why.

Maurice came down from above. As always he was buttoning his coat. But his face was hollow with fear.

"Mademoiselle," he said hoarsely.

She stopped laughing abruptly. "They've come, Maurice," she said.

He looked at her to see what had happened. In his effort to discover what he must do his face twisted into an ugly grimace like pain.

She stifled the impulse to laugh again and made a gesture with one hand. She meant they had gone and that he had better go, too.

He didn't seem to understand her.

She said, "Maurice, don't open the door. Go away."

Perhaps he was made stupid with fear but he gave
no sign of understanding. He clumped down the
front stairs and a moment later she heard him open-
ing the front door.

And then suddenly she had hold of herself again.
She thought, But this is the real thing, the true thing.
The other, the miracle, was not. I wouldn't have
known how to live with that. But I am used to this,
this I can believe.

Chapter XXI

THEIR feet echoed all over the vaulted hall. They sounded like cattle being driven into a tunnel. The first face Françoise saw was that of the young aide to the Kommandant, Captain Hessler. She had seen him the morning before outside the Kommandantur, and once or twice she had been obliged to speak to him about food and medical supplies for the camp for political prisoners. He clicked his heels and bowed. But his face was a mask of gravity: this is a painful occasion, he seemed to be telling her, brought about by yourselves. It was no more than the look of the headmaster.

André was there, and Maurice, who had opened the door and stood watching them all with a dazed look. There were eight soldiers, one a clerk with a despatch case, wearing shining glasses without rims, and finally there was Edouard in bedroom slippers.

They started into the library and there was a slight delay over precedence. Captain Hessler was very formal. He insisted that Françoise go ahead and he stepped aside, bowing from the waist. Then he made up his mind to let the ex-minister and the Vichy representative also precede him, and he stepped aside for them.

At last they were all in. As they arranged themselves Françoise heard more German voices outside. Then there were soldiers around the house. And perhaps they had left more at the stone gate at the end of the drive. But Simon and Blaise could take their bicycles from the chapel and over the stone wall onto the road, without going near the gate or the drive. If they were lucky. If no one was watching at the top of the hill. All this came to her very clearly, very coldly.

Then Maurice came in and she saw he had recovered himself. He had realized after looking them all over that Blaise had got away. And his fear had been for him.

She suddenly realized in its completeness what it means to be a brave man, and to her own courage a little of his was added.

Maurice took his station just behind André and he appeared so much his natural self that he looked sullen and disagreeable, as though he expected them to demand some extraordinary service from him, such as a full meal suddenly prepared, whereupon he would cry, "Oh that, that's too much; I'm not hired to do all this."

With his own solemnity he made ludicrous the

solemnity of this room where the Germans had already begun to spread their order. They were judges come to mete out a death which must be accepted, on their terms and humbly. But Maurice was spoiling this for them already.

Edouard was sitting in his special chair. André stood by the stove. The captain sat by the table and the clerk stood behind him with his papers and a pencil, which he wet slightly at intervals with the end of his tongue.

Françoise looked only at Maurice. He was the only one who mattered now. But she heard Edouard saying something and she listened.

"I assume," Edouard said, "that you had some good reason for coming at this hour."

He was speaking with an attempt at authority. Captain Hessler nodded gravely and said, "I regret, Monsieur l'Ambassadeur, to disturb a house where you are a guest. But — " He made a stiff, formal gesture of regret. His French was very good.

"You have an accusation to make?" Edouard asked.

Captain Hessler said, "Unfortunately, yes. But I wish to state that everything which will happen is a matter of great regret. The German Forces of Occupation find it very painful that this accusation should touch a high personality."

He made a slight bow to Edouard and turned to André. As though he were reading from a paper he went on in a harsh voice, "When the former minister, Monsieur André Galle, came to the military authorities, to intercede for the twenty hostages held in reprisal for the murder of the German noncommissioned officer, Hans Holle, it was assumed by the military authorities that the former minister made these representations in good faith, that he was ignorant of any of the circumstances connected with the crime, and that his sole purpose was to ask for a delay during which time justice could be done."

"That is exactly so," André said.

It seemed also a duty to look at him if only to support him for the moment, but Françoise found she couldn't do it. Even to hear his voice, so high-pitched that it sounded as if it might crack, with even that slight suggestion of a whinny, as when he was about to laugh, that was all she could endure. Even Captain Hessler, she thought, must find something repellent in forcing such a man to speak with such a voice.

The German said, "It has been brought to the attention of the military authorities that the former minister, Monsieur André Galle, was either knowingly or unknowingly sheltering the criminal in his house."

Maurice's face assumed an incredulous expression, as though to say, What bilge is this! And he wagged his head, looking from one to the other idiotically.

Edouard said, "Really, the career and personality

of the minister makes that an insulting and intolerable accusation."

His eyes looked very round and were fixed on the captain. Then he turned them to Françoise.

He is trying to show me that he is doing what he can. But I know he can't do anything. Edouard impotent does not exist.

She saw the captain not looking at Edouard but frowning at Maurice. Then he leaned back and the clerk leaned down to him and they whispered a moment. The clerk nodded several times importantly.

The captain cleared his throat and folded his arms across his chest. "You will now hear the deposition of Yves Mallet," he said.

Maurice strained eagerly forward and cupped one hand to his ear.

The clerk began to read with a strong accent: —

"The following is the deposition of Yves Mallet, taken on the twenty-first of November nineteen hundred and forty-one at twenty-three hours.

"The said Yves Mallet deposes and says that a shotgun of English manufacture was the property of a servant in the house of the ex-minister, Monsieur André Galle, the servant's name being Maurice Garnier. The said Garnier was accustomed to hunt for a few days every autumn with a dog he had. Deponent states that in nineteen hundred and forty, when firearms were required to be turned in to the authorities, the said Garnier remarked that they would never get his. Deponent states that after that he never saw the said gun and he assumed it had been buried or otherwise concealed on the property known as the Manoir du Rusquec.

"Deponent states that he believed said gun was first exhumed about two weeks ago, though he is uncertain of the exact date, but he states that it was used to shoot a hare, which had been observed on the said property."

"Aha!" Maurice exclaimed.

The clerk looked at him over his rimless glasses, frowned, and went on in the slightly different voice of the man who may be interrupted.

"On the fifteenth of November, some time after the shooting of the said hare, it came to the attention of deponent that someone had sawed off part of the barrel of the shotgun, because he discovered the amputated section near the manure heap, which is to the south of the barn and a slight distance from it. It was the opinion of deponent that this was to make the shotgun more easily transportable under a coat or other garment, but he thought no more about it.

"On the night of the sixteenth of November deponent states that he took a cart and drove to town to get a doctor for his wife, who at that time was unwell and seemed to be about to have a convulsion, or some manifestation of a serious character. After he had taken the doctor back he was unable to sleep and sat for a long time by a window.

"Deponent further states that thereafter he observed the following: From this point, which commanded a view of the farm court, he was able to observe a man, whom he believed to be the said Garnier, who came to the court, went to the barn and opened the door. Believing that something might have gone wrong with the cow, as for a day or two she had seemed to be off her feed, though not seriously enough to mention, deponent left his house and went toward the barn to see what was happening. As he neared the door he heard a series of curious sounds, small and sharp, as though someone were striking the earth. As this seemed very irregular he approached with caution and looked through the half-open door. A light showed faintly from one of the stalls, but not the stall containing the cow, who gave no appearance of being unwell at the moment. Retiring to the corner of the barn he saw the man come out carrying something, which he recognized, after some consideration, as the shotgun. This the man carefully placed under his coat and thereupon went stealthily away, followed for a short distance by deponent. At the entrance to the garden the said man took the bicycle, which had been leaning against the wall, and went off, walking beside the bicycle. But deponent was able to observe that the man was not the said Garnier, but the son of the ex-minister, by name Blaise Galle. Deponent then returned to the barn and satisfied himself that something had been dug up."

The clerk stopped to draw breath.

Edouard said, "Are you really going to make us listen to all this? You can surely come to the point a little more quickly."

Not quickly, Françoise thought. Not quickly.

The captain said, "It is necessary that everything be done in order." He signaled to the clerk, who went on: —

"The interest of deponent being now aroused, though he did not as yet suspect that it was a question of anything more serious than a little poaching, he resumed his watch at the window, between intervals of occupying himself with ministrations to his wife. But no one entered or left the court to his knowledge during the next few hours. Deponent states that finally overcome by exhaustion he slept. At half-past three in the morning he awoke. He got up to assure himself that the barn door was closed and all was in order. Approaching the barn he again saw a faint light from a hand torch. Using great caution he climbed to a small window, where he was able to look down and observe the said Blaise Galle burying a gun. While he was watching, his foot slipped and at the slight noise the light was immediately extinguished.

"Deponent states that he did not realize until the next day the full meaning of what he had seen, and even then the habit of loyalty to the family of the ex-minister kept him silent, in spite of the fact that his brother Jacques Mallet, a political prisoner, was selected as one of the hostages to be shot, in reprisal for the murder of the said noncommissioned officer, Hans Holle. Even then he states that he found himself unable to divulge his information. He had been assured that the ex-minister would do everything within his power to prevent the execution of the hostages, and a long habit of confidence in the said ex-minister made him believe he would succeed."

The clerk stopped again and leaned down to the captain. He pointed to something in the paper and murmured in his ear. The captain glanced at the paper and nodded curtly. The clerk straightened up and continued: —

"Deponent states that after two days his anxiety reached a point where he himself went at night and dug up the gun. This gun he found means to show to the Representative of the Vichy Government, His Excellency Monsieur Edouard Schneider, who had come to the Manoir du Rusquec at the request of the said ex-minister, Monsieur Galle. The Representative of the Vichy Government assured deponent that he would do the necessary and advised him to speak to no one."

The captain interrupted icily. "It is assumed that the Representative of the Vichy Government either did not realize the seriousness of the story of Mallet, or that he wished to assure himself further of its truth."

Maurice exclaimed audibly again and smacked his lips, looking at Edouard as though to say, A hell of a scandal for *you*, old boy.

"And finally," the clerk said, running down to the end, "deponent wishes to state that he makes this deposition of his own free will, because he was finally convinced that the said Blaise Galle had forfeited his consideration by a continued willingness to allow others to die in his place. Moreover, deponent states that he wishes to see justice done."

The clerk laid the paper on the table by the captain, took off his glasses, breathed on them, and wiped them on his sleeve.

Françoise thought, By now they are one, perhaps two, kilometers along the road to Douarnenez. This deposition read in the absence of the accused gained two kilometers for them. Her heart had thumped with the strain of their furious pedaling. She had been stretched and drawn over the long road, which was not only a road but a thin, frail segment of time.

What if I should crack now, scream and fling myself at the captain's throat?

She looked at Maurice. He was frowning with a new kind of sadness, a new kind of loneliness. He had been the sad clown always, his loneliness the clown loneliness. He could not live in himself and he could not live in others. Now it was different. Now he, too, was following that flight. He looked at her and raised his eyebrows a little — Be quiet, keep calm, it's all right.

She clasped her hands tightly and sat still.

The captain was speaking again. "I must demand," he said, "that the said Blaise Galle be immediately summoned. It is necessary that he hear the accusation I am about to make and the sentence which is to follow."

André cried out, and his voice pierced her from head to foot, "But this is not a trial! It is simply an accusation to be followed by a sentence." And he added desperately, "It has no legality whatsoever!"

It was worse than that. It was an accusation to be followed by an execution. The proof of its indecency was that Blaise had not killed the man. But they had no recourse against the indecency.

Or rather, they had only one. It was that Blaise was not here.

But even that was a temporary evasion. The indecency was fully backed up and they knew it. They could devour any roads that lay between them. Time and the road would flow back into their yawning mouths.

The captain said, "The legality of what is happening is not dependent on law as it existed in France be-

fore the occupation. That is legal which is conducted
by the orders of the military command. The man murdered was a member of the military forces of occupation. Therefore the case comes under the jurisdic-
tion of the military command."

Françoise heard these words by way of André.
They meant nothing to her or Maurice. But to André
she saw they meant something. They represented the
lesion that had taken place in this man and in the
others who were his kind. It was complete. It had
carried them away from the central trunk. They were
fragments. But then where, he was wondering, did
they get their authority? For this man was filled
with authority. They all were. Their authority had
crowded out everything else. These words, this authority, ruled André's world.

The captain said, "And now, Monsieur le Ministre,
I demand that you produce the accused."

André could not speak. He made a hopeless gesture to Maurice that he should find Blaise, and Maurice, touching his finger to his forehead, at once shuf-
fled out.

When he had gone André said vaguely to Françoise, "He is asleep. At his age they don't waken
easily."

They heard Maurice go upstairs.

Edouard shifted uncomfortably in his seat. There
was a line of glistening sweat on his forehead. "I hope
you will take into consideration," he said, "that the

boy did not run away, that he made no attempt to escape. Also, that he is very young, only eighteen. There is also the long record of his father, which has not been unappreciated in Germany. Any sudden, unconsidered action here would produce a bad effect, certainly in France and perhaps even in Germany."

"I am acting under orders," the captain said.

Maurice came back down the stairs. He stood in the doorway and said, "He is not upstairs!"

There was a stir, a sort of tightening, among the Germans.

André grew whiter. He dropped into a chair. He had instinctively been standing, because to stand on his feet was the last attitude of dignity and resolution of a man. Now he couldn't stand any more.

Edouard said, "He must be somewhere in the house." He looked at Françoise and he saw at once in her face that Blaise had gone. He looked at her with confusion and worry, as though to say, Now you've really done it.

She saw that Edouard was afraid.

"Shall I go on looking for him?" Maurice asked.

"No," the captain said. His voice cut like steel. "We will look."

He gave an order and the five German soldiers in the room went out. Maurice stepped aside for them. In the hall they opened the front door and called to some men outside. Then two of them went upstairs and they could be heard tramping through the rooms. The others began to open and shut doors on the lower floor.

This may take ten minutes.

But one German came quickly back down the hall. His footsteps sounded through a watery, sniveling noise. In the doorway he stopped. He pushed Colette ahead of him into the room. She had her apron up to her eyes. They all looked at her and the soldiers pulled her arm down from her face. It was red and contorted from fear.

"Oh, Monsieur le Ministre!" she cried. "Forgive me! I told them about Monsieur Blaise."

"What do you mean?" André said.

"I told them," she sobbed, "that he had gone away because his bicycle is gone. It was standing just outside the kitchen door after dinner, when I took food to Marie. It was there when I came back. But just now I came down to see what the noise was and it is gone, and this man said, 'What are you looking for?' and I said, 'The bicycle, but it's gone. Monsieur Blaise must have gone.' And I didn't know, Monsieur le Ministre — oh, Mademoiselle, I swear I didn't know, it was for *that!*"

The room filled with the sound of her sobbing.

It was exactly as when she cried over the fish sauce.

Her stupidity extended endlessly, not bounded by any horror that could be created in this world.

The captain said, "If he has gone on his bicycle you must permit me to use your telephone."

He got up.

Françoise sprang to her feet. "Why do you telephone?" she said. "He'll be back any minute now. I sent him into town to get me some medicine. I was sick and needed it very suddenly. He has been gone quite a while and he'll be back."

"You did not tell us this when we began our search," the captain said.

"I thought he had come back. The truth is I felt better and went to sleep. I supposed he had come in and found me asleep and gone to bed."

"How long has he been gone?"

"Oh, a long time. But the pharmacist, Monsieur Costard, died this morning. Perhaps he is having trouble getting it."

As she spoke she felt herself aflame with fear, illumined by it, but her words came clear, high-pitched, and precise. The force of her fear seemed to give them a sort of conviction.

But the captain, after looking steadily at her, said, "With your permission I will still telephone."

Now the road would be sucked back. Simon and Blaise, two flies, two insects, carried on it.

*   *   *

Maurice raised an eyebrow and she thought he was telling her that they would be caught. What a pity, he seemed to say, that we didn't have time to cut the line, because now he will telephone everywhere, to town, to all the towns, to Douarnenez, too. If they don't overtake them, others will be waiting for them as they come in. Well, this is the finish, this is the peak of the nonsense.

"Where is the telephone?" the captain asked.

André said, "Maurice, show him."

Maurice looked sadly at him. His face was sadder than she had ever seen it.

Because at last, once and for all, he had to give in. He had to acknowledge what they had made, those others. He had to face tragedy squarely. He had to say a true thing, and no fooling this time.

"Don't inconvenience yourselves," he said. "I shot him."

"Maurice, be careful!" André cried.

Edouard turned and stared at him. "So it was you." He looked at once relieved and deflated.

The captain, too, stared at Maurice. His eyes seemed to have no lids. He stared so long that Maurice began to blink, as though he were dazzled.

Then Maurice drew the corners of his mouth down and wagged his head from side to side.

"Yes," he said, "it's me. Not so much fun for you, is it?"

Colette had stopped sobbing. She said in a weak voice, "Yes, it is Maurice. *I* knew that all along."

"You're a liar!" Maurice said.

The captain was apparently deciding that it was better like this, after all. To shoot the son of the ex-minister — even for murder — would have raised trouble. And the Kommandant would be rather glad than otherwise to avoid this kind of trouble at this time. Françoise saw his face relax. Everyone, even he, seemed to be relieved that it was only Maurice. It turned it into a simple little affair which they could handle now in a matter of twenty minutes.

While they had not moved, the captain and the clerk, even the soldier standing by the door, gave the impression of having sent at least a part of their attention elsewhere. The other soldiers came tramping back. They were about to report that they had found nothing but the captain silenced them with a lifting of his hand.

He motioned the clerk to write. "Maurice Garnier, repeat after me: I do hereby solemnly swear — "

André interrupted him. "Maurice, don't speak without realizing what it means. Don't confess unless it is the truth. No one can force you otherwise."

"It's the truth all right."

"But the gun," André said, forcing himself, word by word, speaking sternly in the effort he made. "It was Blaise who took it. Yves saw him."

"Yves was crazy," Maurice said. "Monsieur Edouard even has admitted that. It was I who took it. It was mine, wasn't it?"

"Yes," André said doubtfully.

"*You* know, Monsieur le Ministre, that I'm the one. Monsieur Blaise is only a kid. Besides, you know for me it's not the first time."

The captain rapped on the table. He did not intend to have this become an affair to be settled in the family.

"You will repeat after me," he said, "I, Maurice Garnier, do hereby solemnly swear that on the night of November sixteenth I did willfully — "

Maurice said impatiently, "I said I did it, that's enough for you."

The complete attention of the Germans focused on him once more. The soldiers' eyes grew bleak, turning in their heads to rest on the captain. In the silence that followed, the image of the German death again took shape in the room. A solemn thing, monstrous and sacred.

Maurice instantly took an attitude. He thrust his wooden foot forward, folded his arms on his chest, and frowned. He became sterner, more heroic, than they. He mocked their German death.

The captain said, "If you are not willing to take the oath in the proper form your statement will not be conclusive. How do we know, for instance, that you had no accomplices? There are others who might have been capable of helping you."

"No accomplices," Maurice shouted. "No accomplices. Not Monsieur le Ministre, not Monsieur Blaise, not Mademoiselle, not Monsieur Edouard, not Colette, not Yves. Only me — what?"

Colette at the mention of her name burst into tears again. "Oh, my poor Maurice," she sobbed.

Maurice addressed the room in a loud whisper, "But she's incredible, this fountain."

The captain said, "You alone did it?"

"Haven't I said so?" He spread his arms. "Why do you have to go on talking? Everyone wants to go back to bed. I did it. And if I hadn't told you, you'd never have known. That's how bright you are."

The captain said, "Step forward."

Maurice took a step forward, looking to see if his feet were properly placed and resetting his arms, folded across his chest.

"Like this?" he said.

The captain said, "I hereby find you guilty of the murder of the noncommissioned officer Hans Holle and by virtue of the authority vested in me I sentence you to be shot to death."

At the word "death" Maurice grew pale in spite of himself and his jaw, which was bluish already, though he had shaved, Françoise remembered, not more than seven hours ago, locked visibly in the effort to keep it from shaking. Then he managed, without saying a word or moving, to make it appear that this paling, this tightness of jaw, were also a part of the farce, part of the refusal to be anything but a clown, before a race of incompetent imbeciles who merited no more from him.

The captain said, "You have nothing to add?"

Maurice said, "No."

André went to him and put his arm on his shoulders. "You're not sparing us?" he said. "Tell us the truth. Have you nothing more to say?"

For a moment Françoise thought he would openly weaken, that he would say some simple thing, make for once an honest contact, directly with another man.

"You have nothing to say?" André insisted.

"Well — no," Maurice said.

The captain stood up. He had had enough of this. He had conducted many examinations and he knew the moment when they ceased to yield fruit. He knew a hard one when he saw him. He knew a mocker and a scoffer. He recognized a parody.

He signaled to the soldiers and beckoned his clerk to follow. Then he bowed to Françoise, to Edouard, and to André, and they went out.

When she saw Maurice taken away she could not

move or speak. Her lips formed good-by but no sound came.

It was Maurice I ought to have loved, she thought, not Edouard.

"Good-by, Mademoiselle," he said.

Then he went out with them, tramping exaggeratedly, half-swaggering, half-cringing, making a parody of a man going to his execution.

André went with them.

Edouard and Françoise were left. He stood looking at his bedroom slippers. Then without a word he went upstairs.

The camion had left but the car was still there when he came down. He carried his bag. But he hadn't had time to change his shoes. He crossed the hall hurriedly.

He still did not speak, and even his shoes were mute.

Chapter XXII

IN THE darkness water dripped on her from the low eaves. The wet ground, spongy with moss, gave under her feet. The bough of the apple tree answered her with a gentle stirring and finally her hands found the stones of the chapel. The stones were damp and porous. They seemed to breathe.

She found the door but though it hung ajar, the blackness inside was the real obstacle, the implacable final barrier of all hope.

She listened to the silence of the chapel.

Then she pushed the door and the hinges complained rustily.

She turned on her torch and its whitish beam caught the face of the Christ on the chancel screen, caught the precious blood as it fell into the cups.

On the tomb of Jean du Rusquec lay a dark heap of blankets, still holding the shape of Simon's body. Cigarette stubs lay all over the floor. She went quickly and sat down on the cold tomb. She drew the blankets up around her and buried her face in them. She gathered a few stubs, examined them, and

their faint, dead-straw smell tainted the icy air.
But it was useless to search for hope here. There was
none.

She sat a long time. Then she saw the pages torn
from the notebook. They lay neatly in a pile on the
monolithic altar where long ago peasants had offered
tails of their horned beasts to St. Herbaud.

She gathered them up and sat down again to read
them. The little torch trembled in her hand. She
read a page, not knowing what it said. Then she put
her head on her arms and sobbed. Finally she looked
again and read again.

My love —
How much longer must I wait?

A long time passed before she could go on and
when she read again tears kept falling from her eyes.

Today Blaise brought me a pencil and paper. He
says perhaps it will be safe to tell you now and you
may come tonight. But in two more days we'll be
gone.
And perhaps you won't come. Is it possible that
after all you may refuse to come? I won't believe it.

That was one page. The next was more closely
written.

I don't know you now. I don't know what has
happened to you. That woman at Audierne leaning
over my bed — I thought, Is Françoise like that now?

When I heard her feet dragging up and down the stairs I thought, Does Françoise walk like that? And the voices whispering in the house —

If that is what it has been, then perhaps you'll never come.

I went to the house tonight to shave and wash, and I left a drawing in your basket. Did you see it? Will you come?

I know you will because I came to you.

The other pages were crowded with thick writing: —

Blaise tells me things have changed and we must leave tomorrow morning. He says you will surely come tonight.

All this is my fault. If I hadn't been a weak fool and let Blaise and Maurice bring me here, none of it would have happened. The German wouldn't have been killed. You wouldn't be in danger.

And now I'll be taking Blaise away. But that's one thing I don't ask forgiveness for. It's right for Blaise to go. Blaise knows what he must do. And you know too, because you always did know.

Has he told you about me? About the raid, the fire, and the fishermen who picked me up? When I rocked there — and what a long time it was — I knew exactly what was happening to me. I was being brought back to you. That's why I didn't burn in the blazing oil. That's why I didn't drown. I was so sick that after that I forgot. But when I saw Blaise and Maurice I knew again what was intended to be.

Good God — could any man not come! Even if only to see you at a distance and very small. Two days ago I saw you. My face was pressed to the one clear new pane in the old glass. And I saw you walking with your bicycle up the hill.

Can you know what I felt? Or what it was to come back to Rusquec?

It was before daylight when we came. Not a red streak even, only twilight. The shape of the house seemed to have changed. It looked smaller. The trees were leafless and I'd never seen them like that. I remembered the special smell of the place. I saw your window under the roof — wasn't it the third from the end? It was a little open but it was dark inside. I had a certainty that I could make you hear me in some way not yet known. I had a certainty that you had been trying to call me and that I might have come too late.

I asked Blaise if you were ill, if you were in some special trouble, and he said no, you were as right as could be. Whatever you wanted, I'll hear it tonight. And you'll hear my answer.

I don't deserve for you to come. I know it.

I must tell you something. I must tell you what it was like when I left you, and why I left you.

I left because I was afraid.

I was afraid of a spell. And of suffering too much. I thought you loved Edouard, that you were cheating me with Edouard, and that he was rotten. I thought your world, your fabulous world, was rotten, too, and that you loved it. You could only love rottenness, I thought.

So I went home. To be myself again, to be with

my own people. Don't let me say anything false to you now. Don't ever let me be false again. I must tell you that I tried not to think of you. Tried not to know what was happening to you.

All that summer, under the thick leaves, in the blue heat haze in the streets, in the cool house by the shore, through the endless drinks, the slap of the balls on the court, the endless talk, I heard one thing always, very clear — I've lost her, I've lost my love.

I've lost her bright hair, her sweet, dragging voice. I've lost the way she uses her hands. Her wit and grace. I've lost her courage — because she was courageous — I've lost even the little of the love she gave me, because she did give me a little.

I've lost all I felt for her, even the spell. Even the jealousy, the pain. I've lost her.

But then I said, I've got to get over this. People get over this. I was too young. I'm older now. The world is bigger than just that. What happened there is over. I've lost my love: all right, then I've lost her.

I couldn't do anything that was good, not playing, not drinking, not talking to friends, not making love. I couldn't paint. It's good to paint, but it was no good then.

Here were three or four blank sheets. She turned them and the writing came again.

We talked and talked and talked all summer. I went on trying to find out what I'd done when I left you. I thought if I talked to people enough I'd find out. I had to know what I had given up. What I could put in its place. Someone would tell me.

Finally I said, I'm trying to see her still but she doesn't exist. She has become part of a legend so terrible that it has wiped out her living face. But still I saw you. And because I could see you and they couldn't, I hated them as I talked to them — and didn't they hate me!

But still we went on talking. We used our own voices and each other's voices. Everyone's voice. My Aunt Annie's voice, Uncle Jim's, young Jim's, my friends', the man who made a speech in the Senate, the man who wrote the syndicated article, the taxi man, the barman, the woman who sent money to poor old Europe. A collective voice.

But we weren't talking to each other really, though we thought we were. We were talking to the one we are forced to talk to when we wake up and the house is quiet. We were talking to the Enemy, the old Enemy, the one who sits in a tangle of night. He never answered us. It was only our voices. What did we say? We said nothing new, nothing I hadn't heard before. But it meant something to me now because it was my accent and my speech.

We said to him, Congratulations, old fellow. Your Panzer divisions cut them like cheese. I admire your mechanical skill and capacity for success. You make me believe in a mechanistic universe, well run at last. Say, I've got a baseball signed by Babe Ruth — kid stuff of course — and the best little eight-cylinder Ford you ever rode in; want to see them?

And we said, Why the squirrel shooters of North Carolina will be along any minute and will they show you a thing or two. Ever hear of Dan'l Boone? Oh, Pioneers!

And we said, But you disturb all I know of truth and goodness and beauty. So I won't think of you. And God will look after your case.

And we still said, Your case bears examination. The causes go a long way back. There are economic factors, nationalism, the Versailles Treaty, the Haves and the Have Nots. There is more than one side to this question. There are two sides, three sides, there are ten, fifty, a hundred sides.

Ah but, we said, will there be a better world when I'm done with you? Will all abuses be wiped out, will there be justice, true brotherhood, lasting peace? I know there will not. Someone will throw the monkey wrench. And for a less than perfect world I will do nothing. So you can do what you like with me because I'm too smart to be taken in again.

And finally we said, But I *will* do something. I will not spare myself. I will give and give. I'll give old clothes, medical instruments, vitamins, playing cards, flour, and milk. I'll send them trucks, tanks, planes, and guns. I will produce and produce and produce. To produce is all anyone ever asked of me. To ask for more would be an offense against God's creation. It would be like asking a bee to produce something more than honey.

That's the way we talked to the ancient Enemy sitting in the midst of night. Placating, admiring, explaining, questioning. We talked till we talked every word out of us. Till we were bled white of our strength and our honesty.

And he never answered. But suddenly I saw why. That thicket of night was ourselves. That enemy was in us. He was everywhere, in every man. He was in me. We were talking to ourselves, not him.

Why hadn't I known it before? Why had I ever felt that I was empty of this trouble? Even when I saw it in every living man. Even when I saw it in you.

Perhaps men have lived whole lifetimes and never really faced it. But not now. This is the time of every man's test. And it's the time of every man's brotherhood.

The moment I knew that, I knew I hadn't lost you. I knew I could get you back. And I knew what I must do.

I would kill him in me so that he might be killed in all of us. The only way was to give everything. To commit myself with no chance of being let off. To fight without quarter.

Even to write this becomes a little false, a little sickening. It becomes smug and pompous and lousy. That's because nothing is tolerable but to act.

So now I know I'll see you tonight. Not because I deserve you — who knows whether he deserves a blade of grass growing — but because I am not what I was. And you need what I am now. As I looked up at your window, as I saw you at a distance on the road, I knew you needed me. Sick and useless and hunted as I am at this moment, you need me. Have you heard me calling you yet? You will hear me.

If you were dead I'd call you back and make you live.

So now, before we meet face to face, before I speak to you, before I hold you in my arms, let me say this: Whatever you need of me is yours, even if it should be only some lesser gift, even if it should be a thing not peculiarly mine. It is yours, and if it's my whole life then that is yours, too. My life is yours, and I have not lost you. My life, my struggle, my love.

And I ask for nothing more because I have everything already. No man can ask for more than to see his hope.

And to see you living was my hope.

Chapter XXIII

WHEN she went back to the house it was morning twilight, which is purer than evening twilight. In it more things can be seen. The earth was very ancient. She saw Brittany and Cornouailles and Armorica and a land so much earlier than these that it was without a name. And she saw also the land not yet born, but whose shadow lay here, as the shadow of Brittany, of Cornouailles, and Armorica and all that they had brought forth once lay on that older emptiness and namelessness.

In the house she smelled coffee. There was a light in the library and André sat there. She got a little stool and sat at his feet. He poured her coffee from the pot beside him and they drank in silence.

Then he said, "Edouard is dead."

"What!" she whispered. "You don't really mean Edouard!"

"But I do."

"How?"

"I left him in the office of the Kommandant. They shot Maurice. When I went back Edouard was waiting. He wanted to take the morning train. He wanted me to walk to the station with him but I refused. He started out on foot. A German soldier had his bag. As he crossed the square a man shot him from the side street. It may have been aimed at the soldier but I think not."

"He died then?"

"At once."

"But that means it will all begin again! More hostages, more reprisals. More murders, too. It will go on and on."

"Yes, it will go on and on," he said.

"You'll have to fight for them again. You'll have no rest."

"No."

Maurice and Edouard. Blaise and Simon. Only she and André left. Only the endless fear and struggle.

"Blaise has gone," she said.

"Run away?"

"Gone to England."

He put his cup down. She laid her arms on his knees and dropped her head against him.

"He couldn't tell you. There was no time. And he was afraid you wouldn't want him to go."

She did not dare look up. She said in a low voice, "He said to tell you he had to fight."

He made no answer. The room was so still she could hear through the closed wooden shutters the sudden proud, confident cry of the cock.

"He said to kiss you good-by — shall I tell you the rest?"

He made no answer.

Presently I'll tell you everything. That they are safe, Blaise and Simon. With them has gone all we had. But they have left us a new thing — hope.

She felt him shaking under her arms. Then a sob broke from him.

"Thank God!" he cried. "Thank God!"

THE END